'Aumākua Anthology
Book 2

Mo'owahine of Makalike Bridge

Del Aragon

'Aumākua Anthology
Book 2

Mo'owahine of Makalike Bridge

Del Aragon

Moʻowahine of Makalike Bridge

Designed & Created by Del Aragon
Cover Art by Del Aragon
First printing, February 29, 2024

ISBN-13: 978-1-963531-00-8 (Paperback)
ISBN-13: 978-1-963531-02-2 (Hardcover)
ISBN-13: 978-1-963531-01-5 (eBook)
Library of Congress Control Number: 2024900439

Self Published by Del Aragon
Honolulu, HI
arts.delaragon@gmail.com

Printed through KDP

To Kiara.
For always bringing your light into my dark soul and
forever being there to clear my chaotic mind.
I love you, forever and always

Contents

1. Prologue.. 1

2. Friday.. 6

3. Saturday.. 65

4. Sunday.. 128

5. Monday.. 247

6. Tuesday... 330

7. Epilogue.. 335

8. Glossary.. 338

9. Acknowledgement.............................. 340

Mua

The exhausted voice of a young mother of three could be heard calling out to her eldest for help, "Gerry!?" She looked out of the kitchen and saw her daughter painting her nails and occupying the phone line. "Shannon!?"

"Ugh! Hang on a sec, Bev." Shannon glared at her mother, "My nails are still wet, Mom!"

"No, I just wanted you to get Gerry for me. The trash is full and my noodles are boiling over. Could you go get your brother please?"

Shannon could see her mother juggling the cooking and holding her little sister in her arms, "You got it, Mom!" She picked up her brother's baseball mitt and curled it under her armpit, "Bev, give me a minute, my mom wants me to go get Gerry..." Shannon paused for a second and made a face of revulsion, "Oh, my lord, Bev! That's so gross! You wouldn't be saying that if you lived with him, he's a damn pig."

"Watch that mouth, young lady!" The baby girl pulled her mother's hair pick out of her bun causing her mommy's hair to fall, "Now, don't you start acting sassy like your sissy, little missy."

Shannon giggled as she tossed the phone receiver onto the couch and carefully made her way upstairs to her big brother's bedroom.

Gerry's door was cracked open slightly and Shannon could hear the sounds of some kind of creature snarling and grunting as she approached the room. A foul odor slapped her across the face that made the young teen want to vomit. She pressed the door at its edge with her knuckle to avoid damaging her fuchsia colored nails and walked in on one of the most terrifying things she'd ever seen.

"That's disgusting!"

Gerry turned in surprise just in time to see a dark object smack him right in the mouth, "What the heck, Shannon!?"

"Ew, what are you playing?"

"Oh! Isaiah let me borrow his copy of Smash T.V. for the summer, wanna jump in?" Gerry tossed his leather glove onto the unfolded clothes scattered across his bed.

Shannon looked around her brother's room, "I wouldn't stay in here longer than I had to, even if you paid me. It reeks in here, dude!"

Gerry looked confused, "I don't smell anything!"

"Ugh, anyways, Mom wants you to take out the trash," Shannon turned to leave.

"Wait! She wants me to take it out now?" Gerry sank in his chair.

"Uh, durrr, why do you think I came up here? Just to visit your smelly room?" Shannon could see that her brother looked a little uncomfortable. "Are you okay?"

Gerry looked at his window and back toward his sister, "It's kinda dark outside."

Shannon rolled her eyes, "That's usually what happens at night, genius."

"Hey, wanna come help me dump the trash!?"

Gerry's sister looked offended, "Excuse me? That's your job and if you did it before Mom started cooking dinner you would've still had a little light. What's your malfunction anyways?"

"At night, I hear the sounds of some kind of animal sniffing around right outside my window. It follows me through the house, like when I go downstairs to grab a snack. It freaks me out, Shannon." The boy's eyes began to water.

"Oh my goodness, Bev is going to trip when she hears that her crush is still afraid of the dark! What a baby..." Shannon started laughing as she hopped down the stairs.

Gerry flopped into the kitchen and pulled up the rubbish liner. His mother turned around with a zip, "Oh, wait!" She crammed some food packaging into the bag, "Thank you, honey!"

"Mom? Can I wait for Dad to come home before I take this outside?" Gerry tried to bargain.

"No can do, honey. Dad's officiating a wedding in Waikiki and they invited him to stay for the reception." Gerry's mom stuffed a fork full of spaghetti into his mouth.

"Mmm, that's so amazing!" Gerry dripped red meat sauce onto the floor as he spoke.

"So, go and take out the trash so we can eat already!"

Gerry made his way down the slick Futura Stone driveway scanning the street and sidewalk. There were no cars traveling the road and the street light just above the trash area was out. "You've got to be kidding me right now!" The sound of a dog barking in the distance made Gerry's heart race. "Okay, drop the trash and run back to the house." He took a deep breath and pushed on through the darkened walkway. After throwing the bag in the tin can Gerry turned around to bolt back to the house when he bumped into a shadow and yelped.

"Hey, hey, hey, man! Watch where you're going."

Gerry apologized, "I'm so sorry, I didn't mean to bang into you, sir."

The strange man dusted his torn hoodie, "Respect, fool!"

Gerry shook his head and sighed as the perturbed man walked away. Without skipping a beat, Gerry started his way back to the house. As he got halfway up the driveway he heard the odd sniffing sound that creeped him out coming from behind. He turned and saw that the street was empty once more. The pulses of his heart beat inside his ears.

The frightened young man was more than ready to return to the safety of his home. He twisted around at high speed and slammed into another figure that wasn't there a second before. This time it was much larger, a lot more solid and covered in coarse hair from head to toe. Gerry looked up at the strange being trespassing in his yard and its eyes flashed a blazing hot white. He screamed at the terrifying sight, but his call was cut short when his vocal chords were shredded by several razor sharp claws. Gerry could feel the warmth of his blood soaking into his t-shirt. He staggered down the driveway to get away from the creature. He managed to work his way to the road, but was startled when he saw the monster's otherworldly shadow rise up from behind the trash cans. The mutilated young man tried screaming again, only managing to cause gurgling noises to bubble out from his exposed esophagus.

The beasts eyes flashed as it leaped from the trash heap right at the boy.

Friday

‘Ekahi

“Which one I going get!?” Kaimi pondered as he looked at the sun bleached menu taped to the inside of the ice cream shop window. Even though he knew the cost of the sweet treats by heart, Kaimi looked at the prices anyway as he checked his pocket to see if he had enough for a double scoop. He unfurled a crumpled wad of bills from the pouch in his shorts as a breeze caught him off guard causing his wrinkled singles to fall to the pavement.

Kaimi bent over to retrieve his money when a shoe crushed his hand into the cement. He yanked his hand out from its enclosure seeing a bit of his skin torn from the quick gesture. As Kaimi stood up, three older boys cast their shadow over him. He watched as the guy who stepped on his hand reached down for the cash that now had his dirty foot print stamped on it.

“Uh, das my money…” Kaimi squeaked as he reached out his scraped up hand.

The bully scoffed at the smaller boy and quizzed him, “You think this is your money? How much money did you say you had?”

Kaimi started to vibrate uncontrollably as his temper grew. He called back to the punk, "Foah dallah's!" The air from his answer caused the fearful young man to stagger on his quivering legs.

Folding the bills over each other the large boy started to thumb through each note, one at a time, counting them aloud, "One, two, three, *four*, five, six, seven and eight. You were wrong, Bruce, this is my money." The two other boys began to laugh as they turned to walk away.

A tear fell from Kaimi's reddened eyes as he helplessly watched the last of his birthday money heading in the opposite direction of the ice cream parlor.

"Eh, Kaimi! Wassup?" the voice of his older brother, Wiliami, snapped him out of his moment of despair.

Kaimi looked up the sidewalk and pointed at the small gang, "Those guys wen' steal my money, Wili. I wen' ask fo' it back, but da one in da middow wen' trick me."

"What!?" Without hesitation, Wili charged down the walkway and caught up to the thieves. Kaimi watched his brother holding a powerful stance prodding his finger toward the small gang then toward the hand of the guy that stole the money. It didn't take more than a minute when Wiliami made his way back toward his younger brother. "Dea you go, Kaimi." Wili slapped the bills back into his hands safe and snug.

Kaimi, with a huge smile on his face, asked Wili what he wanted from the confectionery, "You like one cone?" Before Kaimi could get an answer he was awoken by a loud banging sound above his head.

"Eh, you betta get up or you gonna miss da skoo bus!" Kaimi's father pawed the side of the door frame leaving his son flopping around in his bed like an ulua. Kaimi could hear his dad going next door to wake up Wili, greeting him with the same announcement.

Kaimi jumped out of bed to get into the shower before his brother could. As he exited his room, he could already see Wili shutting the bathroom door behind him, bouncing his eye brows and curling his upper lip in Kaimi's direction. "Fricken guy! I going eat all yo' spam!" Kaimi slapped the door just as it closed.

Wili's voiced echoed from the bathroom out into the hallway, "Touch my spam an' you goin' get it!"

Recalling his dream, Kaimi gave it a rest and thought, *Wili is so fearless, even when he stood up to doze tree bullies a while back. Da least I can do is let 'em use da rest of da hot watah.* Kaimi decided to keep himself busy while his brother occupied the bathroom.

The boys' father made his way into the kitchen to pour himself some coffee. Its strong delectable scent was found making its way through every nook of the small house. Mr. Lee popped on the television and backed up onto his seat sipping slowly from his steaming mug.

Kaimi wandered toward the savory aroma with his stomach grumbling where he saw his father sitting on his chair, "We get eggs, Dad?"

Mr. Lee slowly bobbed his head in Kaimi's direction without taking his eyes off the television, "Go check! I told you boys if we need stuff you betta let me know befoah I go work."

Kaimi made his way over to the refrigerator. He took a peek in the barely stocked fridge to find an empty egg carton. "Ah, lose money!" Kaimi whined as he carelessly slammed the fridge shut.

Kaimi's dad, taking his eyes off the TV, snapped his gaze at his negligent son, "You broke dat ice box, I broke yo' head!" Kaimi's ol' man slowly turned his attention back to the morning news. Mr. Lee knew he had good boys, but he also knew that he needed to make sure they understood how important it was to mālama pono their belongings, to take responsibility for all of their actions.

Kaimi sat with a bowl of stale cereal sitting in a small pool of water. He reluctantly took a bite while pretending to be interested in what his father was watching. "What, Dad, goin' get storm latah on?"

Kaimi's dad motioned his hand at his son's face rubbing just the tips of his coarse fingers down the boy's lips, "Hāmau! I trying fo' listen." Mr. Lee quieted his son.

Kaimi continued to poke at his bowl while paying partial attention to the monotonous voice that emanated from the speaker of the TV set.

"... And today marks the fifth year anniversary of the missing Lunalilo high schooler, Cheylene Hikina, whose whereabouts are still uncertain. Her disappearance after the ritualistic murders of several other Lunalilo High School students is another dark spot in the history on our small island of ʻĀinapau. Mary Lou Ribeiro, had persisted in her search for her daughter, Cheylene, until she passed away just a few months ago. She believed her daughter had probably suffered a head injury and lost her memory. Cheylene had been spotted at the edge of ʻŌmaʻo State Reserve, but did not respond to her mother's calls. The young woman vanished into the forest and has not been seen since. If anyone has any information we are asking you to please contact local authorities..."

Kaimi's eyes grew as he imagined some terrible fate that could have befallen poor Cheylene. Fear grew in him as he imagined himself becoming a victim, "Brah, pua t'ing her. Da pua maddah nevah even get closure! Died looking for her kid. Das crazy, yeah Dad?"

Just before Mr. Lee could answer, Wiliami jumped on Kaimi, "Yo' turn fo' showah, Kaimi!" His body was still drenched and he only had a towel wrapped around his waist. Wili started to rub his wet, warm underarm against his brother's face, "Eh, shmell good, ah?"

Their father smacked Wili on his left butt cheek, "Eh, knock it off before you get moah watah in yo' braddah's cereal!" He grabbed Wili's towel and yanked it to stop Wili's disgusting act. The towel tie split and Wili quickly grabbed it before it could fall.

Kaimi wiped his face with his napkin, "Ew, Wili! You wen' get yo' stink pubes in my eye!"

Wili ran back into the hallway and made his way toward his room, "At least my pits more clean den yo' face!" Wili shut his bedroom door and silence returned to the small house.

'Elua

Wili and Kaimi hopped up the stairs of the school bus and bid their driver a good morning. Kaimi stopped halfway through the bus where they would both usually sit, but he watched Wili continue onward. Recently, Kaimi's brother would travel all the way to the back of the bus to hang out with a couple of new kids, a guy who flunked a grade and his bizarre sister.

Kaimi moved all the way in toward the window in case Wili changed his mind. He turned around and looked at his brother sitting alone at the back of the bus. It made him think, *If it weren't fo' Wili, I probably wouldn't have had all da experiences dat I had in my life.* Kaimi appreciated Wili for that, which saddened him more to see he no longer wanted to sit beside him on the way to school. *Maybe Wili is sick of always making all of our decisions.* Kaimi shook his head, *Nah, I'm jus' being overly dramatic. Wili loves making da ru'es an' being da firs' fo' do everyt'ing.* In typical Kaimi fashion, the risk would always cause him to withdraw when presented an opportunity. He couldn't think of any reward worth embarrassment of failure.

There were a few risks that surpassed any reward when it came to being associated with those new kids.

From their very first introduction, it seemed like Wili's buddy wanted to scrap and his weird sister, who reminded him of that Wednesday girl from the *Adam's Family* show, couldn't even care less about him or anything else for that matter. Kaimi was never fond of Wili's new clique.

As the school bus pulled up to the De Souza's house it whirred to a stop, Kaimi could see them, Wili's new companions, 'Alapaki and Kenani De Souza. His heart sank as 'Alapaki climbed the steps. His thin fibrous frame was barely cloaked in a faded black hoody with torn off sleeves. The hoodie rested on his head concealing his face in shadow. 'Alapaki slowly looked up at Kaimi with an evil smirk. His white orbs flashed from inside the cover of his hood. Kaimi's pulse began to race when their eyes locked.

As 'Alapaki walked toward Kaimi he cocked back his fist and motioned a punch while stomping his foot, causing Kaimi to flinch. He followed up the juke by stinging Kaimi's arm with a sharp jab.

"Weak," 'Alapaki muttered.

The siblings both continued their trek toward the back of the bus. Wili welcomed 'Alapaki as if he were a long lost cousin. Kaimi shook his head at his inability to talk back to his aggressor, to stand up for himself. *I wonder if Wili saw dat?*

Kenani slowly made her way by following her brother and giving absolutely no recognition to Kaimi.

She gave him the chills in all honesty. Her hair, brown with blonde ends, was voluminous and untrained. Her build was quite similar to her brother's, but she appeared even thinner. She wore denim shorts and jacket, both of which were worn and torn. Her pink tube top had odd oil stains visible across the front of it and she had some of the bushiest arms Kaimi had ever seen on a girl. Truthfully, 'Alapaki and Kenani could pass as twins if it weren't for the amount of hair Kenani displayed proudly on her forearms.

Kaimi lightly massaged the area he was hit and noticed that the De Souza's had left a faint, foul scent, like stale, wet laundry. The smell slowly faded away just like the pain that Kaimi felt in his left arm. It wasn't the first time the wet dog odor lingered in the air while those two were around either. *Perhaps day jus' needed one new washing machine,* Kaimi imagined.

The bus pulled away from the De Souza homestead and as it did Kaimi looked at the house. He always remembered Mrs. De Souza watering her flowers and pulling weeds from her garden. Ever since he started riding the school bus Kaimi would see her head buried in those flower boxes, but he hadn't seen her for quite some time now. It'd been so long that her flowers had all dried up and even the house became quite disheveled. The yard was now overgrown with weeds and wild grass. The place looked dilapidated and unlivable really. Kaimi's attention was pulled to the back of the bus where 'Alapaki was talking loud and laughing louder. It annoyed Kaimi to think his brother could associate himself with such an obnoxious person, but he could only rationalize, *I'm happy if Wili's happy.*

The bus drove through the school's front gate. Kaimi could already see his friend Keoki getting out of his mom's car, and in typical Keoki fashion, he dropped his back pack into the storm gutter where a few days silt had already accumulated into a moist puddle of sludge.

As the bus slowed to a stop, Kaimi wrestled to get off before 'Alapaki could make his way back over to crack him in the arm again. He burst out of the bus's stairwell and headed in the direction of his unfortunate friend.

Keoki was bent over wiping what he could off the bottom of his bag when Kaimi approached him, "Sup, Keoki? Tragedy?" Kaimi questioned in support.

Keoki shook his head, "Hey there, Kaimi. Yeah man, it's just my standard way of life that I have become accustomed to." Keoki let out a huff and stood up to stretch out his back. "Where's Wili?"

Kaimi looked back at the bus and observed his brother being lead by 'Alapaki. "Ah, he stay hanging wit' you know who," Kaimi gripped his arm again.

Keoki just looked at Kaimi and shook his head. "You know, Kaimi, one day you'll need to do something about it. Unless you enjoy being a living punching bag."

Kaimi knew Keoki was right, but he just didn't want things to get worse between him and 'Alapaki. Kaimi believed that in a perfect world they could all get along. "As it is, Keoki, I t'ink I'll jus' have you hang aroun' me moah often."

Keoki beamed a huge smile and squealed with a crack in his voice, "Wow, Kaimi! You really want to hang out with me more!?"

Kaimi glanced sideways at Keoki, "Nah, I just noticed dat I nevah see 'Alapaki come aroun' when I stay wit' you. You must have some kine of 'Alapaki repellent on you." The boys chuckled as they made their way to their homeroom class.

‘Ekolu

“Bye, Kenani!” Wili tried desperately to grab the attention of the indifferent young woman as she turned into her classroom. He cupped his hands over his heart as he and ‘Alapaki continued onto shop class.

“Brah, you gotta put in a good word fo’ me wit’ Kenani. I don’t t’ink da girl can fully appreciate all my grandeur when we hahdly hang out.”

‘Alapaki took a short second to see his sister entering into her homeroom before facing his overly enthusiastic friend. “Braddah Wili, you don’t wanna mess wit’ dat. She will chew you up an’ swallow you whole.”

Wili squished his face, “Don’t chu mean chew me up an’ spit me out?”

‘Alapaki kept pace with the rest of the crowd to avoid getting a tardy slip. “I meant what I said, cuz. Kenani is jus’ like me, minus my sunny disposition. You bettah off not even trying. Besides, dis skoo get plenty ‘ono wāhine.” ‘Alapaki snapped his fingers at Nasmine Chun walking past while signaling Wili with a head gesture.

Wili flicked his hand in the air toward Nasmine to make it clear he was not interested. "No can, 'Alapaki! Dis is somet'ing I no can control, it's feral, it's ancient, it's..." Wili felt a sting on his wrist which snapped him out from his fantasy.

'Alapaki rested his hand back to his side as he frowned at Wili, "It's gross! Stop talking about my sistah laddat."

The two boys made their way to their seats as the first bell rang. 'Alapaki turned toward Wili and asked, "So, talking about hangin', what we going do aftah skoo?"

Wili leaned into his seat with his hands behind his head and asked, "Wea Kenani going be afta skoo?" 'Alapaki gave Wili a terrifying look he had never seen him make before. "Nah, nah, nah I was joking. Cool head, 'Alapaki!" Wili pulled his planner out of his carrier. "I heard on da news goin' have storm. Besides, I get plenty work I gotta do dis weeken'. I might as well get one head staht on 'em tonight."

'Alapaki looked at Wili confused. Then, his eyes lit up like sparkling gems, "If get storm, maybe we go hit Makalike Bridge!"

Wili stopped to think about what happened when he invited the De Souza's the first time to Makalike. *'Alapaki was being really rude to Kaimi las' time we went. If was just me an' 'Alapaki going, no problem, but wit' Kaimi there,* he shook his head unsure if it would work out. Wili knew that the only way he could go hang out anywhere after school was if Kaimi was with him. The boys' father always said they needed to stick together. Wili looked at 'Alapaki and stated, "Let me t'ink about it."

'Alapaki threw his hands in the air as if in complete and utter disbelief, "What's dea to t'ink about!? We jus' go!"

The tardy bell rang and the shop teacher made her way into the workroom. "Alright ladies and gentlemen, we're making a banana hook!" Ms. Horn plopped a curved wooden figure on a work bench. "This project will be a quarter of your grade and it needs to be done before winter break."

Wili shook his head, "Gunfunnit, even moah stress on my plate!" He leaned in to whisper to 'Alapaki, "I'll let you know if can aftah lunch."

‘Ehā

Wili plopped his backpack up against his brother’s hip and followed up by hopping onto the picnic table. Kaimi saw his older brother staring back at him with eyes smiling.

Wiliami finally broke the awkward silence, “Kaimi, we go up Makalike Bridge aftah skoo, yeah?”

Kaimi looked at Wili already with a question forming on his lips, “Who is ‘we’?”

As if offended, Wili’s shoulders pulled away. He squinted at Kaimi with a smirk, “Jus you, me, an’ ‘Alapaki, why?” Wili slapped his hand on his younger brothers shoulder giving it a light massage.

Kaimi brushed Wili’s sweaty meathook away, “Nah, das okay-”

Wili interrupted, “Brah, what? You get one problem wit’ ‘Alapaki?”

Kaimi shook his head looking at his worn down rubber zoris, “I don’t have a problem wit’ anybody, but ‘Alapaki always has beef wit’ me!”

Placing his hand back on Kaimi, Wili continued to massage his shoulder to ease the poor guys worries.

"Brah, 'Alapaki is jus' futtin' aroun' wit' chu, das all. It's nuttin' personal."

Kaimi turned to read his brother's face for a short while. It made him think that maybe he was being overly sensitive about how 'Alapaki speaks to him, his choice of words, his demeanor and tone and even how much rougher he is with him when compared to his interactions with Wili.

Kaimi asked sincerely, "Why do you even hang aroun' dat guy?"

Wili quickly moved toward his little brother's ear so as not to be heard by anyone, "Brah, you know how beautiful I t'ink Kenani is!"

Kaimi belted out an unexpected laugh, "What!? Kenani!? She looks jus' like 'Alapaki but wit' one 'ehu wig!"

Wili reacted immediately, "Eh, shaddap!" He grazed his knuckles across Kaimi's tricep aggravating the same spot 'Alapaki hit him earlier. "Don't chu evah talk laddat about my futchah wife!"

Kaimi gripped his arm and winced, "Easy... Brah, now *you* acking like 'Alapaki! Try move yo' 'okole so I can eat already."

Wili slid off the table top and landed on the bench twisting his legs around until he was comfortably situated. "I'm sorry, bruddah." Wili bent his neck looking for forgiveness.

Kaimi ignored the apology and just reached down for his brown sack lunch to retrieve his can of Hawaiian Sun.

"Ooh! You get Liliko'i!? Like trade?" Wili whipped his can of POG toward his brother. Ice flew from the can's rim and splashed right into his eye.

Kaimi dropped his drink to wipe away the foreign debris, "Babooze, you tryna blind me, oah what!?"

Wili started to brush Kaimi's face when all of a sudden it turned into an unexpected slap.

"What da heck, Wili!?" Kaimi opened his eyes in time to see that 'Alapaki had just joined the table already causing trouble. He saw that Wili was just as surprised at the out of the blue swipe.

"Ah hah, losah!" 'Alapaki raised his hand to give Wili a high five. "So what den, Wili? Makalike Bridge?" 'Alapaki bounced his head in a silent rhythm after Wiliami slapped his hand away.

Wili reluctantly started to decline the afternoon's scheme, "I don't know if today is such a good-"

'Alapaki could already foresee his afternoon being ruined. He blurted, "Oh, Wili, I forgot to mention... Kenani said she like come too."

Wili darted his gaze at his brother. Kaimi could feel Wili's eyes boring a hole straight through his forehead. Without as much as a sound, Kaimi gave in with a slight nod and Wili blurted out almost instantaneously, "We'll be dea, cuz!"

'Alapaki grinned a devilish grin, "Oh, so you coming too, small fry? You shoowah you not sked fo' jump?"

Kaimi bit aggressively into his sandwich as Wili pulled 'Alapaki's attention away from his brother, "If I go Kaimi gotta come too. Das da rule."

'Alapaki slapped the Funyuns out of Kaimi's hand as he stood to leave, "K-den, Wili!"

Wili turned with a huge smile on his face, "T'ank you, t'ank you, t'ank you, Kaimi! You have no idea how much dis means to me!" Wili began to giggle and was giddy at the thought of being with Kenani. "Whoah! Eh, Kaimi, I going see Kenani in her bay-ding suit!"

Kaimi rolled his eyes as he imagined Kenani would just be another witness to him being humiliated at the hands of 'Alapaki.

The second lunch bell blazed through the air letting everyone know it was time to return to class.

Kaimi tossed his banana back into his brown sack and grabbed his books, "You owe me one, Wili!"

Wili's eyes were gazing up into the clouds thinking about Kenani, "Uh huh, yeah shoowah t'ing, Kaimi! What evah you like!"

Friday

'Elima

Kaimi made it to his social studies class just as the tardy bell sang. He went to take a seat next to his friend where he found a dirt covered backpack saving a chair for him. Kaimi tossed Keoki's sack onto the floor and watched as he swirled a freckled finger inside his ear canal. Kaimi saw the girl sitting beside Keoki make a face that read complete disgust. That stuff never bothered Kaimi though. He thought Keoki's uniqueness made for more creative conversations.

Kaimi watched in disbelief as Keoki was going for broke poking his pale, Vienna sausage shaped finger deeper into his ear hole. He started to garner a larger audience. Kaimi intruded, "Eh, Keoki! You busy dis aftah noon?"

Keoki pulled his now stained finger tip out from his ear and flicked away some pia toward the front of the room. He furrowed his brow in curiosity and questioned his long time friend, "Did you want to come over to my place?"

Kaimi shook his head slightly back and forth explaining, "No, my braddah wanted fo' go up Makalike Bridge, but 'Alapaki stay going too. I need you to come help me ignore him." Kaimi eyed Keoki to see if he was game.

Retreating back into his seat, Keoki responded, "How come the only time you want to hang outside of school is when you need me to block 'Alapaki? I'm feeling a bit exploited!" Keoki wiped his finger clean across his lap and continued to grill Kaimi, "You know, 'Alapaki isn't much bigger than you. I guarantee if you sock him in the jaw one time, he'd leave you alone. Or better yet, ask him out on a date! I bet he would leave you alone then…" Keoki pondered the idea of 'Alapaki accepting the offer and tried to scrub the idea from his brain.

Kaimi, getting a bit frustrated, sharply asked once again, "So, you coming ovah owah what?"

Keoki was immediately silenced once Mr. Kahi made his way behind his desk, "Alright gentlemen, class has officially started. Please quiet down."

Keoki distorted his mouth while raising his shoulders which caused Kaimi to grow impatient. Kaimi continued to stare at his friend until Keoki slowly lost interest in their conversation and turned his attention toward their instructor.

"So, as you all remember it was the Menehune or 'Manahuna' that erected these huge ancient structures. What makes it even more amazing is how they were constructed in a single night. If work was not completed by sunrise, the structure would be abandoned, which, from that moment on, would remain unfinished."

Mr. Kahi switched slides as he spoke about each location and discussed their importance in the community. One slide in particular caught the attention of Kaimi. It was an older picture, but the water line of the stream and the shape of the cliff made it easy to see that it was a photo of Makalike. The bridge wasn't as modern as it was today which piqued the young man's interest.

Kaimi raised his hand and Mr. Kahi gave him a look of astonishment. His teacher pointed toward him giving permission to speak, "Eh, Mr. Kahi, isn't dat Makalike Bridge?"

Mr. Kahi was taken aback, he was surprised to see that Kaimi was actually participating in class for once. "Good eye, Mr. Lee! You are correct. It wasn't until the rock slide in '72 that the new concrete bridge we use today had replaced the original wooden one. Here's a question for you all, why is this area called Makalike?"

Kaimi glanced around the class to see if anyone had a response. He saw a petite hand on the opposite side of the class slowly reaching upward.

Mr. Kahi turned his attention toward the student again with the look of shock, "Well, this *is* a surprise! Two of my quietest students willfully adding to our class discussion today. Yes, Miss Agbayani!"

Kaimi sat up at his desk to get a clear look at his classmate. He thought about how Rayna was one of those quiet, mysterious loner types. She would never be seen hanging around campus doing extra curricular activities or cruising down at the local hot spots. Kaimi always had a thing for her, but his dreams of pursuing the girl that was out of his league were dashed the one time Keoki sat beside them. Kaimi's friend squeezed out a loud disgusting fart without remorse. He always believed that Rayna thought it was he who had dealt it. All these strange memories came flooding back to Kaimi as he waited to hear what his crush had to say.

Rayna cleared her throat lightly before speaking, "So, my uncle once told me the story of how there was an ancient creature, a lizard lady, that would abduct children in that area. One rainy day, when my uncle was a kid, he remembered seeing that green lady trying to sneak up on him and his friends. These two huge guys appeared out of nowhere hugging onto the side of the cliffs. They tossed this massive boulder down the stream at her. Unfortunately, they missed the creature and accidentally hit the bridge. The lizard woman fled disappearing into the crevices of the stream."

Being fully immersed in Rayna's tale, Kaimi began feeling the hair on his arms prick upward.

Rayna continued, "Afterwards, my uncle watched those giant, fifty-foot tall men climb up the cliff. They disappeared into the clouds, never to be seen again. Some may say that it was a rock slide that took out that bridge, but my uncle swears by what he and several other onlookers saw. It is also said that the lizard lady seeks revenge on those two men, who were actually brothers, twins. Because the locals witnessed them saving their children, those giant twins were deemed to be heroes. The new bridge was named Makalike, in honor of them. Makalike means, 'Same Face'." Rayna cast her gaze around the class with anxiety. She was panicked until her eyes fell on Kaimi. She could see that he was very much into her story. She smiled at him from the corner of her mouth which made him slowly look back toward the slide with reddened cheeks.

Mr. Kahi raked his finger over his chin stubble as he paced away from Rayna and walked through the light of the projector. "That's a very interesting, and a very entertaining, alternative history, Miss Agbayani!" he responded.

As Mr. Kahi continued to elaborate his thoughts on what Rayna shared, Kaimi focused on her. He could see that she felt embarrassed and had a look that one could only equate to being that of a vengeful mo'owahine. *No wondah she keeps to herself,* Kaimi pondered. *Da firs' time she shares her toughts an' she's greeted wit' skepticism.*

It made Kaimi's ears burn. His hand immediately shot up and this time he spoke before being called upon, "Mr. Kahi, how come da twin giants an' lizard lady are hahdah fo' swallow den da ovah night construction of da Menehune peoples!?" Kaimi's face froze in fear, he immediately lowered his hand and thought, *What da heck jus' got into you, boy!?*

Mr. Kahi 's eyes widened as he blinked them rapidly. "I didn't mean to sound discourteous to you or your friend, Mr. Lee. On the contrary, believe it or not, I was about to share a similar tale to that of the one shared by Miss Agbayani."

Kaimi softened his shoulders and relaxed his posture. He looked back toward Rayna and saw her eyes, that were fixed on him, dart away quickly to look back toward Mr. Kahi.

Their teacher continued, "Look here!" Mr. Kahi pointed toward the cliffs above Makalike Bridge. "Do you see the contour of the mountain face? Before the rock slide of 1972 both of these rock faces looked nearly identical. Many visitors to this valley believed it odd that something so natural could be so symmetrical. They say the area is called Makalike because both of these cliffs were mirror images of each other, like twins."

Kaimi attempted to raise his arm once more but Mr. Kahi held up his left hand to halt the inquisitive teen from speaking aloud. "Now, Mr. Lee, this is what I was getting at. We should look at the history of the area so we can provide an actual explanation to its designated title. I'm not saying that the name is wrong in respect to either what the malihini believe with the bizarre valley formation, or the otherworldly twin supermen mo‘olelo of our kama‘āina. My point is that Makalike is mostly mistranslated because the name was originally Kauaopa‘awai. Looking back at the original place name may help us understand more about the culture in that area or what was important about the location. Now, let me tell you the story I learned when I was your age."

‘Eono

Long before the ancient peoples of this land arrived, there were various tribes of supernatural creatures that lived in their own societies. Each group had their own duty, their own set of skills and their own strengths and weaknesses. Each group also had kapu. One such kapu, or prohibition, had disallowed different species from interbreeding with each other. Breaking this kapu was not only frowned upon, but also had potentially catastrophic side effects. Children born to two different groups could most likely create unknown abnormalities or worse.

One such abomination came when Pa‘awai, a mo‘owahine, fell in love with an entity out of her own class. Their union created two children, twins. Pa‘awai’s lover left immediately after she gave birth without saying a word. These children of Pa‘awai had an insatiable hunger that she tried furiously to quell.

Nothing she fed them made them full. They constantly cried to their mother, “Mama! Mama! Pōloli loa māua!” As they cried the water from the heavens would soak up into the earth. The more they cried the harder it would rain.

She fed them various plants from root to leaf to no avail. She fed them entire animals makai to mauka, yet there was still no relief to their agony. Their cries were so loud that their mother could not bear it. Pa'awai scooped both of her children up and rested them in a cave deep within the valley blocking the opening with a massive limestone slab. Even then their cries could be faintly heard through the thick wall of rock. Pa'awai's heart ached and she cried for her keiki.

It wasn't until one night when the moon was at its fullest, that Pa'awai came across a most peculiar creature. It seemed to have searched for refuge from the storm in the waoakua. This creature she had never seen or heard of before fumbled through the woods exclusively on two legs. It didn't appear to belong to any group she'd ever met. Pa'awai tracked it through the forest for hours to be sure it wasn't another being of greater mana. The small beast finally sought rest and sat up against the feet of Miluakahiwa, who was in the form of a large tree at the time. She knew it was safe to steal away with it as it slept. Within minutes, Pa'awai had returned to the cave with her fare to offer to her children. She placed her quarry at the base of the twins' nest and blocked the cavern's exit. The children's cries ended the moment the little being awakened. The creature felt through the darkness, arms extended, hunting for the cave's exit. With the rain no longer splashing on the ridges of the valley, the panting of the life form echoed inside the chamber walls. It reached through the dark darting from one side of the cave to the other with no success in its search. It confused Pa'awai that this entity had no ability to sense her or her children at all, not even the ability to see its surroundings through the darkness.

Her children emerged from the nest and descended upon their prey. Before the victim could even make a sound the twins tore into it ferociously, devouring every last bit. Her children were completely satisfied and Pa'awai had finally found peace in their repletion.

It worried Pa'awai that she wouldn't be able to find more of this precious food for her little ones and their cries would tear into her soul once more. It wasn't until many moons later that her younglings once again began their torrent of shrills and screaming, "Mea'ai! Mea'ai, Mama!" Pa'awai's heart sank as she realized she hadn't come across the unique food source since that night. Just as the first drop of rain fell there was a sudden burst from the tree tops. Leaves danced all around Pa'awai and her twins, but when they cleared she witnessed her love standing before them.

"Pa'awai, HULŌ! Ua loa'a 'ia'u ko'u 'ohana! It has been so very long, I went to gather mea'ai for our twins and when I returned home you were gone! I feared the worse. They must be starving to death, give this to them quickly!"

Pa'awai, ecstatic at her man's return, presented the items to the youths but they refused to consume them and continued to howl. Lightning cracked and thunder boomed reverberating off of the valley walls like an amphitheater.

Their father, in a confused state, expressed his concern, "I don't understand why they are refusing it.

There is enough mana in this to keep them going for a very long time!"

Pa'awai hid her face behind their children and began to weep, "Auwē! I was tormented by their cries, so I closed them up in the deepest part of the valley behind stone walls. As I searched for food for them, their cries grew more angry and much louder. Forgive me! I tried everything from mauka to makai until I found a creature in the forest, and..."

Pa'awai's husband flashed his wings in the moonlight, "Please tell me you did not feed kānaka to our children!?"

Pa'awai could only weep, "You left me all alone with their hunger..."

Once more he whipped his wings and they snapped in unison with the thunder, "Finding the mana needed for one child is hard enough, twins required me to make haste. But alas, I was not swift enough. Pa'awai, our children have feasted upon man, he kāne! This means they will always yearn for their life's blood! It is kapu for our kind to endanger the kānaka let alone feast upon them!"

Pa'awai stared blankly at her spouse slowly letting his words sink in.

"There are only two things we can do from here, Pa'awai. We flee Hava'iki, never to expose our family to the kānaka ever again, where our children will suffer to die a painful and slow death of starvation..." Pa'awai

began to weep as her love spoke in a soft whisper, "or, I can end their suffering here and now."

Pa'awai's tail thrashed and her eyes burned a glowing scarlet. "Stay back!" she hissed as she coiled around her babies. "I will never let any harm come to them!"

Her husband looked away at the stars and announced, "Forgive me and my wife! There is nothing that I can do but forfeit my life to allow my 'ohana to stay in our birth sands."

A loud, sharp whistle trumpeted through the night sky and was followed by a multitude of voices that sang as one, calling out, "Eō!" This would be the very last time Pa'awai would see her husband ever again. With a white hot flash he was gone.

She gazed up into the tree tops and thought she saw him high up in the canopy, but all she found there was a silent, little creature baring his wings.

"My love, is that you?" Pa'awai called cautiously so as not to frighten this smaller version of her beloved.

The creature opened its large beautiful eyes and looked directly at Pa'awai, responding sternly to her with a single word, "Who?" It opened its wings and flew out of the valley toward the moon.

Pa'awai was grateful for the sacrifice her love made to keep their family safe. She would always remember that. Her children's cries brought her back from reflection. Now it was time to find a way to sustain her children and satisfy their cravings. It was time to hunt for more kānaka.

‘Ehiku

Kaimi’s eye were round as saucers and his mouth was agape. Rayna saw how the story had affected Kaimi and to snap him out of his bewilderment she bellowed, “So, what does the name Kauaopa‘awai have to do with Makalike? What purpose did it serve to change the original name in the first place?”

Wagging his finger and pushing himself off the corner of his desk, Mr. Kahi explained, “Right! Originally the name Kauaopa‘awai, or the rains of Pa‘awai, came from the tears of the distraught mother. She cried because her children had become ‘aikānaka and she needed to keep them alive throughout the centuries on man’s lifeblood. The tales of the lizard lady that would steal away with unattended children from the rivers edge would weigh heavy on the community. Later, the name was changed because of that evil history. They wanted to name it after the cliff faces and their naturally odd symmetry. But ironically, Pa‘awai’s offspring were kupua. As they got older, they were able to effectively hunt for man, and children, on their own.”

Most of the class presented uneasy faces that looked as if they never wanted to travel over Makalike ever again, but Mr. Kahi could see that Rayna still needed a bit more clarification. He added, "Kupua are shapeshifters. The twins have the capability to change their form into any of their victims, Miss Agbayani. So, to get to my long winded point, Makalike doesn't mean 'Same Face', it means 'Shared Face'."

It was at that moment the bell announcing the end of the school day blasted, causing the students to shudder in their seats.

Mr. Kahi spun around and turned on the lights, "Well, class, you can thank Mr. Lee and Miss Agbayani for saving you from homework, but be warned it is coming. Have a fantastic day you're all dismissed."

Rayna made her way over to the opposite side of the class. "Kaimi, I appreciate what you did for me back there…" Rayna's eyes widened as she raised her hand to cover her nose. She quickly and awkwardly headed toward the door at high speed.

Kaimi watched Rayna scurry out of the classroom in a rush. "*What the heck was that all about?*" he thought as he shrugged his shoulders and confronted Keoki once more.

"So? We going Makalike?" he asked his pal one last time.

Keoki was still recovering from Mr. Kahi's mo'olelo, "Brother, let me tell you, that story nearly scared the mud out of me, and when the school bell rang I soiled my drawers!"

Kaimi now understood why Rayna ran off so abruptly. He covered his nose and cried out, "Dammit, Keoki! Not again!"

'Ewalu

Wili snuck up behind Kaimi as he walked along the gravel path from school, "Eh, I heard yo' frien' needed fo' run home an' change his bibadeez!"

Kaimi glanced back and raised his shoulders, "Mr. Kahi gave da class a fright wit' one of his mo'olelo."

Wili snorted and said mid chuckle, "Brah, dat Mr. Kahi has some wild tales! Which one he wen' talk about? Da Night Macha's? Da Menehune's?"

Kaimi huffed, "Da mo'o up at Makalike!"

Wili trotted around his younger brother with knees bent and arms stretched outward, "Ho ho ho! Mr. Kahi wen' bus out da Limu Lady? Brah dat story is classic! Trippy dat he wen' bus 'em out today of all days, yeah?"

Kaimi squinted at Wili as he made a third pass, "Wait, you knew about Pa'awai an' nevah say nuttin'?"

Wili dropped his arms and straightened his frame. He could see that Kaimi was more than unsettled about the story Mr. Kahi shared, "Eh, take it easy, bruddah. No worry beef curry, you not sked of one myt', ah? Look, it's all fun an' games wit' Mr. Kahi. Dat guy jus' shares doze stories fo' help us remembah da facts. It's like, da kine, what dat? Oh yeah! New Mammary Device!"

Kaimi could see that Wili was very proud of himself, "You mean mnemonic?"

Wili popped up like bread from a toaster, "What evahs!" He twitched his head as they continued on their way down the road.

The smell of steamy asphalt caused Kaimi to take a gander at the mountain tops as they turned up Makalike Road. He didn't like the heavy gray clouds gathering about the disappearing summit. Kaimi could make out faint jets of moisture climbing the steep cliffside, weaving in and out of the thin tree trunks covering the mountain as they finally got lost in the billowy mass above.

"I don't know, Wili! Looks like going rain pretty hahd."

As if by coincidence, a light mist started to spray over both of the boys and the air became thicker. It made Kaimi believe that something was attempting to turn them both away to save them from some unknown fate. Kaimi decided to plea once more to his brother.

"Wili, might get flash flood. You t'ink maybe we should come back latahs?"

Wili just kept trucking his way up the hill without slowing, "Nah, if get enough rain, we can safely jump from da bridge! An den I can show off to Kenani!"

Repulsed, Kaimi shivered visually and wondered, *What is it about Kenani dat makes Wili so crazy?*' He continued his thoughts as they went down the bend, *Kenani actually does look like 'Alapaki wit' one 'ehu wig… Not dat 'Alapaki is gross looking, but I mean come on! At some point day goin' be making out an' you mean to tell me not once is he gonna t'ink, 'Sup, 'Alapaki'!?*

They continued around the second curve, finally coming upon the almost hidden trail that led down to the water's edge below Makalike Bridge.

Wili cast his gaze down the steps at first and then scanned across the bridge as if in search of something or someone.

Kaimi questioned, "So what den? Wea stay 'Alapaki dem?"

Wili shrugged his shoulders as he headed down the path bounding from rock to rock. Kaimi kept pace as rain droplets began to form on their hair.

"Eh, Kaimi, try look!" Wili pointed up stream as the waters rose.

Kaimi could see that the water was at a nice depth to safely dive from the bridge. Wili looked over from the edge of the stream and dove into the brisk running waters. He searched thoroughly to make sure that there weren't any random debris or hazards hidden under the bubbling surface of the stream inside the jump zone.

Kaimi focused on where Wili plunged into the water and after about a minute grew concerned. Just before he decided to make a leap in after his brother, Wili's head broke through the rough top of the stream. "How's it!?"

"Puuwah!" Wili took in a deep breath, "Fricken rock." Wili shook his head to get the water out of his hair and eyes, "Brah, had one random stone sitting right in da spot. Guarens ball barrens we would've cracked 'ulu! Had to push 'em ovah!" Wili escaped the current and splashed ice cold water over Kaimi. "But da weirdest t'ing, it look like somebody wen' place da rock right in dat spot on purpose. Buggah was straight up an' small kine lodged between smaller rocks." Wili angled his hands right towards the area the tall rock was fixed.

A third voice cut into the conversation falling from above. "Sup, Wili?! How's da watah?" The boys could see 'Alapaki descending the trail and it appeared as though he already had some annoying quip to unload on Kaimi, "Sup, scrub?" 'Alapaki blurted as he made his way passed. "Eh, Wili, looks like da watah is cherreh! We go up!" 'Alapaki motioned his head toward the bridge. As he turned to go back up the lava rock stairs he shoulder checked Kaimi into a growth of laua'e. "Try move, skid mark."

Wili rushed over to help his brother out of the brush. He made sure he wasn't hurt by looking him over carefully and immediately tailed 'Alapaki. Kaimi followed them up but left some breathing room to allow some time for Wili to question why 'Alapaki was always so nasty to him.

When 'Alapaki and Wili got to the bridge they stood with toes curled around the edge. Wili looked over at 'Alapaki and asked, "Brah, I taught you said Kenani was coming!"

Wili waited calmly for a response, but 'Alapaki just turned his gaze up to the clouds and let the rain pummel his face for a moment. Kaimi made it to the top just in time to hear his brother make no attempt to defend him.

'Alapaki smirked, "Kenani? She'll be hea soon, cuz." He cast his gaze at the jumping spot and back toward Wili. With a crazy look in his eyes 'Alapaki challenged him, "Age befoah beauty."

Wili looked down at the rushing stream and back at 'Alapaki. He let out a shriek as he leapt from the bridge, "Chee-hoo!!!"

Kaimi witnessed 'Alapaki quickly drop to his hands and knees closely observing Wili's descent. In no time there was a giant splash accompanied by what sounded like a boulder falling into the ocean. Patoomba! When Wili emerged unscathed 'Alapaki pressed himself back up to his feet without effort and had a look of utter disappointment hanging from his face. Kaimi thought his behavior was stranger than usual, but his tormenter stood eerily still with eyes widened, focused on Wiliami. After a short moment, 'Alapaki's gaze gradually moved in Kaimi's direction.

He yelled at the meek boy causing him to twitch, "What!?" 'Alapaki felt his power over Kaimi growing, "Go back down losah, we boat know you not going jump."

Even though 'Alapaki scared the heck out of Kaimi, he stood as tall as his spine would allow to even out their height differential. The words of his friend Keoki resonated in his head. Kaimi refused to be a punching bag to 'Alapaki any longer. He scrounged up what little bravery he had within him and walked right over to his aggressor.

"What's yo' deal, 'Alapaki?" Kaimi's voice squeaked causing him to clear his throat. He began to quiver from the combination of fear and ice cold rain dashing against his unintimidating frame.

"Deal? What deal?" 'Alapaki looked back down toward the stream for a minute, watching Wili looking around like a lost puppy. "You know, your braddah has some mayjah mana, I kid you not. But you? You just steal his mana like one mana vampiah! You always need Wili fo' fight yo' battles an' help you out of a tough spot. How is dat fair fo' Wili? Always needing to babysit his scrawny little braddah all da time, you not shame?"

Kaimi was burning behind his eyes and he just about had enough of 'Alapaki's pretentious prattle, "I nevah ask Wili fo' fight my battles, I nevah evah played a victim so he would come running, an' I most certainly do not suck my braddah's mana!"

'Alapaki was a bit taken aback by Kaimi's assertion. He never seen this weak, fragile pest so passionate. The fury was glowing from behind those once immature dewey eyes. He withdrew his intimidating stance and took a step back to take a better look at his opposition.

Wili glanced up at the two young men and tossed an inquiry of concern, "Kaimi! You good?"

Turning away from 'Alapaki he looked down and acknowledged his brother with a nod. Wili immediately remembered that Kenani was supposed to be there soon, if she wasn't there already. He quickly scanned the area to see if she was around to watch him make the leap.

"How was dat jump? Mean, yeah?" Wili tried to play it cool and not sound too desperate as he fished for compliments.

'Alapaki dropped a shaka and turned his attention back toward Kaimi, "Tell you what, you jump from dis bridge an' I'll leave you alone from now on. In fact, I'll treat you moah like I treat yo' braddah."

Without hesitation, 'Alapaki leaned off the side of the bridge and fell into the stream with barely a splash.

He took a while to resurface, but when he did ‘Alapaki had a strange grin emblazoned across his face and his eyes shot through the rain with a menacing white flash that pierced straight through Kaimi’s heart.

The storm grew fierce, with beads of water that had doubled in size pelting Kaimi unceasingly in his already sensitive back. It felt like even mother nature was forcing Kaimi to take the plunge.

“I gotta jump if I want to be free from dis clown.” Kaimi took quick sharp breaths to try to raise his core temperature before making the leap. His body shivered and teeth chattered, but he was determined to finally stand up for himself.

The stream was rushing harder as ‘Alapaki and Wili tried their best to stare up into the falling rain. Both boys awaited Kaimi’s decent into the fast flowing waters with differing expectations. ‘Alapaki decided to remind Kaimi why he was attempting the endeavor.

“Just climb back down, mento. We know you no moah da sacks!”

Kaimi nodded, he had finally convinced himself to leap, *If I jump ‘Alapaki will treat me bettah, if I die I won’t need to worry about his bullying. Either way, I win.* But, as Kaimi was about to step foot off the bridge he could see something moving swiftly from the corner of his eye. Just down the stream, at the edge of the forest, Kaimi saw a large shadow curl around the base of a tree that sat in line with the kahawai. Whatever it was, it was big and it was fast. He stepped back, firmly planting his feet onto the bridge, and focused his eyes toward the bizarre movement. Again, he could see the shadow figure but it was slightly obstructed by the falling rain. He followed it until it crawled its way into the stream heading right toward the two boys below.

"Just come back down already, panty. No need prove yourself!" 'Alapaki continued to goad Kaimi.

Wili finally countered his overly eager friend and called out to his brother, "Eh, Kaimi, pau!"

Wili motioned toward Kaimi with a gentle wave. He pulled his left arm through the stream a few times encouraging his brother to come down off the bridge.

"Kaimi, no need jump. It's okay. You don't have to prove yourself to me or 'Alapaki."

Wili could see Kaimi was looking off somewhere else and not really focusing on him or the dive. Wili turned to observe what it was that unnerved his brother, but he could not find anything out of the ordinary.

'Alapaki saw this as his chance to really dig into Kaimi, "Yup, see!? Yo' braddah gotta come save yo' face again!" The rant ended with a barrage of high pitched yelps. 'Alapaki's cackles harmonized with the sounds of the stream.

Wili splashed a palm full of water at 'Alapaki causing him to stop his laughter. He defended Kaimi by leaning into his comrade, "Enough already, brah!" Wili shook his head and decided to give 'Alapaki an ultimatum, even at the risk of never going steady with Kenani. "You're too much sometimes, 'Alapaki. We're tight, but I'd gladly sacrifice dis friendship fo' my braddah dat I've known since we boat shared ouah maddah's 'ōpū!"

'Alapaki glanced at Wili with a confused look and responded, "You an' Kaimi are twins?"

After that small realization, 'Alapaki threw his gaze back up to the top of Makalike Bridge at the fearful teenager shivering in the rain. Wili was astonished by the look 'Alapaki gave Kaimi and he was startled when his eyes flashed a reflective white, like the eyes of a nocturnal predator.

Standing at the middle of the bridge, Kaimi could see the long dark shadow making its way through the water. He lost sight of it once it got to the deeper part of the stream near the jump zone. Kaimi's fear grew and he lost his ability to speak or move. It was as if he were paralyzed, feeling helpless once again, shivering in the falling rain. His eyes began to tear as he witnessed an inhuman face slowly emerging from behind both Wili and 'Alapaki. The creature finally revealed itself and Kaimi could clearly see a green scaly skinned monster with long dark stringy hair that looked like limu 'ele'ele. His thoughts burst in his head, *She's real! Da lizahd leddeh is real... an' she's looking fo' her nex' victim!*

Kaimi saw its arms rise out of the water and started to reach out toward Wili. *No! Not Wili!* Kaimi willed himself to move and broke free from his possessed state. He bent over and heaved a large rock above his head and took aim down below.

'Alapaki's eyes widened as he saw a completely different Kaimi positioned in a threatening manner. He yelled out, "Wili, is yo' braddah fo' real right now?"

Wili raised both of his arms up to stop Kaimi, "Whoah, whoah, whoah Kaimi! Put da rock down! 'Alapaki didn't mean anyt'ing by it!" Wili tried to plea with his brother not realizing that there was a bigger threat than 'Alapaki's insolence.

Kaimi saw the mo'owahine jet forward with her arms outstretched. Within an instant Kaimi let loose the rock with all his might just as lightning pulsed and thunder clashed. Everything began to move at half speed. Kaimi saw the rock that was illuminated by the electrical discharge slowly growing smaller. His eyes focused on the action below as he watched the mo'owahine grab Wili pulling him into the path of the falling stone. He became terrified at the thought that he just sentenced his brother to death with that astonishingly erroneous decision. Before the rock made contact, Kaimi felt something hit him from the side knocking him down to the ground. Kaimi smacked his head against the bridge and everything started to become hazy. He could hear a muffled voice as his eyes went black. For a brief moment Kaimi could see again. He strained his eyes to see straight and cast his gaze down stream. Just before blacking out completely, he could see Wili's limp body flowing down the red tainted stream.

Friday

'Eiwa

Kaimi's skull throbbed to the rhythm of Wili's voice echoing in his head, "Kaimi, are you alright!?"

He could feel a warm hand slowly and carefully wiping across his wet forehead. The rain had stopped for the time being. The air was still and everything was quiet around the two boys. Maybe a little too quiet. Kaimi opened his eyes and saw Wili smiling a wide grin cradling his head over his lap.

"Whooo, braddah! Dat was one mean fall, no? You feelin' okay?"

Kaimi started to tear and expressed regret, "I'm so sorry, Wili! I nevah intend to hurt you."

Wili gently removed Kaimi's head from his lap and stood to his feet. Laying vulnerable on the cold hard bridge, Kaimi looked up at his brother's deformed silhouette. The sun shined so bright behind Wili that it blinded him.

Wili declared, "Tsa! You'll be alright, Kaimi. As long as I'm around, you'll be alright."

Wili's silhouette slowly dissolved and Kaimi was left with the brightest light he had ever seen burning into his face. He could hear voices softly mumbling in the distance. Pain emanated from his ribs and right side temple. A slow, high pitched beep repeated over and over until he realized where he was.

An angelic voice sang in Kaimi's ear, "Well hello there, young man. Did you have a nice nap? I'm your nurse, Yvonne."

Kaimi's eyes were blurred and could only make out a petite, indistinguishable pink and white shape that moved at a brisk pace.

The sound of the woman's voice spoke once more, "You have some visitors here to see you, Kaimi. Policemen. You haven't been getting into any trouble have you?"

He followed the form around the room until it disappeared behind a brown blob. Soon after, a pair of severe foot steps marched through the same brown hazy shape that Kaimi now understood to be doors.

The smell of stale cologne and cigarette ash wafted through the air followed by a deep raspy tone that was a stark contrast to nurse Yvonne's voice, "Kaimi, I am Detective Barshaw and this is Detective Takao. We have a few questions we'd like to ask you if you are up to it." Kaimi could hear a soft wheeze in the detective's chest.

Before the injured boy could even say a word, he was jolted by a loud slam and the sound of a familiar, yet perturbed voice, "Excuse me detectives, but I don't t'ink it's alright fo' you to come an' bahddah one kid dat just suffah'd some mayjah kine injuries!"

Kaimi could hear his father ranting like a mad man, being all overly dramatic.

Detective Barshaw placed his arm across Kaimi's father's shoulders, "Mr. Lee, we just need to get some closure here. We already have statements from a witness, as well as the young man and his sister your son was at the bridge with. We just need to ask Kaimi a few questions and we'll get out of both of your hair."

Mr. Lee sat in the chair beside Kaimi's bed and watched with scrutiny as the detective questioned his boy.

"So, Kaimi, could you please tell me why you were endangering others at Makalike bridge this afternoon?"

Kaimi could now smell a hint of coffee piercing through the old scent of cologne, which, at the moment was the only way he could identify the detective since his eyes were still pretty messed up.

Kaimi's voice was hoarse, "Ummm, yeah. So, we went up Makalike fo' go swim an' jump off da bridge an' mess aroun'. I saw my braddah an'..." Kaimi stopped speaking, choking back his saliva and stalling his hysteria. He envisioned the shape of his brother's body flowing down stream and began to panic.

Detective Takao came around to the opposite side of Kaimi and rested his hand over his shoulder, "It's okay, Kaimi. When you're ready you can continue."

The warmth of Detective Takao's hand soothed Kaimi and he could feel his heart rate slowing and the throbbing in his head lessening.

Detective Barshaw looked up at Detective Takao and continued with a softer tone, "Kaimi, we know why you all went to the stream. What we don't understand is why you decided to throw stones at the others! We have an eye witness, a Mr. Pacheco, who said you threw a large rock off of the bridge attempting to cause serious bodily harm to one of, if not all of those youths. He said he tried to stop you by tackling you down but he was too late and you had already cast the stone. What was going through your mind? You could have seriously hurt someone or even worse, you could've killed somebody. You do realize that you could be prosecuted as an adult for attempted murder, right!?" Detective Barshaw's eyes were round in seriousness.

Kaimi brushed off the leftover stuttering in his breathing, "Okay, alright, hea's what I remembah. I was at da top, da middle of da bridge. 'Alapaki was teasing me about being too sked fo' jump. Just before I take da leap I wen' see one strange shadow, one non-human shadow, working its way out of da forest moving toward my braddah an' 'Alapaki. I wen' back away from da edge an' picked up one big rock off da ground. Den I tossed it at da monstah before it could hurt my braddah dem." Kaimi began to dry heave as the vision of his brother's lifeless body flowing down stream popped back into his head. He then blurted, "I was hit to da ground an' das all I remembah." Kaimi pressed his head into his pillow avoiding the truth. The truth that he had killed the one person who had always been there to protect him. Kaimi began to sob.

Detective Barshaw pinched his eyebrows together, "Kaimi, 'Alapaki said that you show animosity toward him daily, in and out of school. He said you're jealous of his and your brother's relationship, and you threatened to hurt him to get them to stop being friends." The detective locked his fingers together and leaned back in his stance, "'Alapaki says you threw the rock directly at him."

Kaimi popped his head out from the pillow sounding a bit crazed, "Dat's not what happened!" Kaimi's heart began to pound, "You gotta believe me. Had dis creacha an' it was trying fo' grab my braddah..." Kaimi looked toward the brown and blue blob that sat in a chair beside him, "Dad, you believe me, yeah? I promise, dat's da whole trute!"

The detective placed his hands into his pockets, "Okay then, if this is how your story goes, we'll just need to corroborate your story with Wiliami's once he finally shows up. 'Alapaki and Kenani had a completely different sequence of events that conflict with your statement, but your brother could help us find clarity. Mr. Lee could you please let us know immediately once your son, Wili, shows up so we can get to the bottom of this ordeal?" Detective Barshaw handed Kaimi's father a business card with his number on it.

"Shoowah t'ing, Detective," Mr. Lee took hold of the card.

Kaimi, not fully happy with the conclusion of this exchange, blurted out, "Mistah Detectives!" Both Barshaw and Takao turned to look at Kaimi, "What did 'Alapaki say about Wili? Wea my braddah stay?"

Pulling his chin in toward his neck Detective Barshaw responded, "'Alapaki and his sister both said that your brother took off after he saw you knocked to the ground. Apparently, they said he didn't want to get into trouble too."

"But, dat's not right! I, I saw..." Kaimi had a flashback of Wili's body flowing down stream once more, "I, I saw... I *nevah* saw Kenani at da stream! 'Alapaki told my braddah dat she was coming, but she nevah showed up!" Kaimi began tearing once more.

Detective Barshaw looked at the ground with a shrug on his mouth, "Get some rest young man." Barshaw looked at Kaimi's father and confided, "Mr. Lee, make sure to check in with the doctor about

Kaimi's head trauma. We don't want anything rattling around up there. Have a good evening."

Detective Takao gave a squeeze over Mr. Lee's shoulder, "Sir, please reach out to me if you learn anything new. I am very concerned for you and your boys." He handed Kaimi's father his contact information and continued, "Call me anytime." Detective Takao nodded sincerely as he left the room.

Takao caught up with Detective Barshaw on their way to the lift, "I gotta say, Brent, that boy seemed mighty honest in what he believed he experienced. Waterworks like that aren't very common in liars. Strange story nonetheless, but he sounded so sure of what he experienced."

"He could just be a good actor, but I think you might be onto something, Reed." Detective Barshaw jabbed the down button for the elevator, "It might be a good idea to check on those De Souza kids again once we have a word with the other Lee boy. These testimonies are too different to ignore." The elevator doors shook open and both men entered pondering the possibility that there was a creature roaming around Makalike.

After the detectives had gone, Mr. Lee sat at Kaimi's side waiting for word on his condition. He stared at his son, but Kaimi never made a motion. He seemed deep in thought, and looked guilty about something.

"You know, Kaimi, I'm a little disappointed in your braddah. Why he wen' run off laddat? Bad enough I get da cops accusing you of attempting fo' kill somebody, an' I know you nevah, but yo' braddah just digging out laddat is somet'ing else. It's so unlike him."

Nurse Yvonne walked into the room and handed some paperwork to Mr. Lee to look over and sign. "You should be on your way home soon, Kaimi. After Dr. Lawrence comes back to check on you, he'll give you both some information and you can hand him those papers, signed, Mr. Lee." She began tidying up just as the doctor popped in with some good news.

"Alright Kaimi, we are discharging you soon. How are your eyes?"

Kaimi tried focusing on the doctor's face, but his vision was only slightly better than when he first woke up, "Why everyt'ing stay so blurry?" Kaimi squinted and blinked as if it would snap his vision back to normal.

The doctor pulled up Kaimi's left brow to examine his eye, "It's typical for patients that suffer from a concussion to experience convergence insufficiency." The doctor could see Mr. Lee struggling to understand what it all meant. "So, Mr. Lee, you are going to want to stop by the pharmacy to pick up some Ibuprofen to ease Kaimi's pain. He could use an ice pack on the area of impact to reduce swelling. Do that twice a day. His vision should return to normal, nothing to be too concerned about. I will have the nurse pull a wheelchair around to help you two out to the car." The doctor signed off on a clip board and handed it to the nurse. "Oh! Mr. Lee you'll probably need to help your son into bed when you get home." The doctor looked at Kaimi and patted his knee, "There may be some nausea due to balance issues, I'm sure you'll be more than happy to snack on some crystallized ginger to help with that." The doctor smiled at his patient and winked at his dad as he left the Lee's to gather their things.

Kaimi didn't care the least about his nausea. His heart was being torn apart by the loss of his brother and his brain ached from confusion as to why 'Alapaki hadn't told the authorities the truth about what really happened at the bridge. He thought, *What really happened to my braddah? What happened to Wili?*

Friday

'Umi

Kaimi found himself once more at the edge of Makalike bridge. The rain pelted the skin on his arms, back and shoulders as he held a large rock above his head. He could see the mo'owahine clearly emerging from the waters below reaching toward his brother. Kaimi could hear Wili pleading with him to put the rock down.

He paused for a moment because 'Alapaki had captured his attention. He could see that he had taken on a new form. A form that matched the evil that dwelled within him. 'Alapaki's face stretched and became longer around his mouth, as if he now had a muzzle. His eyes were lit with a piercing white light and he exhibited his spear like fangs. His lips were twitching as they furled over his gums baring long sharp rows of ivory spikes. Kaimi dropped the rock at his feet. His anxiety had taken on a life of its own and became a vision of terror that paralyzed him.

Why do I let 'Alapaki have dis powah ovah me!? Kaimi thought as he remembered all the torment he had let the jerk put him through. The pain of those memories fed the fire within him. It burned red hot like a furnace. Kaimi reasoned, *I won't let da feeyah of being bullied stop me from saving my braddah!*

Kaimi took a slight step back and then lunged forward vaulting himself off the bridge. He aimed his sights down at the mo'owahine that snuck behind Wili to keep her from hurting him, but something stopped Kaimi on his way down.

A sharp, intense pain burned over his left calf as he dangled midair. Feeling the blood rushing to his head, Kaimi screamed in agony as warm liquid exited his body and ran down to his thigh. He looked below to see the mo'owahine pulling Wili's head underwater. 'Alapaki beamed a deranged smile and licked his long tongue over jagged teeth as he looked up at his prey. Kaimi turned to see that there was another creature that looked the same as 'Alapaki, gnawing into his leg. He swung the heel of his free leg into the monster's eye which caused it to yelp. The beast growled at Kaimi relinquishing its toothy grip. He fell head first toward the stream below as 'Alapaki extended the opening of his mouth inhumanly wide to devour his incoming prey. The last thing Kaimi saw was 'Alapaki's jaws shut around his head with the sound of a loud crunch.

Kaimi bolted up out of bed with heavy breath. His head pounded and he felt like he needed to vomit. He reached over to his night stand, tossed a couple of pieces of ginger into his mouth and slowly lowered himself back down onto his damp pillow. Tears fell down Kaimi's cheeks finding their way to his ears and finally disappearing into his head cushion. He said a soft prayer then uttered, "Wili, I'm so sorry."

A strange sensation fell over Kaimi. His heart beat in his chest faster while the shadows in his bedroom teased at his overactive mind. His imagination created some very horrific shapes that flew around in search of any and all unlit spaces to remain ambiguous.

Kaimi could hear footsteps in the grass outside of his bedroom window. He began to reason, *Dat's not my imagination!*

Kaimi pulled himself up to his feet and searched through the darkness for whatever, or whoever, was creeping around in his back yard. His eyes peered through the pitch of night until finally the clouds cleared away exposing the face of the moon. The reflected light revealed what was once invisible to Kaimi's already blurred vision. He saw what looked like a tall, lanky shadow of a distorted person standing under his mango tree. It had long limbs, a crooked spine, and eyes that sparkled from the faint light of the moon. It didn't move an inch. It just stared toward Kaimi's home. The odd visual put the young teen into a quiet panic.

His heart nearly stopped when he heard a loud slam come from next door, originating from his brother's room. Without hesitation Kaimi made his way to Wili's quarters, moving as fast as he possibly could. He stopped a second before entering the door, his heart now pounding just under his jaw. He hoped and prayed his brother would appear before him so everything would be alright again, but sadly, as he pressed the door open, Kaimi was greeted only by a dark, lifeless sleeping area. He could see that Wili's bedroom window was propped back in the open position and the chilly air was blowing through with an odd, sickly smell attached to it.

Kaimi made his way over to the portal to secure it. As he grabbed hold of the frame's latch, he witnessed a large shadow cut through the lawn from right below the window's sill. It ran swiftly toward the mango tree at the edge of their property. Kaimi could now see three glowing orbs dancing in the tree's shadow staring back at the window. The eerie white dots eyed the young man and made the hairs all over his body stand up on end.

"Dis is not real…," Kaimi squealed, as a car made a turn and flashed him in the face with its headlights. When his eyes adjusted to the dark again, Kaimi could see that both silhouettes had disappeared.

Kaimi was left with a feeling of intrusion. His safe place had come under siege by an unknown force that he was not prepared for. He could only think about 'Alapaki and how right he truly was. *Wit'out Wili aroun', I am so helpless.*

Kaimi decided to spend the rest of the night sleeping in Wiliami's bed. He was too miserable to move and felt much more at peace surrounded by his brother's possessions. He could feel Wili's mana all around him and it made him feel safer. Kaimi laid Wili's hoodie over his chest and tried to fall asleep in hopes of not having any more unwanted intruders or being startled awake by night terrors.

The last thing Kaimi thought before dozing off was, *Somet'ing strange is happening... an' I don't t'ink I can handle dis on my own.*

Saturday

ʻUmi kūmākahi

The next day Kaimi woke up to the sound of his father hooting and hollering in a one-sided conversation. He could barely make out what his dad was saying, but Kaimi knew it wasn't a game. His father never raised his voice unless he believed it was important. Kaimi poked his face out of Wili's room to get a better sense of what was happening.

"I need you to do it by today, you understand!?" Mr. Lee hung the phone up and stroked the top of his head.

Kaimi made his way out of the door way, "Everyt'ing okay, pop?"

Kaimi's dad walked over to the sink and grabbed a cup out of the dish rack to fill with some water. "I don't know what da heck is goin' on wit' da boat of you, but I am not happy wit' da current status of dis household!" Mr. Lee took three large gulps and placed his cup back in the dish rack. He took a moment to breathe and ease his heart rate. He could see his boy standing at the end of the hall stabilizing himself against the door frame. "How's your eyes, Kaimi!?" Mr. Lee inquired in a softer tone.

Kaimi squinted a bit and cast his gaze across several textures in the kitchen, "Nah, I'll be okay, Dad. Getting bettah. Who stay on da phone?"

Kaimi's dad shook his head looking down toward his feet, "I hope you not up to somet'ing when it comes to yo' braddah, Kaimi!"

Kaimi's heart started to pound as several questions popped into his mind, *Was it da detectives from da hospital? Did day fine Wili's body? Did day fine only pieces of Wili? Just his bones?* As Kaimi's hand went over his stomach, his dad took notice of the odd behavior.

"I need you to be honest wit' me, Kaimi! I don't know why one of my boys is tossing rocks at people an' da addah jus' flat out takes off an' leaves da addah behine!" Kaimi's dad walked over to the kitchen table and snapped up his car keys and his wallet. "I gotta go in to work today, my boss is taking some family leave an' I need to fill in fo' him until he gets back. I'm sorry I can't keep an eye on you today, but since you're feeling a bit bettah I have peace of mine in knowing you be alright."

Kaimi was a bit nervous being home all alone. He worried that he would have no peace if left with his overactive imagination. He couldn't stop thinking about who it was his dad was yelling at. The stress of it all started to make him feel woozy.

Mr. Lee finally provided some light, "Oh, I told your braddah dat he needs fo' get his 'okole home right away an' help you out today."

Kaimi let out a massive breath and blurted, "Wait, you wen' talk to Wili, Dad!?"

"Yeah! Das yo' braddah, no? Anyways, I told him he needs fo' get his butt home 'cause I need him fo' watch you." Kaimi's dad started for the front door, "Maybe dis 'Alapaki kid is not so good fo' you guys hang out wit'. Making Wili do some t'ings dat I would nevah imagine him doing... an' da way yo' braddah spoke to me! So disrespectful!" Mr. Lee walked over to the front door and apologized for being so loud earlier, "I nevah meant to wake you up laddat, Kaimi." Mr. Lee continued out of the house down the porch stairs and opened his vehicle's door, "Kaimi, just go eat den lay down an' rest. I see you boys latah on tonight." Kaimi's dad slid into his truck's seat and drove off within moments.

Kaimi stood at the front door watching his dad grow blurrier as he travelled down the road. He thought about what he experienced at the bridge and replayed the moment over and over trying to understand how this was possible, *Well, I nevah actually saw da rock smash Wili's head.* Kaimi turned to enter back into his house. *Maybe it was just my imagination that I saw him float down stream.* He felt a load of worry immediately fall from his shoulders and the sinking feeling in his stomach slowly disappeared, *Wili! T'ank you, God. He's alive.*

'Umi kūmālua

Detective Barshaw exited the café and walked over to his car holding onto two cups of hot coffee. He scanned the area to discover that his partner had made his way over to a wooden fence across the road. Barshaw trotted across the empty street and stood beside his colleague as he aimed to catch his breath. Reed stood quietly, with a determined expression fixed upon his face, directly in front of several missing person's posters all of the same individual. They were posters Mary Lou Ribeiro had stapled up of her missing daughter. Some of them had faded a bit and others were a lot more weathered, but Cheylene's face could still be seen clearly in the one Reed observed. The missing teen was a pretty, young woman with the appearance of someone that had it all together.

Barshaw handed Detective Takao a cup of Joe, "Everything alright, Reed?" Detective Takao, as if in a trance, never broke his gaze. Barshaw pressed the back of his hand into Takao's forearm encouraging him to take the drink, "Reed!?"

Takao blinked as he brought his hand to his face smearing his thumb and forefinger across his eye lids. "Oh, thanks boss!" Reed accepted the coffee and sniffed his watery nose.

Barshaw eyed the poster for a moment, "That one there, she had a very good start. Loving parents, active in the community and sharp as a whip. I still don't understand why she would run away like that. Broke her mother's heart, it did."

Takao nodded his head and took a sip from his steaming cup, "Doesn't make a lick of sense, Brent." Reed sucked on his tongue to get rid of the sting, "Maybe her mother was onto something."

Detective Barshaw's eyes wandered slightly upward while he tried his best to recall what Mrs. Ribeiro had said. "Remind me again, Reed."

Detective Takao shook his head swiftly as if moving the pieces of that case to the front of his mind, "Mrs. Ribeiro believed Cheylene had suffered some kind of head trauma. The damage was so great it caused a sort of amnesia."

Barshaw's chest popped up as one side of his face winced, "Amnesia?"

"Well, that's not the point." Detective Takao continued, "She actually witnessed Cheylene traveling through the reserve up north. When she tried calling out to her, Mary Lou said Cheylene looked at her, ducked back into the forest and disappeared. It was the last time anyone had ever seen her."

"Correction!" Detective Barshaw interrupted. "The last time 'her mother' had ever seen her."

Detective Takao furrowed his eyebrows. "Are you insinuating Mary Lou lied about seeing her child, her very own daughter, that day?"

Brent raised his right brow. "Well, sometimes when we go through some terrible events we start taking less care of ourselves and just maybe she hadn't gotten enough sleep, or maybe she imagined that a girl that was around that area could've been her daughter. I'd've been frightened off too if some stranger called out to me by the wrong name." Barshaw rested his case.

Takao slowly blinked while bobbing his head. "Yeah, I suppose you're right."

Detective Barshaw squeezed Detective Takao over his upper arm. "You have a good heart, Reed. I'm sure Cheylene will pop up one day. How far can you go on an island, right?" Brent stepped away from his partner.

Reed heard a voice calling him from the back of his head. It repeated over and over, *Take the poster.* He reached up and yanked the newest copy off of the wall. He folded it gently and placed it into his jacket pocket.

Both detectives made their way back to their car nearly getting banged by a rusty red Toyota truck. "Eh, detectives, you like die oah what!?"

Detective Barshaw was surprised to see Mr. Lee pop up right at that second. "Speak of the devil! Good morning, Mr. Lee." He pat the truck's hood as if it were a large dog.

"Eh, why? You guys stay talking stink about me?" Mr. Lee shrugged his shoulders.

Detective Takao leaned in toward Mr. Lee's window. "No, sir. We were just talking about the children in the area and how they've been running off from the comforts of their own homes. Strange happenings on our quiet island."

Barshaw bounced in and asked, "Sir, did Wili make it home safe and sound?"

Mr. Lee pressed his lips, bending the corners of his mouth upward. "Yeah, yeah. Wili on his way back to da house. I told him he gotta watch Kaimi. Pua t'ing still all mess up from da guy, Pacheco, tackling him to da ground yestahday. Eh, you guys going chahge Pacheco fo' excessive force, oah what!?"

Detective Takao stood up taking a quick glance at his partner. Detective Barshaw helped to clear things up, "Mr. Lee, we have already established that Kaimi appeared to be threatening other children with a dangerous weapon. Pacheco was well within in his right to de-escalate the situation in that manner." Both detectives witnessed the man relax his expression.

Mr. Lee gave Detective Barshaw da stink eye and blurted, "I guess."

Detective Takao continued to distract the upset man by asking, "Mr. Lee, would it be alright if we could stop by your house later on today to question Wili about the incident?"

Mr. Lee replied, "On one condition."

Both detectives looked at each other and back at Mr. Lee, Barshaw smiled and asked, "What is it?"

Mr. Lee shooed his left hand at the detectives and announced, "You get yo 'okole's off da road so I can go work already!" Mr. Lee threw his truck into low gear and pulled away from the detectives who were still mid j-walk.

"Well, Detective Takao. Looks like we can get some closure on at least one of these runaway cases." Barshaw threw his finger at their car to continue their mission to get to the bottom of the Makalike incident. "Maybe later we can head down to Ukulani's deli to grab some lunch."

Saturday

'Umi kūmākolu

Kaimi was startled by a low bass bump that caused the walls in his room to vibrate and the kukui lei that hung from his lamp to sway back and forth. Jumping up off the bed, Kaimi headed out to inspect the unusual movement. He muttered softly, "I wondah if Wili stay." As Kaimi made his way around his house he realized he was still very much alone. The house was eerily calm and lifeless. Even the sunlight that reflected off of the glass and furniture that scattered throughout the living room had lacked its luster. The uneasy feeling made Kaimi's tummy turn. He quickly ran to the bathroom to take care of his issue.

As he rested in his lavatory, Kaimi's ears were roused once again by the same deep thump from moments earlier. It was accompanied by shuffling and knocking sounds that emanated from the other side of the bathroom door. He then heard the tell tale high pitched squeak that came from Wili's closet being opened. *Dat must be Wili,* Kaimi thought as he cleaned himself and flushed the toilet.

The rustling from outside the washroom had ceased because of the banging caused by the pipes stuttering under the house. Kaimi washed his hands as quietly as he could when a loud crash shook the young man to his core. He called out to who he believed was his brother, "Wili!? You alright?" Kaimi dried his hands on a towel as he exited the restroom calling out once more, "Wili!?" Still, he received no answer. Kaimi knocked three times on the door to the tumultuous bedroom before slowly peeking in. "Wili, you okay?" Kaimi was surprised when he was presented with an empty room. He couldn't remember if he had knocked Wili's clothes onto the floor or if something else had moved them about, but something was off about how the room appeared. It seemed different from a moment earlier. On exhale Kaimi recalled his current physical malady, "Okay, maybe you wen' bang yo' head a little too hahd on dat bridge."

A cool breeze blew into Wili's bedroom window causing the young man to come to his senses, "Wait a minute! I know I wen' close dat puka las' night!" Kaimi scurried over to the window and looked outside. He was startled to see a young girl standing in his yard just under the mango tree. It was in the same spot he saw the tall crooked shadows standing last night. The pretty, young girl just stared at Kaimi and gave him the most peculiar feeling. He recognized her, but he knew she wasn't a student that went to his school.

"Eh! You need somet'ing?"

At that moment, a loud bang and a set of heavy footsteps ripped out of Wili's closet in a hurry. Kaimi spun around just in time to see a large shadow turning out into the hallway. The bedroom door slammed up against the doorframe causing Wili's stereo to go flying from the shelf. Kaimi looked back out the window to see that the strange young woman had vanished. He quickly shut the bedroom windows and ran out into the living room trailing behind the trespasser. Kaimi arrived at the front of the house, a bit dizzy, when he witnessed a shadow moving just outside the front door. He ran to the entry, turned the knob and flew the door open whacking Detective Barshaw's coffee onto his shirt.

"Geez, son! What are you thinking!?" Detective Barshaw snipped as he flicked at his shirt. "Ugh, do you have a towel I could use?"

Kaimi immediately identified the angry old man. He remembered the sound of Detective Barshaw's voice and he still had that nasty old cologne scent lingering on his person, surrounding him like an aura.

"Sorry detective!" Kaimi looked around Detective Barshaw to see Detective Takao making a face of disgust at the whole ordeal. "Eh, you guys wen' see anybody running outta da house just before...?" Kaimi eyed the detective's soiled white shirt.

Barshaw laid his tie down with his eyes widened, iris' fully exposed, wondering if the boy had heard his request earlier. "No one came out but you, Kaimi! Hey, you know what? It would be really great if I could get that towel."

Kaimi pushed the door back so the detectives could make their way into the house. He walked into the kitchen still on high alert, eyes darting from one part of the room to the next. He pulled a dish towel off the oven's handle,

"Heeyah, detective."

Barshaw snapped the towel from Kaimi's hands and began patting it over the drenched surface.

"Sorry." Kaimi was very apologetic and offered, "You guys like somet'ing fo' drink?"

Detective Takao glanced down at the brown stain forming on Brent's shirt. "I think we've had enough. Thank you, Kaimi." Detective Takao could see that Kaimi was wired. "Why are you so jumpy, young man?"

Kaimi took a deep breath and eyeballed the hallway. "I was jus' home alone waiting fo' my braddah come back. I went to da lua an' I heard funny kine sounds in my house. I taught Wili was home. I went fo' check my braddah's room, wea da noises stay coming from, an' nevah have nobody. His window was open so

I wen' shut 'em an' I saw dis girl outside in my back yahd." Detective Barshaw looked at Kaimi and stopped wiping his shirt. "I called out to her an' somet'ing wen' chahge outta Wili's closet. I wen' chase 'em into my living room an' taught I saw it outside an' dat's when I accidentally smash into yo' cup…" Kaimi glanced at Barshaw's shirt. "I so sorry, detective."

"Enough already!" Barshaw took a look around the room. "Wait, so, is Wili home or not?"

Kaimi shook his head. "I dunno! It might be him playing pranks, but dis isn't somet'ing he does typically." Kaimi rubbed his hands together.

There was a loud pop that came from Wili's room that all three men heard clearly. Detective Takao's eyes darted toward the hall as Detective Barshaw stood up tossing the damp towel down onto the couch.

"Okay, enough of this. We need to talk to Wili." Barshaw walked over to the room and looked in. No one was there.

Kaimi glanced into Wili's room and saw the window was wide open once more. "I swear I wen' close dat window!"

"I do *not* like these games, young man." Detective Barshaw examined Wili's bedroom, opening the closet and pulling up the mattress. "Wili!" Barshaw bellowed, covering the small room within seconds. He called out again, "Wili!" Both detectives headed back out into the hallway.

Detective Takao put his hand on Kaimi's shoulder. "Where did you see this girl?" Kaimi pointed toward the mango tree out back. Both men followed Kaimi out of the house. Takao tailed Kaimi as they marched toward the mauka side of the home.

Barshaw took a right down the porch stairs and made a sweep around the makai side of the house calling out for the other Lee boy. "Wili!"

Takao walked slowly around Kaimi to keep him safe as they made their way toward the mango tree. He turned back to look at the house and could see Wili's bedroom window that was still in the open position.

Kaimi stood closely beside Takao looking up into the tree and at the brush surrounding his home. "Detective, I don't t'ink dat was Wili playing around. Dat girl I saw doesn't go to ouah skoo..." Kaimi dug deep into his memory, "but, she wen' look familiah. I jus' can not place wea I know her from."

Detective Takao could see Barshaw making his way around the house still calling out for Wili. He observed that Kaimi was visibly shaken by what was happening and he knew this was no act. He asked the unnerved teen, "Kaimi, you said this girl looked familiar... I need you to think hard about where you recognized her from, okay?"

Kaimi stood there trying his best to recall where he saw the strange young woman. Detective Barshaw met up with the two as he struggled to catch his breath.

Kaimi felt embarrassed for Detective Barshaw and his serious health condition. "I don't mean fo' be rude, detective, but maybe you should try fo' quit smoking."

"I've tried to get him to quit for years," Detective Takao responded while resting his hands on his hips.

Detective Barshaw did not look like he was in a good mood. He placed one hand on his chest and pointed a finger at Kaimi's chin, "Look, I need the truth! What are you boys hiding? Your father said Wili was supposed to be here watching over you, but here we find you supposedly all alone. This isn't a game, Kaimi. I don't find any of this amusing. It's an abuse of our time and obstruction of justice. What are you Lee boys refusing to tell us!?" Detective Barshaw took a deep breath and exhaled slowly awaiting an answer.

Kaimi began to weep, "I'm sorry I nevah told you earliah. But, I did see somet'ing aftah I wen' trow da rock." Kaimi sniffled while Reed patted him on the back. "I saw dat green mo'owahine grabbing fo' my braddah an' I wen' try whack da monstah wit' da rock, but it pulled my braddah into da rocks pat'. I got hit from da side an' buss my head on da bridge. Before I wen' black out, I could see my braddah floating down stream. I taught I wen' kill Wili. But my fada said he wen' talk to Wili on da phone an' told me he was coming home today to keep one eye on me!" Kaimi stopped with stuttering breath.

Detective Barshaw eased his stance and searched Detective Takao's face for answers. "Reed, what's your take?"

Detective Takao asked Kaimi, "Assuming your brother is healthy, where could he be right now?"

Kaimi just shrugged nonchalantly, "I'm gonna be honest detectives, we nevah go sleep ovah friend's house. Most da kids parents at skoo no like kids like us at deah place. It's like day t'ink bumbai we going steal sometin' or wreck da place." Kaimi's face looked as if he were in pain. "I guess he could be hangin' at da De Souza's. But dat place is a mess."

Detective Barshaw gazed up into the mango tree and let out a huff, "Damn kids these days, running away."

Kaimi tilted his head with a look of contemplation, "Detectives, I t'ink I remembah wea I wen' see dat girl." The two men stood by as Kaimi elucidated, "She was da girl I seen on T.V. yestahday morning!"

Takao had a confused look on his face. "You saw her on the T.V.? Like an actress?"

"No, not on a show." Kaimi recalled hearing on the news that it was the anniversary of a missing person.

"Had dis girl on da news dat went missing like five yeahs ago… Sharla? Shayla? Cheyenne…"

Detective Takao's eye's brightened up with a flash, "Cheylene? Cheylene Hikina!?"

Kaimi seemed a bit unconvinced, "Maybe das da name I heard, I t'ink so."

Detective Takao pulled the poster that he took off the wall of Cheylene out of his pocket and unfolded it carefully. He handed the announcement over to Kaimi to take a look at. "Is this the girl you saw?" Takao asked anxiously.

Even though his eyes were still a bit fuzzy there was no mistake. Kaimi jumped, "Das da one! It looks like her anyways. I t'ink das even da same pitcha!"

"Brent," Takao showed Barshaw the missing person's poster. "It's Cheylene."

Detectives Takao and Barshaw looked at Kaimi and realized this whole situation just got a lot more complicated.

Saturday

ʻUmi kūmāhā

Detective Takao pulled up to the curb of the old De Souza home. On approach, he could see that the house was in some pretty bad shape. The walkways were hidden by overgrowth causing the lower sections of his pants to become a resting ground for a nasty bunch of burs. As he got closer to the house he could hear coarse wheezing coming from the window of one of the rooms. He tried his best to isolate where the noise was coming from. It started to sound like a large injured animal whining in pain. Reed peeked in through some cracked jalousies but the screen was covered in a thick gray dust. The whimpering was followed by short quick breaths, like panting. A foul odor wafted out of the windows and clung to the detective's nose making him gag. Takao's foot slipped off of a loose brick and his shoulder hit the side of the house with a hard thud. The sound of the animal had gone from hurt to angry, conjuring up a formidably deep growl.

An out of place monotonous voice caught Detective Takao by surprise. "Be careful."

The detective leaped up to his feet and found a lanky young woman leaning against the corner of the lanai with her dainty, but hairy arms folded. She gave the detective an indifferent look with half mast eyes.

He dusted the old powdery paint off his shoulder and apologetically responded, "Oh, hey! I didn't see you there young lady. My name is Reed Takao, I am a detective with the HPD."

Takao made his way, high stepping out of the brush with his hand extended. The young woman continued to stare blankly at him.

"Kenani, right?"

The teenager slowly shut her eyes with lids that were lined with long dark lashes. She gave an impassive nod but still did not reach out toward the detective.

"Ah, okay." Reed lowered his hand and got straight down to business. "So, yesterday my partner, Detective Barshaw, took a statement from you and your brother 'Alapaki. I came to do a follow up." Kenani continued to look at Detective Takao apathetically. "Now, I understand that you, 'Alapaki, Wiliami and Kaimi were at Makalike Bridge yesterday around three-thirty in the afternoon. Do you remember seeing what happened to Wiliami Lee after his brother, Kaimi, threw the rock?

Has he come around here? Stayed the night? Contacted either of you?" Detective Takao gazed at the bizarre teen awaiting a response for an uncomfortable length of time.

Kenani pushed herself off of the house's frame with her elbow. "I think Wili and my brother are messing around somewhere in town. Probably went to go get a bite." She turned slowly away from the detective and pulled the front door open. The door made a hellish shriek as it shut behind Kenani and clashed when it shut.

Detective Takao considered that to be the end of their conversation. He pulled his phone from his pocket. "Brent! No luck at the De Souza's." Takao took a quick glance back over his shoulder. "Kenani, the girl with the sunny disposition, says the boys went into town for a bite."

Detective Barshaw's voice could be heard on the other end, "Go check town and if you find Wili bring him back here to the house."

Detective Takao pulled open his car door, "Got it boss."

Barshaw continued, "Oh, and could you make a quick stop at Ukulani's? Go pick us up something to eat." Brent's voice became muffled but Reed could still follow the conversation, "Kaimi, you getting hungry?" Takao strained his ears trying to make out his partner's words and jumped when Barshaw came back at full volume. “Grab something for Kaimi while you’re at it, and Wili too… if you find him.”

The detective rubbed his ear and nodded as if his partner were right beside him. Reed closed his cell, jumped into his car’s seat and drove away from the De Souza’s property.

ʻUmi kūmālima

The loud hum of idle semi-trucks filled the air in a bustling loading zone. A high pitched voice sailed effortlessly through all the commotion, "Kalena! Eh, Kalena, telephone!" A short round shape wandered back into the work office as the flimsy plastic door slapped shut behind her.

After a minute, a second taller shape pushed into the office, "Aloha, dis is Kalena Lee, shiff managah, how can I help you?" Mr. Lee caught his breath from running up the steps to the office.

A soft, quivering voice climbed out of the receiver, "Hey, Dad, it's me, Kaimi."

Mr. Lee hugged the phone closer to his head, "Eh, Kaimi. You doing okay? Yo' braddah keeping watch?"

Kaimi ignored his father's query and immediately passed the phone on, "Try wait, Dad, here's Detective Barshaw." Kaimi handed the receiver to the detective.

"Mr. Lee, Brent Barshaw here. Just stopped by the house and wanted to let you know that Kaimi is doing okay, I will be with him until Wili gets home." Detective Barshaw winked at Kaimi.

The twin's father blurted out an angry growl, "Detective, you mean to tell me dat Wiliami hasn't come home yet!?" Mr. Lee turned his face away from the phone looking at the office staff and muttered, "Damn kid going get it!"

The detective could hear Mr. Lee's annoyed tone and assured the angry father, "That is correct Mr. Lee, however, Detective Takao has reason to believe that Wili is out with his friend, 'Alapaki, hanging around town. I have my partner on his way to pick him up as we speak."

Mr. Lee hissed, "Tsa! When dat boy gets home, you get my permission fo' slap him upside da head, detective!" Mr. Lee gave a short pause, "Detective Barshaw, mahalo fo' being dea wit' Kaimi. I know if was Wili home, no problem. Kaimi is a little moah sensitive, yeah. So, I appreciate it."

"No worries, Mr. Lee. I'll have Wili call you when he gets home. I just wanted to keep open communication." Barshaw rubbed his hand over the fresh stain on his shirt.

Mr. Lee explained, "T'anks fo' da heads up, detective. But today stay real busy, an' I cannot keep coming into da office fo' answah calls all day. Tell da boys I call 'em on my break."

"Sounds good, Mr. Lee. I'll let you go now, sorry for the bother." Detective Barshaw placed the phone back onto its seat. "Well, Kaimi? You wanna talk about it?"

Barshaw witnessed Kaimi scanning the living room trying to find a random subject to talk about. "Look, Kaimi. Everyone has troubles. Even the most put together individuals have some dark secret they don't want to let out into the light of day. So, let me have it!" Barshaw lightly slapped Kaimi's shoulder with the back of his hand, "I'm all ears."

Kaimi just sank into his seat, "I mean, what is dea fo' me to say? My braddah actin' pūpule, I seeing t'ings an' da guy, 'Alapaki, terrifies me."

Barshaw bounced his finger in Kaimi's direction, "There! I don't get the feeling that you are the type of person who could be threatening. It doesn't even seem like you have a bad bone in your body, Kaimi. My bet is that 'Alapaki and his sister are the one's up to no good, and it seems like they're bullying you. Am I wrong?"

"Actually, detective," Kaimi began to confide, "it's just 'Alapaki dat pushes me aroun'. Kenani no kea eidah way. I nevah seen Kenani really kea about much. I no even see her at da picnic area during lunches." Kaimi looked at Brent with a furrowed brow, "In fact, I nevah remembah seeing Kenani at da stream yestahday."

Detective Barshaw cocked his jaw to the right, "Why do you think Kenani lied about being up at Makalike yesterday afternoon?"

Kaimi tossed both of his hands up, "I dunno why she making up stories, detective! But what I do know is dat 'Alapaki was goading me on. Taunting me fo' jump. It was really weird." Kaimi's eye's popped open wide, "Detective, do you t'ink you can take me to Makalike Bridge?"

Barshaw nodded, "Sure, Kaimi. But let's eat something before we head up there. Detective Takao should be back soon with your brother."

"Sir," Kaimi said in a soft panic, "If it is what I'm imagining… I don't t'ink da Detective will be bringing my braddah home." A tear slowly fell from Kaimi's left eye.

'Umi kūmāono

Detective Takao circled the town a few times making small stops at the local hot spots. He swung by the high school, a couple of nearby parks and even took a drive by the strip mall. No sign of the Wili, or 'Alapaki, anywhere. He decided to hop out and go by foot. He walked into the shops and food places asking the where about's of his quarry, still nothing. He found a couple small groups of teenagers hanging about, but when he questioned them, none could recall seeing either of the boys since Friday afternoon at school. Everywhere seemed like a dead end, as if he were sent on a wild goose chase. Reed decided to end his futile search and made his way into Uku Paila Deli to pick up some local kine grinds.

As Reed entered into the shop he was bumped in the shoulder by an older gentleman that was on his way out, "Oh excuse me, sir."

The old man turned and looked at the detective, "Reed?"

Detective Takao was stunned by how different Frank Hikina appeared. He looked much older, the lines on his face were deeper and his hair completely white like the snow on Mauna Kea.

"Oh, hey Mr. Hikina! Good to see you." He backed out of the deli to follow Frank outside. "I'm sorry again for your loss, Mr. Hikina."

The old man waved his hand in Takao's face, "Call me Frank, boy." He placed his package on the newspaper dispenser and pressed his hand down on it for balance. He gave a slight chuckle, "You know, I always thought Mary Lou would out live me. After my first wife passed, I never thought I'd find someone who would put up with me like that ever again. When my Lou-Lu came around, even though she was much younger, I was fortunate enough to find that love once more and, as if by a miracle, I received that love a third time when our little princess was born."

Reed looked down at one of his shoes and gawked at the dry, chalky paint that came from the De Souza's house which had scuffed over the toe. "We're still keeping an eye out for your baby girl, Frank. Now more than ever."

Mr. Hikina took a deep breath that had heavy phlegm resonating from his chest. "I don't think that's a fruitful use of your time, detective," Mr. Hikina coughed and wheezed for a minute. "I had a dream of my Chey. She came to me, you know? She held my hands." Mr. Hikina took in another raspy breath, "She tells me, 'Dad, no worry about me. I am here with Rosie.' Boy, I wen' cry. When I woke up, I felt at peace though. Mary on the other hand, she wouldn't give up, even after I told her about my dream of Chey. My lord, that sweet little angel had gone through so much in her short time here with me an' Lou-Lu. It seemed as though the devil himself was hunting after our girl. Too good for this earth is what I reckon."

Detective Takao didn't have the nerve to tell Frank that he may have a lead on his daughter. He thought, *It's better to get something tangible before revealing anything that may give false hope.*

To offer some comfort, Takao added, "If there's anything you need, Frank."

Mr. Hikina bobbed his head as he grabbed his lunch sack off of the newspaper stand, "Okay, boy. See you." Frank walked away slowly hacking up a lung as he crossed the road.

Detective Takao made his way back into the deli with a new found weight on his heart. He hoped that Kaimi was right and he had actually seen the young Hikina girl. He wanted so badly to present Cheylene to her father and return her to her family. He knew Frank didn't have much more time. His health seemed to have gotten worse since his wife's passing. Eating out at Uku Paila Deli everyday didn't help his well being either. Takao stopped at the counter still pondering his recent encounter.

A spirited and sultry voice popped Reed out of his stupor, "Eh, good aftahnoon Detective Takao. Wea stay my boyfrien'!?" Aunty Ukulani raised her right brow and pursed her red smothered lips toward the same side.

Reed just shook his head and smiled, "I'm here to pick up some lunch for us and a couple kids."

Aunty Uku smacked her kisser, "What he like? His usual?" She wiggled her brow and shook her hips in a suggestive manner.

Reed, now uncomfortable, just squished his nose, "Maybe we'll try something different."

"Get spesho today, detective! Kalua pig pancakes topped wit' chilled applesauce." Aunty Uku pointed at the sign next to the cash register. The word special was spelt, S-P-A-C-I-E-L.

Takao gave a look of surprise, "No, no, that's okay." He quickly scanned the menu items that were listed on the wall behind her, "We'll just take three hot pastrami sandwiches."

The deli owner frowned, "Gotta substitute ham, we all outta pastrami. Okay?"

Detective Takao presented his wallet while thinking about the kalua pig pancake special, “Yes, that is perfectly fine.”

“Okay!” Aunty Ukulani disappeared into the grill area to prepare the order.

Saturday

'Umi kūmāhiku

Detective Takao pulled into the Lee's driveway. He could see Kaimi searching the car with optimism from the living room window. On completion of his sweep, Kaimi's face transformed, reflecting dread. Reed spoke softly to himself, "Oh boy, what happened now?" He put the car in park and turned off the engine.

Detective Barshaw was already standing in the driveway as Reed pulled up. "No luck finding the boys?"

Detective Takao stepped out of the vehicle holding a brown paper bag, "No luck boss."

"Aw, damn." Barshaw pressed his hand over the top of his head, smoothing out his white hair. He side eyed Kaimi who had just retreated away from the window. "The boy said he had a gut feeling that you wouldn't find Wili. He wants to go to Makalike Bridge because he believes there may be a clue to Wili's whereabout's."

Detective Takao slammed the car door shut and accompanied Barshaw back to the house, "You'll never guess who I saw at the deli."

Detective Barshaw snickered, "Okay, have a laugh at my expense."

Reed bumped Barshaw in the shoulder, "No, Brent. I saw Frank Hikina."

Detective Barshaw cast a puzzled look. "Did you happen to tell him about possibly having a lead on Cheylene?"

Takao shook his head, "I couldn't promise anything substantial, so I just kept the conversation light."

"Good idea." Detective Barshaw opened the Lee's front door and Reed stepped into the house. The air felt different as both detectives entered the domicile. They witnessed Kaimi's posture collapse as he began to fall into a trance.

"Kaimi!?" Takao placed the brown sack down on the coffee table and tended to the boy.

Kaimi just kept shaking his head, "I need to know. I need to know what happened. My braddah nevah deserve fo' get hurt." Kaimi's arms began to tremble. He couldn't control his physical movements any longer. The adrenaline had spiked so high it rendered Kaimi useless. He just needed to breathe and relax.

"It's okay Kaimi, Detective Barshaw and I are here for you." Reed could only assure Kaimi that he didn't need to face whatever this was alone. Again, he was subjected to the same conditions as before, not wanting to deliver false hope. He could only sit back and be there for the young man. "Maybe you should eat. It might make you feel a little better, Kaimi."

The teen just nodded. He took a hot ham sandwich from Detective Takao and held it between both of his palms. The warmth from the sandwich gave Kaimi some comfort and helped to calm his jitters.

After several minutes of watching Kaimi trying unsuccessfully to pull himself back together, Detective Barshaw tossed his meal down. "Maybe we should just go already. It doesn't seem like Kaimi will find peace of mind until he unearths what it is that he's looking for. Besides, this ham sandwich tastes like burnt rubber."

Detective Takao agreed and helped the boy to his feet. "Let's take you back to Makalike."

Saturday

ʻUmi kūmāwalu

Kaimi didn't speak a word on the way to the stream. The memory of that infamous Sunday morning years ago, when those three older boys stole his money in front of the ice cream shop, shot back into his mind. Seeing Wili stand up to not just one older kid, but three older boys made him look like a superhero. Kaimi had so much love and pride in his big brother. Everything Wili did looked so effortless. These thoughts made Kaimi feel better, but it also made him think about the words ʻAlapaki said in regards to him being a mana vampire.

Why do I keep t'inking about dis!?

In frustration, Kaimi slapped the side of his temple catching the attention of the older detective. He knew exactly why he kept returning to that traumatic event. It was the overwhelming feeling of despair in making decisions that would have terrible repercussions on him, on his family or anyone else he cared about. He wished he could turn into a bird and just fly away from everything that gave him even the slightest discomfort.

"You alright there, Kaimi?" Detective Barshaw asked with a beguiled look. He turned his gaze toward Detective Takao expecting there to be some follow up statement of concern, but there was nothing. Reed continued to drive unfazed by Kaimi's odd behavior and Brent's uneasy inquiry.

As the squad car pulled around the corner of Makalike Road, the helpless young man just stared out the window replaying the walk from school to the bridge. He thought about how different the scenery was from just one day prior. It amazed Kaimi how some diffused light and drops of moisture could change the atmosphere of an area so dramatically.

Detective Barshaw spoke a bit louder to catch the young man's attention. He was most curious as to what Kaimi may have discovered on his own back at home. He was hoping the boy could shed some light on their little journey.

"Kaimi, you want to give us some insight into what it is we're looking for up at the stream?"

Kaimi just continued looking out the window, lost in thought.

Barshaw threw up his hands and huffed, "I guess not."

The police vehicle pulled up right before the bridge where there was a small shoulder just big enough to park a few cars. The road was still wet and there was moss present. It was growing all over the edge of the road. The neon green patches accentuated by the wet, dark asphalt made it appear as though they were standing in a different world.

"Watch your step as you get out, Barshaw. I don't know if I'll be able to pull you back up this hill if you fall." Reed surveyed the trail heading down to the edge of the stream. "I think it should be okay, boss. The steps aren't too steep."

Kaimi hopped out of the detective's car and ran to the spot where he was knocked unconscious. He studied the stream below and realized there was a significant drop to the water level. It wasn't low enough to find what he was looking for though.

By the time Detective Barshaw made his way to the bridge, Kaimi had lunged toward the path that lead down to the stream's edge.

"Kaimi, hold up!" Barshaw barked as he observed the overly eager child hopping down from one flat rock to the next. Brent was a lot more cautious, taking his time going from step to step, trying his best to follow Kaimi's decent sequence as if he were unlocking a secret pattern for safe passage. The elder detective could only hear a voice repeating, perhaps it was his conscience, *You're getting too old for this, you're getting way too old for this.* Brent arrived at the edge of the stream just as Kaimi yanked his t-shirt off.

"Takao! What's he doing!? Kaimi, wait a second!" Barshaw's words continued to bounce off of the Lee boy. "Tell us what's going on, young man!?" Kaimi splashed into the fresh, cold water just as the detective finished his probing.

Takao filled Barshaw in, "When the Lee's got to the bridge, they were surprised to see 'Alapaki and Kenani hadn't arrived. Wili took it upon himself to dive in to check the landing zone for any deadly hazards. Very smart..." Takao studied the stream keeping a close look out for the boy. "Kaimi said, Wili took a long time to surface because he found that a large stone had been propped up, square within the diving spot, intentionally. So, he wanted to come back here and see something for himself."

Barshaw squinted through the sunlight reflecting on the surface of the rushing water, "So what then?"

Detective Takao shook his head, "That's all he told me on our way down the these rocky steps. He jumped right in afterward."

Both men stood by awaiting Kaimi's return. The boy had been submerged for a good amount of time. Takao began to unbutton his shirt in preparation to go in after him when he could see a scalp rising out of the stream.

Kaimi resurfaced and Detective Barshaw could see he was not happy. "Whoah, whoah, whoah, Kaimi, is everything okay!?" The sound of the rushing water made it difficult to communicate clearly, so Barshaw put up his hands to halt the upset teenager.

"I going kill 'em!" Kaimi clenched his fists as his eyes turned red.

Detective Takao's concern for Kaimi returned, trying his best at being impartial yet supportive, he inquired, "What did you find? Who are you going to kill?"

Kaimi pointed out toward the middle of the stream. "Look ovah dea! Da rock wen' return to da same spot. It stay wedged, propped up by smallah rocks." Kaimi dusted his hair with both of his hands, raining water droplets down onto the river stones.

"Aftah Wili wen' push da rock ovah, 'Alapaki wen' convince him fo' jump firs'. I remembah seeing 'Alapaki drop down to his hands an' knees as Wili dove from da bridge. I noticed 'Alapaki was disappointed when he saw Wili pop back out of da watah." Kaimi pulled his t-shirt over his head and yanked it onto his body. "Aftah dat, 'Alapaki wen' dive off da bridge. He wen' disappeah long time, but wen' he came up he had dis real sinister looking smile on his face. It gave me da creeps." Kaimi began to put together all of the information he had uncovered, "Das why he wen' try get me fo' jump! 'Alapaki wanted me fo' karang my ala's."

Kaimi took off, back up the hill. Takao and Barshaw ascended the uneven trail at their own pace and caught up to Kaimi standing once more at the center of the bridge.

"You see ovah dea?" Kaimi pointed at the tree line that was set several feet in from the actual stream. "Right ovah dea is wea I wen' see da mo'owahine. Da lizahd leddeh!"

Barshaw placed his hand on Kaimi's shoulder as he continued to focus on breathing. "Son, is it possible that you could have been imagining this creature?"

Kaimi pulled away far enough for Barshaw to lose his grip on him, "I saw what I saw, detective. She came up an' grabbed Wili!"

Detective Takao tried to help Kaimi not sound too far fetched so that his partner wouldn't write him off as certifiable. "Okay, Kaimi. What does all of this prove?" Detective Takao paced the bridge. "You're saying that 'Alapaki first planned to hurt your brother but failed. Then, because Wili avoided his trap, 'Alapaki focused his malice on you, which made him prop the rock back up? For what reason?"

Reed hadn't even gotten to the most ambiguous part of the reveal, the existence of a mythical being, a half human, half dragon woman that abducts young children from the river. Reed's head began to swim.

Detective Takao tried his best to organize the facts of Kaimi's portrait, "I'm having a difficult time trying to follow all of this, Kaimi. Was it 'Alapaki or the creature that was here to hurt you and your brother?"

Kaimi was just as stumped. He replayed the events back in his mind, *I know 'Alapaki wen' set up da rock maliciously, not once but twice! Was it just by coincidence dat dea was one fah worse predatah lurking aroun' da stream at dat very same moment?*

It took Kaimi a little while to find his way around the small dark room in his mind. All of it began to frustrate him until a window cracked open letting in a sliver of light.

"Detectives!" Barshaw and Takao waited for Kaimi to divulge his revelation. "What if 'Alapaki's sistah, Kenani, *was* hea aftah all!? What if Kenani *is* da moʻowahine I saw!? 'Alapaki was da one dat wanted fo' come up Makalike yestahday! He was bringing us up hea fo' feed his sistah, dat suckin' moʻopilikua!" Kaimi nodded in all certainty, but the detectives just weren't seeing it from his perspective.

Detective Barshaw exhaled and looked down while resting his hands on his hips, "Okay, Kaimi. That's enough. I think it's about time for us to go home now." Barshaw signaled to Takao to get the car started.

Kaimi stood in disbelief as he watched all of his credibility disappear in Barshaw's eyes. "Wait, you gotta believe me, man! It makes sense, no?" Kaimi shouted at Reed's back, "Detective Takao, you believe me, right? But da rock!"

Takao opened the door to the back seat and prompted Kaimi to get in with a gesture of his hand, "Let's go home, Kaimi."

Saturday

‘Umi kūmāiwa

On the way back to the Lee residence, the car was in complete silence, except for the humming coming from the police radio that was always kept at a low volume. The detectives could see Mr. Lee's truck parked in the driveway. Brent fumbled around the seat buckle's switch and pulled the door's latch open before the car could come to a standstill.

"I'll go walk Kaimi in and talk to the boy's father. Don't shut off the engine. Just sit tight, I'll be back in a moment." Barshaw barked toward the backseat, "C'mon, Kaimi!"

The young man exited the running car feeling dejected. He moped alongside Detective Barshaw all the way up to the porch. Mr. Lee set foot out of the house to receive his son.

"How's it, detective?" Mr. Lee appeared exhausted.

Detective Barshaw eyed the back of Kaimi's head and raised his eyebrows.

Mr. Lee watched his son pathetically ascending the steps, "Kaimi? What's up?"

Kaimi just continued on his way into the house. "I'm still not feeling well, Pop."

Mr. Lee pinched his brows together, "Go lay down. I come check on you aftah da detective an' I wala'au." Mr. Lee squeezed Kaimi's shoulder as his body slid away into the house. The concerned father turned back to speak with the detective who appeared annoyed.

"Awright, well at least I know Kaimi's okay. Now wea stay Wili?" Mr. Lee peeked over Barshaw's shoulder to see if another body was emerging from the vehicle.

Detective Barshaw pulled Mr. Lee from the frame of the door and whispered, "Mr. Lee, I think we may have a serious problem." Barshaw could feel Mr. Lee trembling slightly in his light grip as he released his arm. "I'm so sorry, I don't mean to alarm you, but there are some very suspicious things going on."

Mr. Lee looked up at Barshaw with eyes that were reddened and shiny. "Is Wili okay, detective?" He finished with a slight sniffle.

Barshaw stretched a knot out of his neck by tilting his head deeply. "I don't have an answer for you at this time about Wili's whereabouts. Detective Takao spent the morning searching the local hot spots and couldn't find any trace of Wili or his friend 'Alapaki. The kids in town said the last time they saw either of them was before they left school and went up to the bridge." Barshaw peeked in through the living room jalousies for movement and leaned in closer to Mr. Lee. "Now, when we focus on Kaimi's history of what went down at Makalike, we know he's sincere and his words feel genuine, but his story is completely off the rails. The truth from the De Souza's? Well, it is just as crazy when we try to piece it together because there seems to be too much misalignment. Wili is the key to making any sense of this whole dilemma because nothing seems to fit!" It almost made Detective Barshaw believe in the craziness Kaimi deduced earlier at the stream. Almost. He couldn't let the idea of supernatural beings and murderous teenagers win in his logical reasonings. He decided to let Mr. Lee know what was exactly on his mind, "Or… there could be something else going on with Kaimi."

Mr. Lee sat peacefully on the bottom step of his porch, he began watching some ants make a path around an exposed root. Reluctantly, he agreed to hear more of what the detective had to share, "Okay, shoot! Give me da details."

Barshaw stood in front of Mr. Lee keeping his voice down in a hushed tone, "Kaimi swears that he saw this mo'owahine, this lizard lady, at the stream yesterday." Barshaw's expression tried to evoke some reaction from Kaimi's dad.

Mr. Lee looked at the detective waiting for the part of the story that was too crazy to be true. "An' den?"

The detective, a bit taken aback, followed up, "Mr. Lee, your son has fears that he and Wili had attempts against their lives. He believes 'Alapaki was trying to lure them into this creature's den so it could feed on them!" Barshaw now stood with his palms toward Kaimi's father as if he just deployed an enchanting magical finale.

Mr. Lee looked closely at the detective and began to understand what he was going on about. "Kaimi has unreal integrity, detective. If he says something, one hundred percent going be true. He has no reason fo' lie, evah." Mr. Lee cupped one hand over the other indicating its irrefutability.

"I get it, Mr. Lee." Brent swung around and took a few steps away from the boys' father. He dramatically turned back once more to put an end to beating around the bush. "If we look at all the information laid in front of us, we either have a story that seems factual coming from individuals who are untrustworthy, or we get an incredibly imaginative narrative that's coming from your boy!" Barshaw's voice was now loud enough for Kaimi to hear, but he felt it needed to be said. "Maybe it's a health issue? Maybe Kaimi has something going on upstairs that is causing him to hallucinate? All I know is that none of this is making any real sense Mr. Lee, and the only conclusion that I can see is that Kaimi's mental state may be a bit fragile."

Mr. Lee just bobbed his head, "Da clinic stay closed tomorrow so maybe I'll take Kaimi on Monday fo' go see one terapist." Mr. Lee raised his right hand.

Detective Barshaw could see Mr. Lee had heard enough about the issue. He scrunched his mouth and took hold of Mr. Lee's hand. "We'll bring Wili straight home when we find him. On the other hand, please let us know the moment he walks through this door." Barshaw reversed away from Mr. Lee and spoke aloud, "Take care, Kaimi. Let us know if you need anything." Brent nodded and excused himself, "Good evening, Mr. Lee."

Kalena yanked himself up and went inside. He walked over to Kaimi's bedroom where he found his son gazing out the window. He walked around Kaimi's bed and lowered himself slowly onto its corner.

"So, dis 'Alapaki guy, he making up stories?" Kaimi gave no response. "I believe you, son. I believe you saw what you saw. But we gotta stay strong an' figyah dis out togedah." Kaimi made several visual passes of his family homestead. "What should we do, Kaimi? Dis is some real hamajang you experiencing, no? We need to fine out what's happening wit' yo' braddah too." Mr. Lee grew in concern about Kaimi's distant behavior and Wili's willingness to abandon his 'ohana. "We go doctah on Monday, okay?" The exhausted middle-aged man hiked himself back up to his feet. "So, tomorrow we should visit wit' yo' maddah. She know what do."

Kaimi's father left the sullen bedroom to make some calls to the neighbors and a few shops that he believed Wili could be cruising around. He got the same results as Detective Takao. No one had seen Wili since the day before. Mr. Lee leaned back in his seat and exhaled, "Akua, watch ovah my boys."

Mr. Lee nearly jumped out of his skin when the silence of his home was disrupted by the blaring of the house phone. The ring continued to echo through his ears as he answered the call, "Lee residence." Mr. Lee started to curse and scream, "Wea da hell have you been, boy!? We've been worried sick about you!"

The commotion had snapped Kaimi out of his trance and he took off out of his room, down the hall and straight into the kitchen. "Dad, is dat Wili!?"

Mr. Lee halted Kaimi from speaking, "Look, da fricken detectives had to watch yo' braddah today because you nevah show up, wea you stay!? I come get you *right* now!" Mr. Lee jingled his keys by the receiver.

Kaimi could hear Wili's faint voice coming through the ear piece, but he sounded different, unlike himself.

"Dad!" Kaimi tried to get his father's attention. "Dad, try ask Wili if I can eat da las' of his spam!"

Mr. Lee frowned at Kaimi, "What!?"

"Dad, just ask Wili if I can eat da las' of his spam... please!" Kaimi had a plan and this was one way to solve one of his conundrum's.

Mr. Lee turned back to the phone and asked, "Kaimi goin' eat da spam, okay?"

Kaimi's dad looked back at him and nodded with a look that it was alright. Kaimi's eye's grew and his hand immediately gripped onto his dad's shoulder rocking him with quick motion. Unfazed, Mr. Lee continued to speak sternly to his wayward son.

"Look Wili, you bettah get yo' 'okole home now!" There was a small break and a short vibration resonating from the phone. Mr. Lee shouted in response, "What!? Wili I'm not going to..." as Mr. Lee spoke he heard the receiver click and the phone was lifeless. He leaped up to his feet and hollered, "Kaimi, I going pa'i yo' braddah!"

Kaimi jumped up to calm his father. "Dad! Dad, dat wasn't Wili!"

Mr. Lee's wild gaze pierced Kaimi's eyes. He slowly settled down with a look of bewilderment. The boys' father's voice warbled, "Yeah, you right Kaimi. It wen' soun' like him, but nevah *soun'* like him. Wili would nevah do dat to me, to us." Mr. Lee wrapped his arms around his son. "Who or what was dat?"

Kaimi saw that his father was finally on board with the notion that something very strange was happening to their ʻohana. "I was honest wit' da detectives, Dad. I saw one moʻowahine. She grabbed Wili. Now I feeyah da worse fo' him."

Mr. Lee squeezed Kaimi and held him close. "We need some help, but who going believe us? All dis stuff sound nuts!"

Kaimi broke free from his father's grip. "Detective Takao believed me! I'm shua he would help!"

Mr. Lee wiped his face and nodded in agreement as he patted his pockets to retrieve his wallet. He found both detectives' business cards and tossed Detective Barshaw's card onto the table while pinching Reed's between his finger and thumb.

"Okay, we'll get Detective Takao to come back and help us, Kaimi. If you trust him, I trust him."

Iwakālua

Back at the station, Detective Barshaw discussed the case with his superior, Captain Roger Lalau, highlighting his efforts throughout the day. The captain, a man of mild temperament, large frame, and sweet face, sat comfortably in his chair with a despondent look.

"So, the Lee boy has not yet been found?" The deepness of Captain Lalau's voice caused the room to pulse.

Barshaw reassured the captain, "Sir, Detective Takao and I have reason to believe he is just a runaway. Unless we get information to tell us otherwise, we remain confident the boy is just hiding out with friends. It seems as though he wants to avoid getting in trouble with his father, who, may I add, is a pretty intense guy."

The captain raised an eyebrow over his silver framed lenses as he eyed Brent's shirt, "Confident?"

Barshaw tightened his jacket to hide the coffee stained remnants. "Yes, sir. I'm sure Wiliami Lee will pop up safely sooner rather than later."

Captain Lalau extended his hand. "Good work, Barshaw. Get some rest, we will see you tomorrow morning, bright and early."

Detective Barshaw shook the captain's thick fingered hand. "Yes, sir. Have a good evening."

He left his superior's office and traveled down the hall into the detective's work station. Brent could see his partner sitting at his cubicle hanging up his cell phone as he approached.

"How's that report coming, Reed?"

Startled, Detective Takao sat straight in his chair. "Almost done boss! You ready to head out?" Reed stuffed his phone into his shirt pocket in haste.

Barshaw grabbed a couple of his belongings from inside his desk drawer. "Yeah, just gonna stop off at the deli before heading home. How about you?"

Takao clicked his computer monitor off and spun around in his seat. "I may take one last look around town before heading home for the night. New movie came out this weekend, I may catch Wili making his way into the theater."

"Well, if you see the kid, grab him and take his butt straight home. Alright, I'll see you tomorrow." Detective Barshaw did a slight hop and skipped off the work floor.

Takao shook his head as to what kind of treat Barshaw was looking forward to ordering from the deli. Aunty Uku's luscious red lips popped into Reed's head for a second and that was enough to cause him to dry heave. Reed took the final sip of his vapid coffee and chucked the empty cup into the trash. He grabbed his jacket off the back of his chair and made his way out of the building.

Detective Takao had gotten to the lot's exit just in time to see Barshaw pulling out. Brent gave Reed a thumbs up as he drove by.

"Good luck, boss," Takao muttered reverently while walking toward his car.

As Reed sat waiting for the engine to warm up, he thought about an effective route to make the best of his time and energy. *The theater will be selling tickets at six o'clock and they will probably be seating their customers at around six thirty. That means I can drive past the school and park before heading through town.* Takao drove off of the lot and decided to start at Lunalilo High School.

Reed saw one white car driving cautiously through an intersection far up ahead. He drew out a long breath, "Where is everyone tonight?"

As he searched the town, the detective started to think it odd that the streets were so empty, *The high school ended up being a ghost town, no illegal gatherings or loitering of any kind, Waena park only had a small group of seniors practicing Tai Chi, and the state reserve was completely dead. Not even the Kamaka's were there enjoying their usual weekend picnic.* The lack of any form of life caused Reed's throat to tighten. *If this kid doesn't show up at the theater then he must be holed up at a friend's house, or…* The story Kaimi told him and Brent came up like a bad case of acid reflux. *What is going on in this town? Why was Cheylene at the Lee's house?*

Reed pulled up to the town theater and saw a nice long line of children and young adults, none of whom looked like Wili, ʻAlapaki, or Kenani. After a few minutes the theater workers started letting in the patrons. The lack of any sign of the missing Lee boy frustrated Detective Takao. Kaimi's story whipped back to the front of his mind. *If the moʻowahine grabbed Wili and hurt him, it could be possible the De Souza's provided care to him and brought him back to their home in a medical capacity… could it have been Wili that was making the hurt animal sounds coming from the window at the De Souza's?*

Takao let out a laugh and shook his head. "This crazy story is getting to you, Reed," he blurted out loud with little doubt to his denial. He started up the car and made his way out of town. Reed dialed the Lee's home and the phone was answered by the boy's father.

"Mr. Lee!? I did a drive around town and no luck. There's only one other place I can think of, so I'm heading over to the De Souza house to see if Wili is up there. I'll contact you when I find out more."

Detective Takao could hear that the boy's father had become more anxious, "Okay, detective. An'... t'ank you fo' doing dis for us."

"No problem, Mr. Lee. We'll find Wili soon. I can feel it." Detective Takao hung up with the concerned father and continued on his way to the De Souza's house with the feeling that he would indeed find the missing boy there, but the question in his mind was, *In what kind of shape will Wiliami be in?* He shuddered at the thought.

It was already dark and the roadways didn't have the best lighting. Flying up through the zigzag turns of the shallow valley walls, the trees flying past his window were exhibiting eerie forms that taunted him with their terrifying silhouettes. At one point, he swore he could even see things moving through the forest. Perhaps his imagination was getting the best of him, perhaps it was a fear for Wili's safety. An ominous feeling started to wash over Reed's entire body. His heart began to pound and his head began to ache. As he made the corner to the intersection of the De Souza's residence a large, fast moving form vaulted into the middle of the road causing the detective to temporarily lose control of his automobile. He swerved to and fro until the car expelled a tremendous pop. The vehicle skidded to a stop and the detective stared wide eyed out the windshield, panting uncontrollably, "What the heck was that!?" He glanced in the rearview mirror and saw a dark empty street.

Reed peered into the dark woods and observed the bizarre shadow making its way toward the De Souza's street. Detective Takao pulled forward to pursue the dark figure, but his car was dragging and his wheel pulled heavily to the right. He got out of the vehicle and found that his tire had blown out. Reed hopped back in the driver's seat, pulling the car further off to the side of the road, to avoid an accident. He continued to the De Souza's address on foot and ran as fast as he could.

Takao approached the somber homestead. The sinister feeling had returned to take hold of Detective Takao's rationale. Every hair stood up on his body as he traveled through the dark. There were absolutely no lights on at the De Souza house or on the empty street for that matter. It appeared that the street lights were not operational. Judging by the shattered glass below the telephone poles, they appeared to have been deliberately impaired. He trampled through the De Souza's yard and fell against the wall he had heard the whimpers and cries from earlier in the day. Again, a putrid smell could be detected pouring out of the sooty, pitch black window. Detective Takao raised his mini torch up to shine its feeble beam into the inky room.

"Wili! Wiliami Lee are you in there?"

He could faintly make out the deep, hoarse breaths that he recalled from before and he yelled out once more, "Wili! It's Detective Takao with the HPD, do you need medical assistance?"

The detective was paralyzed instantly by the appearance of two glowing orbs shining from inside the dark chamber staring directly at him. A booming growl shot through the window breaking the silence. It was accompanied by a hot, thick jet of steam which fell onto the detective's face. He snapped out of his trance and darted away from the house in fear.

Reed could hear crashing and banging as he ran away, like all hell broke loose inside the De Souza residence. The clamber made its way toward the front door where it slammed open with a heavy impact that echoed through the blackened street. Detective Takao tried to make his way back to his car to get hold of his weapon, but was viciously snagged and pulled off the road. His body sailed effortlessly through the air from the brutality of the throw. The powerful force chucked him right into the forest where he landed with a thud on a bed made up of a mixture of leaves and fresh mud. Shaking off the strike, the detective was able to pull himself back up to his feet.

The moon had emerged from the heavy cluster of clouds revealing his assailant that was blocking the path to his car. Standing up on two legs, right in the center of the road was a tall, slender form with long fingers, baring sharp claws. It looked very much like a tall, hunched over malnourished person. Once more, Takao's attention was seized by the two glowing orbs set into its deep eye sockets. He was finally subjected to the unimaginable horror of the creatures visage. The monster possessed the head of a wild dog, its brindled hair covered its entire body and shimmered in the pale moonlight. It cast its gaze up to the heavens and let out a fierce howl.

In disbelief, Detective Takao turned and ran as fast as he could through the deep, dark woods holding his small Maglite above his head to illuminate the maze like surroundings. He could hear the sounds of heavy trampling gaining on him. Twigs and branches were snapping and cracking ferociously under the beast's feet. It seemed as though the evil entity was fast approaching from the side, too fast for the man to out run. The detective did not stop, not even to catch his breath. He kept running, dodging, and jumping until he safely circumvented the pitch black forest to gain some ground on the creature. It was as if he used some unknown ability, like a sixth sense, to avoid all the dangers the living woods threw at him. Reed kept going until his lungs caught fire which forced him to involuntarily come to a stop. He begged for the pain to cease and after a short while it sounded as though he was no longer being pursued. The ruckus that followed him had halted and there were only chirps of crickets and croaking of frogs moving through the chilly night air.

Taking refuge in the roots of a massive banyan tree, Takao finally found a place of sanctuary to catch his breath. *Deep, slow, quiet.* Detective Takao repeated these words like a mantra in the silence of his mind. His heart pounded so hard and so fast that he could see lights in the darkness flashing in his eyes with each throb. He calmed himself to the point of being able to hear the faint hush of a waterfall in the distance. The sound of the rushing stream began to fill Takao with inner peace. The adrenalin began to wane as it made its way through his body causing his limbs to involuntarily jerk and spasm.

"Okay, Reed. Get a hold of yourself."

He shook his head and massaged the pain emanating from his arm. He could feel the warmth of his blood trailing downward and dripping at his wrist. With the help of his mini Maglite, Detective Takao could make out two rows of puncture marks wrapping around his upper arm. It appeared to be teeth. His mind was about to explode. *Kaimi was right all along!*

The detective no longer had any doubt about the credibility of the Lee boy. Although the creature Kaimi described was not the same as the one that he saw attack Wiliami, Reed knew that Kaimi was being one hundred percent honest about the strange creature he saw.

Detective Takao pulled up Detective Barshaw's number on his cellphone and pressed the dial key. His hand shook as he held the phone against his ear. He thought, *I need to tell Brent that the boy was right…* the phone blurted a loud flat beep. "Ugh, no signal!?" The detective raised his hand upwards to see if he could get reception. *I need to make my way out of the forest quickly and quietly,* Reed reflected and continued to press his way through the darkness making slow gains to avoid attracting the aggressive beast.

As Takao stepped over a gnarled tree root, he was shocked to his core when he heard the sobbing of a young woman. It echoed from somewhere in the dense forest. Out in the distance, the faint voice of the woman could be heard calling out into the lonesome night.

"Help me!"

The detective froze in place. His eyes widened to allow himself to see through more of the pitch black environment. Scanning the dark woods for signs of the one in need, Takao rotated at his neck and waist.

The voice pleaded, "Somebody, anybody!? Please, help me!"

For the sake of both of their lives, Takao knew he needed to find this person to get them to quiet down. It was too dangerous for them to be so exposed with that ferocious creature stalking them. Again, Detective Takao's adrenalin began to spike as he searched through the gloom fighting to hold his composure.

Reed came upon the shape of a young woman that was laid bare in a small sink hole with her arms raised above her head. The detective just looked at the girl perplexed, while instinctively removing his jacket.

"I'm not going to hurt you. I'm Detective Reed Takao with the HPD. You can lower your arms, miss."

As the young woman dropped her extremities, the detective could finally make out her face in the faint glow of his torch. He nearly choked when he realized who it was that called out for help. It was Frank and Mary Lou's missing daughter.

"Cheylene!? Cheylene Hikina!?" Reed covered her naked frame as best as he could. He began rubbing the stranded young woman's arms to warm her up.

"Miss Hikina, where have you been all this time? We've been looking for you everywhere!" Reed helped Cheylene up to her feet and pulled her out of the rocky hole. She trembled and whimpered as her arms draped around Reed's neck. The detective held her close as they made their way with caution through the woods.

"We need to get you out of here, my dear. I need to get you back to your father."

They made their way aimlessly through the blanket of night staying close to each other with every cautious step. Masking the severity of their current situation, the detective had become a bit more vocal than normal to add some levity to their dire situation.

"We are going to be okay, Cheylene. Everything is going to be alright."

Takao held true hope within his hands. Bringing loved ones back together is what Reed truly loved about his work. He could already picture her glorious homecoming. *Cheylene's return is going to mean the world to Frank. It would be the day the smile on the ol' man's face would return. A miracle, no doubt about it.*

"Without the efforts spent searching for Wili, I would've never crossed paths with you, Miss Hikina. I thank God that you are safe." The detective continued in thought, *Now, I just need to keep her that way and get her out of this jungle.*

A smell began to irritate Detective Takao's nose and throat. He could hear Cheylene's breathing becoming labored as her chest began to vibrate with a deep quiver.

"Cheylene?" Takao could feel the young woman slowing down. "Yeah, okay. Maybe we should take a short break. Let me see if we have reception out here."

Reed released his grip on Cheylene, holding his light up toward the girl, he was startled to see she was gone. The enormous dog like creature that chased him into the woods was there in her stead wearing his police jacket. The monster snarled and slashed the cell phone out of Detective Takao's hand. He grabbed his wrist and winced. He tried desperately to communicate with the missing girl.

"Cheylene!? Wait, stop, don't do this! Let me help you!"

The dog faced monstrosity lunged at the detective causing him to accidentally slip backwards falling down a steep ninety foot drop.

The brindled half-animal moved to the edge of the dark abyss and growled at the chasm below. It looked upward at the radiant moon glued onto the deep blue canvas above and let out a savage howl that echoed down the mountainside and along the valley walls.

Iwakālua kūmākahi

Mr. Lee stayed up all night sitting beside the house phone and keeping a close watch on his driveway. The light from the television began to compete with the dawning of the rising sun. His mind started to move into a dark place. *Dis is not da time wea no news is good news. Please don't let us down, Detective Takao.*

Kaimi had fallen asleep on the couch with a light blanket covering his legs. He rolled over to see the T.V. was on, but muted.

"Dad? Eh, you was up all night?" Kaimi rubbed his eyes to see the stress on his father's face.

Mr. Lee wiped his cheeks with both hands blinking slowly as he stared far away. "I'm sorry, Kaimi, I don't mean to seem distant. Yo' mama would know exactly what to do in dis situation. She would know what to say, how to comfort you and keep me calm."

Kaimi could understand exactly what his father was trying to express, but he didn't believe he was the one in need of the support. Just by looking at how his father had physically changed in one day helped Kaimi understand that his pops deserved that solace.

"Dad, dea's no reason fo' be sorry. Dis isn't somet'ing you need to carry all by yo'self. I t'ink dat it's time dat I finally take chahge an' become moah like you." He tried his best to sound like Wili.

Kaimi's father began to laugh hysterically. It scared and worried Kaimi to see his dad display this behavior.

"Boy, you already too much like me! What you need to do is be moah like yo' maddah! I nevah had any worry wen' it came to da safety of yo' mama. She could handle. In fac', she fought moah den a few battles fo' yo' old man!" It was nice to see his dad smiling again, he began to chuckle as memories of the twins' mother clearly returned, but soon his smile slowly faded and he began to sob, "Yo' braddah, he reminds me of D, yo' mama. Not knowing wea he stay is killing me. It feels like losing her all ovah again."

Kaimi started to understand now why his father would always dote over him, yet he would allow Wili to do the most precarious things. Kaimi remembered the one time his dad let Wili go up on the roof to clean the swiped mangoes from the house gutters, but threw a fit when he found out that he followed his brother up the ladder. It also explained why he always wanted them both to be together. It was like the relationship his mom and dad had with each other.

"It'll be alright Dad. Wili will make it home safe an' sound. Guarens!"

The ol' man's face was in doubt, "Dis world is a terrifying place, my boy. Terrifying. Did I tell you how yo' maddah an' I firs' met?"

Kaimi sat up on the couch and shook his head with the edges of his mouth pulled to the floor.

"I was hangin' wit' some of my frien's from skoo. Day wanted fo' go ova to da protest's up at 'Ōma'o State Reserve. It was during a time befoah da state wen' actually grow one conscience. My frien's wen' tell me get da 'ono kine grinds up at deez events, cuz da Hawaiian's really know how fo' trow one mean pā'ina! When we got dea, had governmental's all dress up in riot gear, laddat. Da kānaka was hootin' an' hollerin' an' chantin', all kine kahiko going on, it was nuts. Da head governmental was sitting on one scaffold, holding dis megaphone yellin' at da lāhui fo' go away. I gotta admit, Kaimi, yo' faddah was sked. I didn't even know why I was dea. It was getting pretty bad, pretty fas'! Like I said befoah, terrifying." Mr. Lee flashed his hands toward his son, "Den, I see da most beautiful creacha emerge from da crowd, a young girl about my age wearing one red an' yellow sarong, standin' up tall an' just started yellin' moah loud den da rest of da addah's, 'I mua kākou, I mua! Mālama pono kēia wahi!"

Mr. Lee could already see his story telling was moving a bit too fast. Kaimi's face compacted as he tilted his head, "I mua kākou? What do doze words mean, Dad?"

Mr. Lee nodded at his son's request to speak clearer. "It means to do better, son. So anyways, dis powerhouse of one wahine, yo' maddah, was calling out to deez militants to return to da old ways. To be kama'āina, people of da land, you see? Too much haolification too fast was killing da 'āina. Da Hawaiian's believe if you take kea da land, da land take kea of you. Live pono. Day believe da 'āina needed a voice, an advocate fo' proteck her. Da hā'ole's was bussin' her up fo' make crazy money, greedy buggahz. An' deez kānaka maoli knew dat aftah da rape of da 'āina, da hā'ole's would leave da Hawaiian's fo' clean up all da 'ōpala." Mr. Lee checked his son to make sure he was still in a comfortable place. "Anyway, yo' mama jus' ran up into da valley right pass da line of māka'i. Den all da army ants followed aftah, but all da extra stuff on dea body made it hahd fo' dem keep up wit' yo' mama."

Kaimi began to squirm, "So, what happened? Was Mom okay?"

Mr. Lee nodded, "Moah den okay, yo' maddah wen' fine one of da most important ancient sites on dis island. She found da entrance to one lava tube hidden in one fern grotto. Da cave was massive an' what was moah important was da contents dat remained inside fo' hundreds of yeeahs."

Kaimi was quite literally on the edge of his seat, "What was it, Dad? What was in da lava tube?"

Kaimi's father pointed to a photo on the bookshelf, "Cave drawings, artifac's and bones of da ancient peoples."

Mr. Lee could see his son struggling with new found inquiry. Kaimi stood up and walked over to the picture. "I always tought dis was jus' one photo of Mom at da museum. You mean to tell me dis was what she found, an' dis is how it looked when she found it!?"

Kaimi's father nodded. The morning sun shined off of his moistened eyes, "Every single one of us dea, da kamaʻāina an' malihini, who evah was at da reserve dat day, got to experience goin' inside dat lava tube. Da whole mood changed aftah dat. All da kānaka was singin' an' da governmental's… well, day had to leave."

"Wait! Why did da guys need to leave?" Kaimi gave his father a perplexed look.

Mr. Lee explained, "Da place was now historical, an' no can build on historical land. But you wanna heeyah somet'ing real chicken skin, Kaimi? I wen' fine out latah dat dose suckin' hāʻole's went back up da reserve fo' go try steal all da artifac's, fo' buss up da kiʻi pōhaku an' try trow away da iwi so day could continue workin' on dat site, but when day went back up, day couldn't fine da lava tube. No one could, evah again. Da business guys wen' mess up though, da baboozes. See, no one would've found out what day was up to if day nevah go pay one local moke fo' help dem fine da cave, doze dummies."

Kaimi asked in bewilderment, "So, wait, da entire cave jus' vanished!?"

Mr. Lee shrugged, "Da buggah wen' jus' evaporate. If it wasn't fo' da witnesses dat day an' all da photos day took in an' aroun' da area, guarantee 'Ōma'o State Reserve would be one suckin' resort!" Mr. Lee watched Kaimi internalize what he had learned. "You okay, boy?"

"Pop, I was jus' wondering," Kaimi placed the picture frame back onto the bookshelf, "how did Mom know wea fo' look to find dat lava tube in da first place?"

Before Mr. Lee could say another word the phone blared and startled him and his boy, "Good morning, Lee residence."

A monotonous yet intense voice broke through the headset, "Am I speaking with a Mister Kalena Lee?"

Kaimi sat with eyes concentrated on the phone's speaker. A terrible feeling fell over him and he could tell this call was not going to be beneficial. The lines on Kaimi's father's brow bent and caused the wrinkles on his forehead to accentuate. "Dis is Kalena Lee. Who may I ask is calling?" Mr. Lee awaited an answer in a similarly direct tone.

"Mr. Lee, this is Detective Wilson with the HPD, Homicide. I need you to come down to the station. We have a few questions that we'd like to ask you about a detective that is assisting with your son's whereabouts." The detective made no noise on the other end after giving his introduction and making clear his intentions.

Mr. Lee got a foreboding vibe but he agreed to come down to the police station, "Give me fifteen minutes, Detective Wilson. I'll be dea." Mr. Lee hung up the phone quietly and explained to Kaimi he was going to be gone for a short while, "Apparently, I gotta go down to da police station now."

Kaimi had a look of worry. He remembered the strange girl under the tree and the shadows slamming around the house. It worried him that they might make an appearance again when he was all alone. "How long you gonna be gone?"

Mr. Lee took in a deep breath, "I don't know, son. Da guy on da phone said he's a detective wit' homicide."

Kaimi's heart raced, "Oh no! Is it Wili!?"

"Hang on, boy! It's not about yo' braddah. They jus' had some question's to ask, okay!?" Mr. Lee tried to calm his son before making his way down town.

Kaimi just shook his head with an aching in his heart for his brother, "Wili is so fearless. You said he was moah like Mom, yeah Dad? Was dea evah a time dat Mom was afraid?"

Kaimi's father smiled and sat back on the chair with his fingers interlaced. "Once." He looked up at his boy and could see he had the same look of concern that his wife made when she was hāpai with their boys. "She was nervous about childbirth. She heard about how painful it could be, an' it worried her. A lot. When she foun' out dat it wasn't just Wili swimmin' aroun' in her 'ōpū, an' dat you was in dea too, she wen' burs' into teeyahs. I was at a loss, boy!" Kaimi's dad started to laugh hysterically again. "I nevah knew what fo' do, I nevah know what fo' say. It's da one time yo' maddah said somet'ing negative to me. I'll nevah forget it." A tear fell from the eye of Kaimi's dad. He sniffed and looked directly into his son's eye's, "Yo' maddah wen' call me one wuss." A huge smile came over the old man's face, "I raised my arms like dis," He imitated the look he made over a decade ago, "I taught you wen' marry me fo' my chahm an' good looks!" Kaimi's dad slapped his hands together making a loud pop, "Yo' maddah jus' laughed at me uncontrollably fo' a good ten minutes straight, pointing directly at my face. Huuu! Yo' maddah had a beautiful laugh I tell you." Mr. Lee could see that his son looked a bit better off than before, but he decided to offer him to come for the ride,

"Will you be okay, Kaimi? Did you want to come wit' me?"

Kaimi sat up tall, "It's cool, Dad. I'll be alright. It'll be me an' Mom until you get back."

Kaimi's father stood up and cleared his chest with a deep cough. He grabbed his keys and wallet then pushed the front door open, "K-den, I'll be right back, boy."

The young man watched the front door slam shut behind his dad. He heard his father's clunker struggling to come to life and after a few clicks it finally turned over. With a pop from the muffler and the crunch over the gravel driveway, Mr. Lee made his way onto the road. The young man watched the family transport roll off the property, and even though that dirty old truck pulled away from home stealing away with his father, Kaimi did not feel alone. He looked back at the photo of his mother standing in the lava tube and smiled, "Okay, Mom. Whatchu like fo' breakfast?"

Iwakālua kūmālua

It was a reasonably quiet morning at the police department, with the exception of stern voices being hushed by thin plaster walls and large glass windows. Captain Lalau was in the middle of pushing procedure onto one of his senior detectives.

"I understand Reed was your partner, but from what Detective Wilson described *and* what was found at the scene, you need to take a step back and let Kenneth and Rush work this case." Captain Lalau drummed his finger tip on his desk as he spoke to emphasize his point.

Detective Barshaw hunched over the captain's desk to assert his earthly seniority over Detective Wilson. "With all do respect Captain, we don't know if Reed is dead! At the moment he is just missing, and that's my job, to find missing persons. So, let me find him!"

The captain stood to show Barshaw he wasn't in the mood to deal. "Don't you already have an assignment? Shouldn't you be out looking for Kalena Lee's son?"

Standing upright Detective Barshaw concurred, "Yes, Captain Lalau, but I believe the reason for Detective Takao's sudden disappearance is because he was working the Lee case after we left for the evening last night. At least let me tag along with Wilson to see if we can come to a definitive conclusion! Please, Captain... Reed isn't just a partner, he is my best friend."

Captain Lalau looked down at his desk eyeballing a photo of his golden retriever, Milky. "I know what it's like losing a good friend and partner on the job, Brent. Look, you ride along with Wilson as long as he is fine with it. The moment you locate Detective Takao you get a hold of me immediately, do you understand?"

Detective Barshaw's posture became stiff as a board, "Yes, sir! Thank you, sir!"

"Don't thank me yet, detective," Captain Lalau began his descent back into his black leather throne. "Just remember, I was trying to do right by protecting you. I know all of my officers. I know their families. I know what you're going through. Just don't make me regret this decision. Keep a cool head, detective."

The captain flicked his face toward his office door. Detective Barshaw opened the entry allowing Detective Wilson to exit first. Barshaw looked back at the captain as the door closed behind him reading the expression on his face. The prospect of finding Takao alive had become awfully grim.

As Detectives Wilson, Peters, and Barshaw made their way to the motor pool, Wilson gave his "Who's in charge" speech.

"Don't touch *anything* at the scene! I run a *very* tight ship around here, just ask Peters." Detective Peters nodded wide eyed to express the seriousness of Wilson's warning. Detective Wilson continued indulging in his declaration, "I would expect you to honor that or we will have a problem, and I *will* send you packing back to your captain. You *see* something, you tell me or Peters. You *smell* something, you tell me or Peters. You *hear* something, you tell me or Peters. Any conclusions or thoughts that materialize in that crusty head of yours…"

Brent interrupted, "Let me guess, tell you or Peters?"

Wilson waved his arm in front of Barshaw pressing into his shoulder, stalling him in place, "No, you *tell* me. You being here right now is a favor to Reed, Detective Barshaw. He was there for me when we went through training. He's a good guy. So let me make myself clear,

I am also just as invested in finding Detective Takao as you are." Detective Wilson lowered his arm and put on his sunglasses.

"Get in!"

Wilson popped open the locks on his all black Ford Mustang. Detective Peters gripped the front passenger door handle.

Barshaw put both hands up at chest level, "Look, as much as I enjoy riding Ms. Daisy, I think we'll all be a lot more comfortable if I drove my own wheels." Brent walked over a couple of lanes and hopped into his vehicle and pulled his sunshade down. He looked into the eyes of the old man in the reflection of his rearview mirror and sputtered, "Lord, help me."

Iwakālua kūmākolu

Detective Wilson pulled his car over about sixteen yards behind Takao's abandoned vehicle. Barshaw pulled up alongside the two other detectives exiting their ride, "Are we taking a shuttle the rest of the way?"

Detective Wilson rolled his eyes toward the crime scene and shook his head. "If the walk is too hard for you old man, you could always turn around and go back to the station for your mid-morning nap."

Barshaw reversed and paralleled behind Wilson's transport, slightly tempted to bump into the back of it as Peters fumbled out of the car with their work duffle.

Barshaw blinked slowly and whispered, "Well, here we go." He secured his automobile and met up with Wilson and Peters. "So, what exactly happened here? How did you two come to the conclusion someone died?"

Brent needed hard evidence to convince him it was a homicide. Detective Wilson squatted while directing

Barshaw's attention toward Takao's back tire with an extended pinky finger. The elder detective bent his torso to get a closer look.

"Okay, the tire popped. That doesn't spell certain doom."

Detective Peters threw a nervous look at Barshaw then watched his partner give out his signature "Wilson exhale" typically made when Peters would make mistakes. He was relieved to know that Barshaw was not immune to his superior's off putting retort.

Wilson looked back at Barshaw and squinted his eyes, "Do you need to go back to your car to grab your glasses, grandpa?"

Barshaw glared at Detective Wilson as he straightened his body. "Your rookie might be used to your condescending attitude, but you need to start showing me a little more respect, or this investigation will suffer. Reed doesn't deserve half-assed service! At least not at the expense of belittling me."

Detective Peters took an audible gulp catching the attention of his higher-up.

"Okay, you're right," Detective Wilson chewed at the corner of his mouth and pointed at the tire once more. "It's hard to see, but there is a bit of blood splatter here on the tire wall." Wilson stood up and jogged over to the side of the road. "Peters found a partial imprint here in the soft earth. It looks as if the victim fell pretty hard in this spot. We also found footprints just there." Wilson moved with a quick pace around the impacted area and faced the road. "The prints suggest the victim had gotten up and stood just here, making eye contact with their assailant, then pivoting and putting all effort into getting away." Detective Wilson squatted down again to show Detective Barshaw the depth of the leading foot. "But, this is where it gets very strange."

Detective Barshaw was astounded to see that there was a second set of footprints in the mud. These impressions were large, smeared prints of some kind of animal. Brent searched for a definitive explanation.

"So, what!? Where exactly does this lead!?"

Detective Peters glanced at his training officer and darted a look back at Detective Barshaw. "Sorry, Brent. When we called in all of our findings, Captain Lalau communicated to us directly to halt investigation. He had us come back to base before we could do any more digging. This was as far as we got. In all honesty, sir, we only made our way out here because we got the call earlier this morning from a Mrs. Durante. She initially saw Takao's car sitting in the ditch last night on her way to her kids house, but she realized there was something amiss when she saw it a second time after she left her family this morning. Our supervisor called us back to the station because Captain Lalau wanted to see us."

"Halting investigation to come back to the station? For what reason!?" Barshaw placed his hands on his hips and grunted, "In any case, why did you decide to wait this long to continue the investigation? Reed could be out there right now suffering! We've wasted too much time, it might already be too late. We need to do a search of these woods now!"

Iwakālua kūmāhā

Mr. Lee pushed his way through the station's front doors and was greeted at the help desk. "Hi, good mornin', my name is Kalena Lee. I was asked to come down an' talk to a Detective Wilson."

The officer at the front desk pointed at the waiting area, "I'll let the detective know you're here, Mr. Lee. Please take a seat."

After about ten minutes of waiting, Mr. Lee was greeted by a young female officer, "Good morning, Mr. Lee. I'm officer Lisa No'eau. You can follow me this way." They both walked over to the elevator and the doors popped open just as they approached.

Lisa reminded Kalena of his beautiful, late wife. She exuded a strong, yet feminine, disposition. Her hair was neat and tidy, she walked tall with long strides that went as far as her short legs would allow. Trying not to sound creepy, yet still paying a compliment to Lisa and honoring his wife, Mr. Lee attempted conversation, "I could imagine if my wife had become an officer of da law, she would pretty much look jus' like you... but much oldah, of course."

Lisa looked at the older gentleman's sweet innocent face and smiled, "Thank you. What does your wife do Mr. Lee, if you don't mind me asking?"

Mr. Lee rubbed the back of his neck thinking of how not to make things awkward, "Oh! Haha, she mostly just watches over da twins."

Lisa's brow arched up high, "Ah! A stay at home mom!?" She placed one hand in front of the other and rotated back and forth at the waist in a delighted manner. "It all starts at home, right Mr. Lee? And, values are best taught when a parent not only teaches but leads by that example! How old are they?"

For a moment, Mr. Lee thought he was having a conversation with his wife. When he noticed Lisa standing there frozen he realized he needed to get a hold of himself and offer her an answer. "How old? ah?" Mr. Lee reached his ear toward Lisa as if the question was asked in a foreign language, "Oh! My boys!?" Lisa smiled and gave quick short nods. "Haha, I'm so sorry, Offisah No'eau. Dayah fifteen. Sophomores dis yeeah."

"Oh!" Lisa placed her right hand over her vest and continued, "There is nothing more honorable than taking care of 'ohana, isn't that right Mr. Lee? What a blessing for you both."

The elevator beeped and the doors opened to reveal a work area that contrasted with officer No‘eau’s personality. Mr. Lee thought the floor was a drab and depressing space. The young officer walked Mr. Lee over to the captain’s office and had him sit at one of the desks just outside the door. He could see the captain on a call through the picture windows, so he just sat back and waited patiently.

“Okay, Mr. Lee. It was a pleasure meeting you. You have a very nice day.”

As Mr. Lee waved good-bye, he started to wander in his memories of the days when the boys were little. It made his eyes tear up thinking about their mama, and not seeing Wili for this long was making him very concerned about this particular meeting.

After a short while, the glass door of the office brushed against its metal frame. The large mass of Captain Lalau eclipsed the fluorescents that once filled the entire floor with forlorn luminance.

“Mr. Lee?” his booming voice caused Mr. Lee to jolt. “Please, come inside.”

Mr. Lee sat and looked around Captain Lalau’s office. He had all kinds of ancient weapons decorating his walls. They all had a sheen to them, like they were recently reproduced in a factory. On closer inspection he could see metal name plates attached to each one. Apparently, they were commendations and awards for outstanding leadership. Mr. Lee thought, *I guess his stature wasn't da only t'ing about him dat was quite impressive.* He looked down at the captain's desk and saw a photo of officer No'eau in a koa wood frame. She was wearing a stack of lei and a huge smile. She was already a young woman but the photo made her look even younger.

Captain Lalau snapped Mr. Lee's attention straight back to him, "My daughter. At her graduation from the academy."

Mr. Lee blinked from the surprise of the captain's sudden declaration and how odd it was that this petite young lady had a full grown bear for a father.

"No'eau?"

The captain found his seat and exhaled, "My first wife. Her maiden name was No'eau. My daughter took her name so it wouldn't show nepotism in the department. It doesn't matter either way, she would've become an officer regardless of who her parents were. She's very skilled. You can see the irony."

What Mr. Lee could see was that the captain had strong family ties, which is probably why Lisa did too. Mr. Lee was no slouch when it came to 'ohana either.

"Captain Lalau, why was I called to da station? Is dea new information about my son, Wiliami?"

The captain leaned forward and put his elbows on the desk while weaving his fingers together. "A problem may have come up in your son's case. I may need to reassign your missing son to a different team."

Mr. Lee was confused, "Wait, I'm not following. Did Barshaw an' Takao drop my case? Did day give up on my boy?"

Captain Lalau shook his head, "It's nothing like that, Mr. Lee. Inexplicably, one of my men went missing yesterday evening. He hadn't checked in this morning and then we got a call from a civilian about finding a vehicle abandoned up Pu'u Uila. As you may or may not have already deduced, the car belonged to the officer that has not checked in. The detectives that were on the scene have found evidence of foul play. They're currently looking into it."

Mr. Lee rested his face in his hands thinking about the craziness that had cropped up in these last couple of days and the safety of his family. He sat up in his chair and asked, "Captain Lalau, what in da name of all t'ings holy is goin' on in dis town!? Do you have any idea of who it was dat went missing?"

Captain Lalau stuck out his lower lip and pushed it up toward his nose, he breathed deeply and spoke on exhale. "Detective Reed Takao."

Mr. Lee's face began to burn and his heart sank, "Oh, my God." He felt like he needed to vomit.

"Hey, are you okay, Mr. Lee?" The captain stood up quickly to attend to his visitor. "What's happening?"

Holding his hands up above his head, closing his eyes and pressing his chin into his chest, Mr. Lee stalled Captain Lalau. "I'm fine, Captain. I'm just very, very concerned. I spoke to Reed last night. I wen' ask him fo' help wit' our situation because it required a bit more understanding, somet'ing we weren't getting wit' Detective Barshaw. Detective Takao agreed to take a look around town on his way home. He taught Wili might show up wit' his friends at da strip mall or movie teayatah. He called me at aroun' a quartah to seven to let me know he was going ovah to da De Souza's an' dat was da las' time I heard from him."

Captain Lalau looked at Mr. Lee and stood unnervingly still. The expression on Captain Lalau's face began to frighten Mr. Lee. He stared over his eyeglass rims, his gaze resembling that of a lioness stalking its prey. The room's temperature dropped and the walls began to darken. Mr. Lee's heart began to thump like a rabbit's.

"Captain?"

The captain's face changed into a heartwarming smile and then everything in the office illuminated and warmed back up to normal.

"Mr. Lee, I have a wonderful idea!" Captain Lalau strut around his desk and snapped up the phone. His large fingers poked at the key pad wildly while he nestled the handset between his neck and shoulder.

"Wilson! I am going to send Mr. Lee, the father of the missing boy, to come and help with the search. Uh huh. Yes. Alright! He will be down there soon." Captain Lalau smiled again as he hung up the phone, "Mr. Lee, I think you may want to join the team at Pu'u Uila street. They are currently investigating near the De Souza's. Maybe you'll be able provide a different perspective. Bring the search for your son to a close?" The captain could see Mr. Lee's hesitation, "Or not Mr. Lee, if you don't feel up to it. I can call Detective Wilson right back and let him know. I just figured your being there would make it easier for Wiliami to come home and help bring about a safe and sound ending."

Mr. Lee stood up and patted his pockets to make sure he had all of his belongings. "Yeah, s-sounds good, Captain! I t'ink I going h-head out to, uh, what was dat street name again? Uh, Pu'u Uila, no? Okay, I be on my way. Mahalo, again captain."

Captain Lalau stood beside his desk and watched Mr. Lee lumbering off to the elevators. Mr. Lee was too nervous to turn around. He pressed the button to the lift and it opened immediately.

"T'ank you, elevator!" Mr. Lee blurted as he jumped inside and knuckled the L button. He took a deep breath and shook his head, "What da heck is going on!?"

Iwakālua kūmālima

"Reed!" Detective Barshaw's voice soared above the forest canopy. He called out once more, but his voice began to crack from over use. "Reed!"

Wilson and Peters could be heard off in the distance also calling out for the missing detective. Because all of the tree's large roots were overlapping and tangled, it was difficult to pin point in what direction Detective Takao went.

There was a steady cool breeze flowing high above the tree tops that pushed the clouds swiftly across the sky. Detective Barshaw could see the midday sun sparkling through the tree's branches, causing the shadows from the leaves to dance along the forest floor. Barshaw tried desperately to understand how Reed could have possibly navigated the woods in the dark. He had a hard enough time trying to catch his bearings at high noon. The hush of the leaves made Barshaw feel as though the forest was keeping secrets.

The eerie nonchalant whistling high in the canopy gave him the notion that they had already run out of time.

Peters could be heard calling out to the two other men. Detective Barshaw negotiated his way through the uneven terrain. He found Peters examining a blood trail that traveled north-west of their position.

Barshaw barked, "What are we waiting for? Let's go!"

The new found vigor in all three men had them racing to find the end of the trail. Each detective hoping it would lead to a successful rescue of their injured colleague. After only a few minutes, they were stopped near a small pit where a larger quantity of blood had settled. Wilson halted them from moving on.

"Hey, guys! Look here." Barshaw and Peters eyed the stain that Wilson inspected. "It looks like the victim hung around here for a while… but, why?"

Wilson proceeded up and away from the sink hole. He could see there was a larger space between blood spatter. His thoughts moved through his lips, "The increase in blood and change in pattern suggests the victim decreased the speed that they traveled. Why did the victim decide to slow their momentum while being chased by a large predator?"

Barshaw interrupted, "Look, Wilson, can we stop saying 'victim' and just say Reed? We all know it's his blood."

Wilson could see Detective Barshaw was more than annoyed with the use of proper terminology. "Okay, Brent, but my question still stands. Why would Reed slow down if he were being hunted?" Wilson continued to track Takao's movements while Barshaw and Peters followed closely behind.

"There!" Barshaw dabbed his pointer finger at a tree root. "A partial!"

Kenneth kneeled over, "Good eye, Brent! I guess your vision isn't as bad as I thought it was." Detective Wilson thought as he inspected the toes and ball of the incomplete print. *Huh? Small...* well, I guess it could be a young woman's print or a teen-ish boy..."

Barshaw's eye brows flexed, "Wili!?" Peters looked back toward the older detective out of curiosity. Brent elected to clarify, "Our current case had a teenaged boy gone missing. Might be why Reed came out here last night. Maybe he got a lead."

The story began to take shape. Wilson started to connect the pieces, "So, Detective Takao was trying to protect someone. A young male or a woman that was hurt or incapacitated?" Wilson got up and continued on. He carefully examined the area around each drop of blood. "Did he just happen across this individual? Did he know they were out here?"

They could all hear the faint sound of water flowing nearby. Peters declared, "Careful gentlemen, there may be more sinkholes like this in the area. Stay together."

It wasn't long after finding the new pattern of gore that their journey had finally come to a head. As the detectives pushed their way through a thicket, they found an HPD issue flip phone laying in the dirt with arterial fluid spattered over it.

Brent turned away and wiped his hand across his forehead, "Damn it!" The two other detectives looked at Barshaw seeking an explanation. "It's Takao's cellular. He put that damn rainbow sticker toward the top." The two other detectives eyed the reflective decal. "It was given to him by a little girl, the sister of one of our cases. We never found her brother, but Reed became close to her. She's up at a university in California now." Barshaw jumped to a thought of the young girl returning home to find out that while she was away she had lost her second big brother.

The three men scanned the area for more important hints. Peters bent over to get a better look at the soil when he felt a sharp tug on his right shoulder, "Easy, detective!" Wilson pulled Peters away from the edge of a steep cliff.

"Holy cow!" Peters looked down to see a far drop, "Thanks, Ken."

Wilson patted Peters on the back, "You need to keep a better eye, Rush." The lead detective continued to search through the overgrown area to find more clues and called out once he found something of significance. Standing up from a squat he exclaimed, "There you are!" Kenneth pushed some brush off to the side and stated, "Our culprit."

Barshaw looked under the low foliage to find an unobstructed shot of a clear set of large footprints made by an animal of considerable size. "Can't be a bear…"

Wilson squinted his right eye at Barshaw and held him in contempt for even thinking about the possibility of someone being attacked by a bear in Hawai'i.

Peters came over to share his expertise, "Hmmm, that's canine. An unrealistically big fella too, and even *that* is an understatement."

Barshaw rubbed his jaw, "So, a wolf?"

"Not at all," Peters traced his finger on the outside of the impression. "These prints are wide which would indicate that it's your standard breed of dog. Although, a very, *very* big dog."

Wilson scooted over to test his subordinate, "You're missing one detail, Detective Peters."

The rookie looked even closer, "I'm sorry Ken, I don't follow."

"You're too close, take a step back," Wilson explained. He held the bush in place to make it easier for Peters to examine the footprints unhindered.

"There's no way!" The young detective's voice was shaken. His face reflected fear as he shook his head in disbelief, "This is something else!"

Barshaw snorted impatiently, "Not a dog!?"

Peters skin became paler than normal. He shook his head and explained his reasoning, "This thing, it can't be a dog. It's walking around on two legs!"

Sunday

Iwakālua kūmāono

Mr. Lee's nerves had him on high alert. His attention was divided by the storm clouds looming above and his meeting at the police station. He was still pretty freaked out at Captain Lalau's reaction when explaining that he had contacted Detective Takao before he disappeared. Mr. Lee began to rationalize the response, *Wouldn't I be upset at dat news too? I probably trew da captain fo' a loop when I provided dat information.* Mr. Lee shook his head and began to accept that Detective Takao probably went missing all because he asked for his help. He thought about how insensitive he was being. *Ah! Deez guys just tryin' fo' help us out! Why am I being so unappreciative? Donna wouldn't ack laddat, D would probably be out dea lookin' foah ouah son wit' out hesitation!* Wiliami popped into his mind and he started to feel terrible.

"I'm coming, son!"

Rain began to sprinkle down as a light mist. The sound of tapping could be heard coming from the roof of Mr. Lee's truck. He switched his wipers on and the dust from the work yard that sat on the windshield mixed with the light smattering of rain. It caused a layer of mud to smear across his windshield like jam over bread. A dark sheet of clay blocked out all forward visibility. Mr. Lee quickly rolled down his window and stuck his head outside to avoid getting into an accident. Suddenly, a torrential downpour pounded his poor rusty clunker and drenched his face. Mr. Lee yanked his head back inside the cab and rolled up the window. He immediately wiped the water from his eyes to clear his vision. The mud had vanished off of the windshield, but the huge amount of water that was falling remained a safety concern. It caused the worn down wipers to bow and flex beyond its structural ability.

Mr. Lee began to grumble, "How da heck are we supposed to search fo' Wili an' Detective Takao in dis mess?"

From the corner of Mr. Lee's eye he could see a swift, inhuman shadow slipping in between the trees that lined the side of the road.

He blurted out in hysterics, "What da heck is dat!?"

Casting his attention toward the roadside, Kalena witnessed the shadowy form lean up against a tall pine tree further up ahead. As he got closer, Mr. Lee could make out a tail flicking and flailing at the back of the mysterious figure. It stretched its rear legs and braced its arms against the tree causing the thirty foot fir to come crashing down with a heavy thud. The fallen tree laid across the entire street blocking the path in both directions. Mr. Lee yanked the steering wheel hard to the left causing it to hydroplane. The truck slid to a halt and Mr. Lee took a look out the passenger window to see his vehicle had come within mere inches of striking the collapsed fir.

The rusty wagon began to shake and vibrate aggressively as the bed was being pressed down with an immense weight. Mr. Lee looked into the rear view mirror and observed the otherworldly creature climbing into the back of his truck heading toward the cab. Mr. Lee slammed the gas pedal down hard causing the machine to spit out a bang from the muffler. Its wheels spun freely over the slick surface making no gains in distance. When the tires finally gripped the asphalt, it launched the truck uncontrollably off the side of the road and down the grassy hill. The truck stopped with a loud crash just as thunder cracked from the heavens above.

Iwakālua kūmāhiku

With a flash of lightning and roar of thunder, water fell from above with intense power. Detective Barshaw squawked, "Where the hell did all this come from!?" He hugged up against the trunk of a large banyan tree using it as a make shift shelter.

Peters eyed up above with a puzzled expression. "The sky was clear just a moment ago!"

"We're experiencing some very peculiar weather, gentlemen." Wilson scooped a portable poncho out of his coat and slipped it on at high speed. "We need to be prepared for anything."

Wilson, Peters, and Barshaw scrambled to get out of the forest. The rain poured down with so much force that the leaves up in the canopy provided no defense against getting soaked. None of the men stopped, they continued moving quickly until finally they made it back to the street near their vehicles.

Peters recounted their speed on return, "It felt like we were a lot deeper into the woods then that!"

All three men jumped into Wilson's Mustang to make a plan. Barshaw sat resentfully in the backseat inspecting the car's sleek interior. Even the oh so fresh smell of the car made him annoyed. "So, Kenneth, what's next?"

Detective Wilson looked at Barshaw through his rear view mirror, "This isn't looking good for your partner, Brent. I'm thinking recovery."

Detective Barshaw shook his head in disbelief, "I can't give up hope, Wilson. He wouldn't!"

Wilson cast his eyes up at the falling rain while still communicating direct and to the point with Brent, "It's just another step, detective, you know that. If we find no trace of remains, hope is restored for us optimists. But, if we recover him, at least we'll have closure."

Detective Barshaw thought of himself as being cold and calculating, but Wilson was on a whole new level, almost teetering on psychopathic. "Where was your first location of interest?"

Detective Wilson nodded at Barshaw's acceptance, "We covered these woods pretty well. Location A should be at the base of the cliff where we found Takao's cellular. It's quite possible he could've pulled a Peters and slipped by accident. My bet is his body will be at the bottom of that cliff." Detective Peters looked at

Wilson from his periphery feeling slighted. "Location B is the housing in this area. We canvass these homes to find anything or anyone suspicious. We find out if anyone had seen or heard anything strange last night. Detective Takao can't be far from this region, with or without a teenager in tow. If Takao made it out of these woods, he would've sought medical attention for his wounds. Our final location would be island wide with the focus on hospitals and clinics. It's possible a civilian assisted Takao and his companion. Someone could have given them a ride to a medical facility."

Barshaw nodded making a choice in his head, "Okay, I'll call in for a search party to go to the base of the cliff. Then, I will stop off at all of the after hours clinics and the main hospital to see if we can find him there with his plus one. You two can go door to door to see if you can find any clues."

Detective Barshaw hopped out of Wilson's black Ford and quickly got into his vehicle. Brent turned on the heater and contacted the station as he watched Wilson's brake lights glow. After a moment, Wilson and Peters slowly pulled away, turning onto Puʻu Uila Street. Barshaw called in for the search and rescue.

Takao's car sat calm and alone as the rain and loose leaves sprinkled all over it. Detective Barshaw pulled his gear shift into drive and turned around to make his way back down the mountain. As Brent carefully managed his way through the rain and around curves of the road he unexpectedly came across a downed tree. He pulled his vehicle over to the shoulder and stepped out to survey the situation. “This weekend keeps getting stranger and stranger by the moment.” Brent could see the tree hanging another ten feet off the side of the town bound lane.

"Hey!”

Barshaw was startled by a voice cutting through the shower. He turned to see a man holding an umbrella standing on the opposite side of the fallen evergreen.

“Hey, you got a cell phone, buddy!?”

Detective Barshaw yelled over the splashing noises, “Yes, and a radio!”

The man dropped his hands to his side and turned his ear, “What!?”

Barshaw tried to raise his voice over the falling rain, “I have both!”

The man twitched and reported back, “Ha, ha very funny, buddy! The water isn’t high enough for that!”

Barshaw’s expression looked as if he wished he’d never stepped out of his car. He swiped his finger in the air back and forth, “Other than the tree, do you need assistance!?”

The man just stood there shaking head, “What!?”

“This guy is giving me a migraine already,” Detective Barshaw murmured as he got ready to give it one last shot. He took the deepest breath he could and spoke as loud as possible just as the rain coincidentally stopped, "Did you need assistance!?" Barshaw cast his gaze upward to see that the sky was now burning a bright blue.

The motorist stood with rounded eyes, "Yeah, there seems to have been an accident."

Barshaw, already fed up with this back and forth, asked for clarification, "Other than this tree here, is everything alright on your side?"

The man turned slowly and looked over to the side of the road, "There's a truck at the bottom of this hill."

The detective ran quickly to the guard rail and leaned over it to get a good look. He could see a very familiar red pickup truck busted to pieces at the base of the hill. What was left of the motor vehicle was lodged between a tight cluster of pine trees.

"Oh, lord! Kalena!" Barshaw made his way back to his car to report the downed tree and the accident. "Dispatch, send fire rescue to Lunalilo Highway west, near marker niner-two-six, civilian vehicle is at the base of the pike near a downed tree blocking all lanes in both directions."

Not wanting to waste time the detective made his way to the road's edge and carefully started to descend the slippery hill. The wet grass made the slope very difficult to navigate which caused him to contemplate just sitting down and letting gravity do its work. Instead, he just took one step at a time and with each step he chanted, "Lord, have mercy."

When Detective Barshaw got to the base of the hill he dashed over to the wreck. He observed that all of the windows were completely blown out. The front end, including the engine, had caved into the cab, which was now so crushed he couldn't tell if Mr. Lee was still inside the vehicle or not. He moved to the driver's side with a worried heart. It was then that the detective could see that Mr. Lee's body was not present in the vehicle. He turned to inspect the area in front of the truck to determine if his body had ejected through the front windshield. There was no evidence he had. Brent started to move back up the hill keeping an open eye for Kalena's body laying amongst the incline of the hill. He found nothing.

The motorist had met Detective Barshaw halfway down the hill to help him back up to the top. "Perhaps you should've waited for the police to show up, buddy! You could get seriously hurt trying to be a hero like this."

The motorist yanked Barshaw back up to the road as the detective struggled to catch his breath. A sharp ringing sang in his right ear as he inhaled a deep breath to show his appreciation, "Okay, thank you for your help… Whoo!"

Barshaw placed his hands on his head. His jacket lifted up revealing his badge to the motorist, "Oh! officer, I'm sorry. I didn't know you were part of law enforcement."

Detective Barshaw waved his hand as he gulped down oxygen, "It's all good. I have already contacted dispatch. They're sending help."

As the detective and the motorist awaited aid, Barshaw decided to do some investigating. Brent aimed his way over to the base of the downed tree and he could see that even though it was partially termite eaten, there was some freshly splintered wood. Rubbing his thumb against the recent break he softly added, "I guess it's possible the heavy rain could've convinced the tree to give way." He looked toward a couple of other firs standing nearby to compare their durability.

A patrol car whooped and caught the detective's attention. The officer parked parallel to the downed tree with the light bar flashing. A young man exited his squad car and began setting out traffic cones. When he placed down the last cone, the footman made his way over to Brent.

"Detective Barshaw, I'm Officer Kūpau and I'm here to relieve you as first responder. Is there anything you need to pass down?"

Barshaw pointed over to the edge of the road, "Besides this downed tree, there was a motorist that drove his truck over the edge of the hill. The truck is smashed to bits, but there were no remains at the scene. We need a recovery vehicle down here to tow the wreckage back up." The detective cast his gaze back up at the sky, "Let's hope there isn't another freak storm."

The officer reached his finger under the back of his hat to scratch his head, "Another freak storm, sir?"

Barshaw turned and looked at the officer, "Yeah, the freak storm that made this road wet. What, it didn't rain at the station?"

"Sorry, detective," the officer straightened his cap, "I was posted up near the high school, and it didn't rain a single drop there."

Brent just nodded and furrowed his brows. *The high school is even closer than the police station. How did this guy not see any rain?* He glanced at the patrol car and realized it was bone dry.

Detective Barshaw left the officer and walked over to the motorist to provide some insight. "It's likely that we won't be able to go through this way for at least an hour."

The motorist shook his umbrella and contemplated the information. "I guess I could head back into town to do some shopping."

Barshaw looked at the man and asked, “Say, you wouldn’t mind helping out the HPD, would you?”

The gentleman smiled at the prospect, “What did you have in mind?”

Barshaw explained, “That truck down there belongs to a friend of mine and his son is home all alone.” The motorist just smiled quietly and awkwardly at Detective Barshaw, “Well, I thought since my car is stuck on the other side of the tree you could give me a lift over to see the boy. We can let him know what’s going on with his father.”

The motorist agreed to help, “Oh! Yeah, sure. Hop on in, buddy,” he invited Detective Barshaw into his automobile.

Brent jumped into the man’s passenger seat. There was some kind of pastel colored knitted fabric covering his dash board, and sitting right in the middle was a bobble head of Christ the Savior. Barshaw smiled as an airy half hearted laugh rose from his lips.

“What’s this, buddy?” The motorist questioned as the engine to his station wagon roared to life.

Ignoring the awkward moment completely, the detective introduced himself, “I’m Brent Barshaw, a detective with the H.P.D.”

The motorist extended his hand while pulling onto the street, “Marvin Mutter, but you can call me Mutt, buddy.”

The detective shook Mutt's hand and apologized for the mess his jacket was making on his interior. "Nice to meet you, uh, Mutt. Sorry about the mess…"

Marvin interrupted the detective, "Hey now, don't you worry about that. Water dries, it's no muss." He beamed a radiant smile that made Brent a little uncomfortable.

Barshaw frowned at his brow and cleared his throat, "Well, on behalf of the department I would like to say, 'Thank you for your time and assistance in this urgent matter.' I understand your time is important, so thank you."

"This is so exciting for me!" Mutt looked out his windshield still grinning from ear to ear. "I always wanted to be a policeman, like Riggs and Murtaugh, you know from *Forty-eight Hours*? I always found those stories to be so exhilarating! But, then I heard that police have a high divorce rate, and it quickly changed my mind."

"Ah! Mr. Mutter, how long have you been married?" Barshaw asked with endearment.

Marvin soured his expression for a short second and immediately went back to his unsettling smile, "No, detective, I'm not married." Mutt began to laugh a bit frantically, while shaking his head, as if it were a big joke. "No, no. At the Mutter residence it's just me and my Joel."

The detective did a double take, "Oh, so, just you and your son?"

The driver began to laugh even heartier, "Oh, goodness no, detective. Although Joel does behave like a child more often than I care to admit, when he upsets me I just boot him out of our bed, straight to the dog house."

Barshaw nodded in understanding, "Respect, it's very important nowadays."

Mutter turned to look at the detective and rubbed the side of his nose as he winked. The two men continued their conversation on their way to deliver the tragic news to a very lonely boy.

Iwakālua kūmāwalu

Kaimi grew impatient. His father said he'd be home shortly, yet three hours had already passed since he left the house and there was still no sign of his dad's red pickup. He contemplated calling Detective Takao's cell phone, but he didn't want to disturb the investigation. Kaimi just sat wishing he wasn't so helpless.

He thought back to when his family was whole. He remembered how there was a role for each person in the ʻohana. Categorizing always made things simple and neat to Kaimi. At a young age, it formed his perceptions of the people around him and helped him to accept why people would do things they'd do even though it seemed to be too difficult, monotonous, or down right dangerous.

He would observe his father and how hard working and responsible he was. Kaimi recalled how his dad would take care of any troubles that came up around the house, everything from electrical problems to monsters hiding under the bed. *Typical dad stuffs,* Kaimi snickered.

He watched how his mother could handle the house finances, interpreting paper work that would otherwise ruin their father's sanity. She would even help him and Wili with their schoolwork. He shrugged, *It's what a good mama does!*

It reinforced a falsehood that men be strong and protective, to be providers to the 'ohana. The other side of the same coin falsely painted women as just house wives and cooks, preprogrammed to be caregivers that are tender and loving. It wasn't until his mother was diagnosed with cancer, that Kaimi realized that both of his parents had the potential of being both sides of that coin. Categorizing people only limited the scope of the individual that perceived them that way. That neat little box didn't truly respect an individual and their unique skills and talents.

He remembered how his father needed to take care of the debts and paperwork that was piling up. *Dad struggled, but in da end he figured it out.* It was amazing that his dad also helped him and Wili with their school work. On top of that, both of them had a better understanding in their studies. Kaimi could only think, *Way to go, Pop!* He was so very proud of his dad and could only imagine that it must've been such an uncomfortable affair that he assisted him and Wili with.

He also remembered how challenging it was for his dad to show affection and comfort them when they yearned for their mama after she passed away. It was the most difficult time in all of their lives.

Before that, his mother showed incredible courage and strength when she fought her ravenous disease. She never complained, no matter how much pain she was in. When either he or Wili would search for her attention, she gave it without fail and always with a smile. The roles had flipped and Kaimi no longer believed that his father could be only one way or that his mother could only be one way. They showed him that through strenuous times either of them could pick up the slack. Both of his parents were brilliant and both of them had the strength of an ox. Both of them fought to protect and love the the people in their home and it wasn't because that's how they were built.

Kaimi decided he didn't want to be placed in a neat little box. He felt he could be just as strong, smart, and skilled as his dad, his mom and his brother. The scope of those ambitions caused fear to set in and made him wonder, *How would I evah reach dat goal? What would I need to do to be moah confident in myself?*

Kaimi believed he was not equipped with the tools necessary to be successful in his aspirations. He held his head in his hands, frustrated by his current state. *What's wrong wit' me, Mom? It must be like explaining color to a blind person.*

Kaimi continued his train of thought, *Wili was always sociable. He could make frien's anywea, an' he could make doze people fall in love wit' him jus' laddat. He was reckless, but it always seemed dat everyt'ing worked out fo' him no mattah how dangerous his decisions were. Wili seemed charmed. His choices made him look so mature an' purposeful. Why couldn't some of dat care free attitude rub off on me? Me an' Wili are twins aftah all.*

Kaimi still felt he was a baby. It made him angry that 'Alapaki could see that and even angrier when the guy threw it right in his face. Kaimi started to realize he used his youth as a crutch, because with age comes wisdom and strength, or so he thought. Everyday he prayed that his time on the earth would gift him with new attributes. The confused youth did not know that what he needed was a serious wake up call, a trial by fire, a moment of struggle to snap him out of his ignorance and self delusions. He had those gifts he yearned for inside him all along. The time was nearly upon him to emerge from his cocoon and spread his wings into the bigger world of self reliance.

From the corner of his eye Kaimi could see a shadowy profile making its way to the entrance of the house. The strange figure stomped its way up each step. As Kaimi moved over to the window to see who it was, he nearly had a stroke. He could see his brother standing on the landing right outside the house, motionless. Questions began to swirl in Kaimi's mind. *Why didn't he jus' come insai? Maybe it wasn't really Wili, but how was dat possible? He could clearly see him, plain as day!* Kaimi studied the solemn form as best he could through the window's screen. *There was no denying it, it sure looked like Wili.* At that moment, Kaimi didn't know if he should be happy or fearful. Either way, his heart thumped heavy and deep.

Walking as quietly as he could, Kaimi made his way to the wooden door and grabbed onto the handle. He opened the entry slowly not knowing what to expect. Upon pulling the door open, a small creak vibrated from the portal which caused Kaimi to cease all motion. He could make out his brother's contour through the narrow crack in the door frame. He noticed Wili remained unmoving. His breathing was rasped and heavy. There was a slight wheeze that turned into a rumbling growl that accompanied each one of his labored breaths. Kaimi carefully reached for the handle of the exterior screen door. As he turned the lever, the latch popped and made a sharp click which caused Wili to halt his breathing with a snort. Kaimi's body jolted as he gazed at the thick yellow liquid oozing from Wili's nose down to his mouth. He hesitated in disgust and was frightened back when Wili snatched the door handle away from him and slammed it open with ferocity.

Wili turned toward Kaimi with foam dripping from his mouth. Baring his teeth, he snarled, "You!?"

Kaimi's eyes bulged when he surveyed the right side of Wili's face. It was indented and looked as if it were smashed in by a large rock. His right eye was sealed shut with dried blood and puss. The skin around the area of impact looked like grated meat. Kaimi could see fly larvae crawling about the cavity of Wili's shattered cheek. The hurt young man stepped into the house. A maggot dripped from his chin and fell flat on the floor. Kaimi shook his head, backing away from the living horror movie. *I must be having one nightmayah! I fell asleep right dea on da couch an' I'm dreaming.* Kaimi glanced at the couch where he had been sitting in hopes that he was indeed having a nightmare. *I'll wake up once dis scab faced version of my braddah attacks me or kills me... I guess.*

Still hesitant to just let it happen, the fearful young man continued to retreat backward while chanting, "Wake up, wake up, wake up!"

Kaimi raised his arms in a protective fashion while letting out a scream as Scab Face Wili lunged toward him, grabbing Kaimi by the shoulder and taking hold of the waist band of his shorts. Wili threw his sibling across the living room, sending Kaimi's body soaring through the air until it was stopped by the bookshelf that was held fast to the wall. Blood started to pour from Kaimi's hairline and his vision began to blur. He shook his head, and pressing himself up off the floor, turned to see Wili smiling with his left eye glowing a fierce white. The disfigured boy leaped across the room and landed directly over Kaimi, knocking him back down to the floor, square onto his back. The photo of his mother fell from the shelf and crashed onto the ground beside him. The glass from the frame projected shards outward slicing Kaimi's face.

"You!?" Scab Face Wili took hold of Kaimi's neck with both hands and began squeezing. Warm saliva began dripping from his mouth falling onto Kaimi's face.

Kaimi had never seen his brother so irate, so vicious. Wili's hands grew tighter and tighter around his neck. Kaimi tried to pry his grip apart but it was too strong. He reached up toward Wili's right eye and scratched his fingers deep into the socket. Wili's stranglehold loosened as he clamped one hand over his wound. Warm blood sprayed down over Kaimi's chest drenching his neck and shirt.

Wili snarled. Baring his teeth inches from Kaimi's face he screamed again a high pitched shrill, "You!?"

Gripping his brother's soiled shirt he lifted Kaimi's shoulders off the floor and slammed him back down on the ground. Over and over, Kaimi was bashed into the wood panels of the floor. Wili then pressed his weight into Kaimi and looked up to the ceiling while letting out an ear-splitting howl. Wili's face tore open, his skull transformed right before Kaimi's eyes. His mouth then extended outward and his teeth grew into sharp spikes.

It brought Kaimi back to his nightmare at Makalike Bridge. His brother's appearance began to resemble 'Alapaki's face just as he chomped down on his head in that dark vision. Kaimi, in defeat, turned his head and squeezed his eyes shut to avoid witnessing his own demise.

A soft voice filled the young man's ears, "Kaimi! I mua! I mua!" It was the sound of his mother calling out to him. When he opened his eyes, he could see the photo of his mama. The story of her courage shot to the front of his mind. This small, young kanaka standing up to the fully armed might of a massive foreign government bent on destroying freedoms, life, and culture through fear and aggression. Kaimi's heart began to burn.

He looked directly at the creature he now believed was in no way his brother and shouted, "I mua kākou, I mua! Mālama pono kēia wahi!"

The dog-faced monstrosity furrowed its eyebrows and growled menacingly.

Kaimi swung his right fist into its jaw, knocking the brute back into the kitchen table with a loud smash. The beast whined and scrambled back up to its feet. His focus shot toward the front door where a voice could be heard shouting. The monster peered at Kaimi rising to his feet with fists clenched and a look of determination on his face. Scab Face Wili shot through the hallway turning into Wili's bedroom.

Detective Barshaw burst into the house with his gun exposed, "Kaimi!" He turned to see the young man covered in blood shaking as he eyed the hallway. "Kaimi, are you hurt!?" Barshaw made his way over to the boy to inspect his injuries.

Kaimi pointed toward the hall as his lower jaw chattered against his maxilla, "It's in Wili's room!"

Detective Barshaw made his way carefully toward the room's entry. He kicked in the door to see that the bedroom was uninhabited and the window was wide open. The detective ran over to the window and stuck his head out. He witnessed the car that drove him over to the Lee's house taking off down the street in a panic.

Barshaw shouted from the window, "Hey! Wait!"

Brent pulled his head back into the opening and flew to the porch. As he stepped outside he could see Mr. Mutter standing at the base of the steps shaken and confused.

"Mutt! What happened!?"

Marvin turned with his arm extended out in the direction his vehicle disappeared in, "You got out and I waited in my car like you asked when I heard terrifying noises coming from the house." His arm slapped down to his side as he made his way over to the detective. "When I saw you disappear into the house and let out that scream, I jumped out of the car to see if you needed help. Then, this kid with a messed up face threw me down and stole my automobile! What, in all things holy, is going on!?"

The detective looked at the ground shaking his head while rubbing his fingers over his eyes. "That's just perfect."

Iwakālua kūmāiwa

After the rain stopped, Detectives Wilson and Peters split up to start their questioning in the area. Both men moved unsuccessfully door to door trying to find the answers to Detective Takao's whereabouts. Several of the residences in that area were occupied by seniors, most of whom lived alone. The homes with full families hadn't noticed anything strange or unusual from the night before.

Peters continued house to house in hopes of giving his superior good news. Wilson just wanted to find something that would lead to Reed's safe return. No one had any information for the inspectors. That caused them both to fear that they may never find the truth of what happened from the night before.

Wilson made his way up the walkway of the De Souza's place, already believing the home was vacant. The house stood quiet and still, but it didn't stop the detective from knocking on the door's paint chipped frame. After a few minutes of waiting for some kind of reply, he turned to head over to the next home. As Wilson stepped off the lanai he was halted by the sound of something falling inside the run down home.

"Hello!? Detective Wilson with the HPD. I have some question's I'd like to ask if that would be alright."

The unkempt household remained eerily still as the detective stood patiently awaiting a response. He then saw a shadow flow past the window.

"Hello!?" Wilson walked over to the wall and peered through the darkness, "HPD, please open up. I just want to ask a few questions and I'll be on my way."

A putrid breeze poured out of the window and nearly choked the detective. The smell of rotting flesh filling Wilson's nose was more than enough cause to enter the domicile without a warrant. He removed his firearm from its holster and lined himself up with the entrance of the home.

"HPD, you have ten seconds to open up or I will kick in this door!" Wilson placed his right foot back in preparation to strike below the door's knob, "One! Two! Three!" The detective's heart sped up in his chest, "Four! Five!" Wilson could have sworn he heard activity behind the entryway so he paused his countdown for a moment. The sounds came to a stop, "Six! Seven! Eight! Nine!"

The inner door popped open a few of inches with a loud crack causing Wilson to terminate his countdown. He fixed his eye's on the dingy entrance as his heart beat even faster.

"Open the door and come out with your hands where I can *clearly* see them!"

The door disappeared as it swung into the dank room. It appeared as though there was a shadow standing beside the frame's siding, concealing itself from the light of day. Dust particles coasted through small strips of sunlight that could be seen through the opening.

The detective spoke sternly, "I said to come out, now!"

The outer door pressed open toward the detective and the obscured individual stepped out of the shadows onto the patio. Detective Wilson's face turned sheet white and his heart felt as if it stopped. His eyes became saucers and he slowly shook his head as he lowered his gun.

"Reed?"

Kanakolu

"I said, what in the name of the good Lord is going on here, detective!?" Mutt asked while looking out of the Lee's living room window in hopes his car would be on its way back to where it was stolen from.

Detective Barshaw sat the couch back upright and began picking up the items that fell off of the kitchen table. "I'm so sorry that your car was taken, Mutt…"

The unhinged assistant interrupted, "Call me Mr. Mutter, Detective Barshaw!"

"Look! I am sorry, but obviously there are bigger things going on here, Mr. Mutter." Barshaw grabbed the broom and dustpan to sweep the broken glass off the floor. "Even I am having difficulties with what's been happening with this poor family. Within the short span of three days, this young man has lost his brother *and* his father…"

Again the detective was interrupted mid sentence, "Wait, my dad stay missing!?" Kaimi had just come out of the bathroom from showering when he overheard the detective's heart wrenching news.

Detective Barshaw leaned the broom and dust pan up against the back of the couch, "Kaimi! I didn't mean for you to find out like that." Brent dusted his hands off on his shirt and guided Kaimi's attention toward Mutt. "Kaimi, I want you to meet Mr. Marvin Mutter. He found your father's truck at the base of Pu'u Uila Hill."

Kaimi walked over to Mutt and shook his hand, "Pleasah fo' meet you. So, you foun' my dad's truck?"

"It's a pleasure to meet you, young man." Marvin smiled at the boy. He felt terrible about the condition he was in. "Yes, Kaimi. I noticed your father's truck at the base of the hill when I saw tire tracks leading off the highway from a downed tree. It was actually Detective Barshaw that discovered it was your father's truck and most importantly that he was not amongst the wreckage."

Barshaw looked at Kaimi and provided more clarity, "Your father's truck was completely totaled at the base of that hill, but upon inspection of the area there was no evidence that your dad was injured in the accident." Barshaw straightened Mr. Lee's favorite chair and sat down while motioning Kaimi to sit on the couch nearby. "I can't tell you where your father is or in what condition he's in, but I am quite focused on finding that out, Kaimi. Finding him, and your brother, both in one piece is my main goal."

Kaimi began to experience that typical panic attack wash over him. He stood up in defiance of the emotion and stated, "Detective, I no longer believe dat my braddah, Wili, is okay. Jus' before you got hea, Wili had shown up on da steps, only it wasn't Wili. He was all hamajang. Da rock I trew at da bridge hit my braddah in da face an' wen' mess 'em all up."

Mr. Mutter pointed his finger toward Kaimi while widening his eyes at Barshaw, "That's what I saw, a boy with a face that was smashed! He's the one that stole my car!"

Kaimi tried his best to explain what he experienced before Barshaw burst onto the scene. "Da Scab Face Wili showed up on da front steps all mess up, an' angry! It was all my fault."

Barshaw squinted at the young man, "Your brother, Wili, was here!? You actually saw him?"

Kaimi nodded with a look of disappointment, "Da t'ing dat attacked me look like Wili, but nevah ack like Wili. It wen' buss me up an' made all dis mess." Kaimi double checked the detective to see if his story hadn't made him discount the rest of his experience. "But, dis was da unbelievable paht, detective." Kaimi could see Barshaw had already gotten his fair share of unbelievability for one day, but he continued his story anyway. "Wili transformed into some kind of monstah. Like one Wea-wolf!"

Mr. Mutter's mouth fell open, while Barshaw quickly added to Kaimi's story hoping to make sense of this madness. "Kaimi, we found very big footprints in the woods today. They belonged to some kind of huge canine that stood up on two legs!"

Mr. Mutter's mouth fell even more. Kaimi smiled, the cuts on his face had clotted and purple bruises magically appeared all over his body making it look like the spots on a dog. "I'm so happy dat you stay on board wit' what I've been saying, Detective Barshaw! Now you an' Detective Takao can work togedah to solve dis mystery!"

Brent clasped his hands with fingers pressed to his lips. He looked at his feet and took a quick moment, "Kaimi, Detective Takao was the reason we went into the woods today."

The wounded young man had a puzzled look on his face, "Detective Takao needed help in da woods?"

"No, Kaimi." Barshaw looked directly toward the boy, "Detective Takao did not report to work today. His car was found abandoned on the side of the road last night. There was evidence of a struggle near his car and ultimately the detectives' blood was scattered throughout the forest. We also recovered his cellphone from inside the woods near the edge of a cliff. I was on my way to the hospital when I came upon Mr. Mutter, the downed tree, and your father's truck. Mr. Mutter was nice enough to bring me here and regretfully had his car stolen."

Mr. Mutter looked as if he were about to faint, his skin became pale and shiny. Barshaw took notice, "Mr. Mutter, are you doing alright?"

"No! I am struggling to understand what is going on! This poor child was attacked by some smashed faced kid that was supposedly his own brother, but it then changed into a werewolf!?" Marvin looked as if he were going to lose it.

"Please remain calm, Mr. Mutter." Barshaw tried to inject some stability by coming up with a plan. "My duties still stand. First and foremost, we need to get a hold of transportation. I'll call the station and have a squad car brought to the house."

Marvin interjected, "What about my car!?"

Barshaw bobbed his head, "I'm sure your vehicle will reappear sooner or later. Unfortunately, that's not our main priority right now, Mr. Mutter. If we find fake Wili we will probably find your car, but we have no idea where the, um, other Wili has disappeared to."

Kaimi blurted, "Scab Face Wili!"

Barshaw gave a look that questioned Kaimi's state of mind, "Scab Face? Alright, scab face... okay, I guess. We have no idea where Scab Face Wili drove off to. It's an island and we know the car's make and color. It will turn up." Barshaw looked at Marvin with a hopeful stare, "Mr. Mutter, could I ask you another enormous favor?"

Marvin looked at Barshaw and vocalized how he detested helping the detective again. "Harumph! What is it this time, detective? You want to commandeer my house too!?"

The detective grimaced and then nodded at Mutt's response. "I can't bring Kaimi with me to investigate because it's too dangerous. He can't stay here because it's too dangerous. You've been such an amazing help thus far, would it be possible to babysit the boy this afternoon? The attacker has no idea where you live, so Kaimi will be safe until I return for him."

Mr. Mutter again looked at Kaimi and how his heart ached to see this kid hurt and alone. "Okay, fine! I'll watch Kaimi at my place. Joel will be there to help keep him safe too." Mutt looked over at Kaimi, "Maybe we can order a pizza and watch a movie. How does that sound?"

Kaimi dipped his head in agreement, "Dat sounds fun, Mr. Mutter. T'ank you!"

Marvin stopped the young man, "You can call me Mutt, buddy. And, you can thank the HPD and Detective Barshaw for the acquisition of our evening's musings."

Detective Barshaw went into the kitchen to contact the station and have them send out a car.

Kanakolu kūmākahi

The sun began its descent and the air grew cold. Peters decided to head back and meet up with his partner. He hoped that Wilson or Barshaw had better luck finding Detective Takao or at least had some kind of clue of how to locate him. As the detective strolled back the way he came, he realized that the area had changed from its lush colored atmosphere into a grim unsavory locale. The street became less vibrant and grew ominous with the setting of the sun. He began to feel quite unwelcome as the shadows grew long. It seemed like each home came alive and watched his every step closely, sensing the detective's fear and unease. Peters' pace quickened and he avoided eye contact with the houses. The residences that he received no answer from felt more foreboding, their mouths tightly shut to the whereabouts of his fellow law enforcement officer. Detective Peters was ready to leave the grim neighborhood behind if it refused to offer any support.

Rush ended up all the way back at the car and found no sign of Detective Wilson. He spun around looking for inlets or cul-de-sac's that he may have missed on exiting the eerie stretch. As he reluctantly started to walk back up the road, a sinister feeling made its way back into Detective Peters' chest. His heart beat forcefully and could be felt throbbing inside his ears. He brought out his cell and sent an alert to Detective Wilson's phone. He called to see if he should stay back at the car or meet up at a specific home. A second later, Detective Peters heard Wilson's ringtone close by. He jogged up to where he thought he heard the sound coming from, following it until the tone finally ended. The signal chimed from a dilapidated house with an overgrown yard. He walked up to the front door but couldn't see anything or anyone on the property.

Peters knocked on the door and called out, "Kenneth, are you in there!?"

No sound came from the menacing homestead. Peters circled around the house checking each portal as he came across one.

"Ken!?"

Rush made it all the way around to the back of the house and still there was no sign of his partner. He thought, *Did he go inside?*

The detective made his way up to one of the windows and tried to take a look, but it was too difficult to make anything out through the darkness and the sheet of nastiness covering the screens. He noticed there was a foul odor coming from a window of the house as it seemed to exhale.

"Good grief, did something die in there?" Peters mumbled.

He tried scratching at the screen to remove some of the soot that blocked the light from penetrating into the room. Peters felt a hand grip tight to his left shoulder which caused him to jump.

"Holy cow! Wilson, are you trying to give me a heart attack!?"

Detective Wilson looked at Peters as if he were overreacting. "Find anything interesting?"

Rush concentrated on willing his heart to withdraw from his throat. "I didn't find anything. Well, there was an older lady from one house around the corner that said she thought she heard a woman crying for help in the woods last night. When she went to get her husband, she found him fast asleep in front of the television that was playing a horror story." Detective Peters stepped out from the tall grass and weeds, "I don't know, Wilson. It just doesn't seem like the people around here get out much. Seems like this is more of a community for the retired."

Wilson just looked at Peters as if he were awaiting some ground breaking information that would help to resolve Detective Takao's bearings. But nothing of use flowed from his rookie's prattle.

Peters asked, "Did you happen to come across anything that could help us find Detective Takao, sir?"

Wilson rolled his eyes and walked away from the De Souza's house, "Nope, not a thing."

Peters shook his head, "Well, I hope Barshaw had better luck on his end."

Wilson remained quiet as the couple returned to the black Ford Mustang that sat out of place in the sullen town. The rookie detective positioned himself beside the car and just waited for his partner to pop the locks open. Wilson stood at the back of his car with hands clasped waiting for some kind of magic to happen.

Peters looked at his training officer befuddled, "Say, Kenneth, are you going to unlock the car so we can get the heck out of here?"

Wilson quickly patted at his pockets finding the car keys in his jacket, "Hey, you want to drive?"

Peters eyes snapped open, "Really, Ken?"

Peters had always wanted to drive his partner's Mustang and asked him on a few occasions, but would always be greeted by the Wilson exhale that was typically produced when Peters made mistakes. He never believed in a million years the day would come when Wilson would allow him to drive his baby. Ken tossed the keys in Rush's direction and both men jumped in. Peters rubbed his thumbs over the smooth surface of the steering wheel.

"So, where are we off to, sir? Shall we join the search at the base of the cliff?"

Wilson looked at Peters from the passenger's seat. "I think it would be best if we went back to the station."

Kanakolu kūmālua

Brent and Kaimi straightened up the house as much as possible. The broken furniture was moved to the front of the yard for collection and the floor was mopped to remove all of the blood. Mutt sat quietly on the couch observing the two men working methodically from one end of the home to the other. He couldn't help but watch a small, off white colored grub crawl from one side of the room to the other without either of them disposing of it as they passed it by. He saw that Kaimi almost stepped on the thing twice and Mutt could have sworn Barshaw looked directly at it, but made no effort to get rid of it. The immature fly wriggled closer and closer to where Mutt rested, the larva's movement caused his skin to crawl. Kaimi hopped in front of Mutt and bent over toward the maggot giving the nervous gentleman a sense of relief. Kaimi stood up from retrieving the picture of his mom. Holding the busted frame between his fingers, he walked it back over to the bookshelf, but the immature bug remained on its path to the disgusted man. It slinked closer to Marvin and his skin pricked which caused his hairs to stand up all over his body. Mutt could here the sticky skin of the infant bug rubbing up against the surface of the floor as it squirmed a mere foot away. He could feel his throat starting to gag, but he fought to keep from retching at the wet trail the moist skin of the infant fly left behind.

"Hey!" Barshaw bellowed as he looked out of the living room window.

The loud yell shook Mutt and sent him over the edge, "I can't take it anymore!" He flew off of the chair and scurried into the kitchen to grab something to drink.

Barshaw swooped over to the jalousies in the living room and called out, "Officer No'eau!" The detective pushed off of the back of the seat and clapped his hands in a quick tempo, "Okay! Mr. Mutter, it's time to go. Kaimi go grab your overnight bag and your school work too. We won't be coming back here tonight. I'll go outside and inform the officer about our plans."

Detective Barshaw approached Officer No'eau as she exited the squad car. "Hey, Lisa. Thank you so much for coming by."

Officer No'eau smiled and folded her arms on the roof of the police vehicle. "It's no problem, Detective. It seems you have the entire station buzzing around like a wasp's nest. What's all the hubbub?"

Barshaw stroked his jaw realizing he'd need a shave soon, "There's something *huge* going on, I mean '*Friday Night Frights*', '*Twilight Zone*', '*Night of the Living Dead*' kind of freaky stuff!" He scratched his finger around the rim of his ear. "Look, this kid that lives here, Kaimi Lee, he's had some very bad luck recently."

Lisa tilted her head and arched her eyebrow, "Is this Kalena Lee's residence?"

Barshaw's face elongated, "Yes, Kaimi is Kalena's son. You know the guy?"

The young officer shook her head, "I just met Mr. Lee this morning. So, what's going on with the boy?"

Barshaw laid down the facts, "Where do I begin? Well, first of all, his brother went missing the other night. We found his father's truck smashed to bits at the base of Pu'u Uila just this morning, and he was just attacked by a home intruder." Detective Barshaw looked at Lisa a bit befuddled, "Why was Kalena called to come to the station?"

"He came down to speak with Captain Lalau, that's all I know." Lisa cupped her hands over her chest, "That guy! He is such a sweet man and father. Did he get seriously injured?"

Barshaw raised his hands, "I don't know, Lisa. I looked for evidence of Kalena over the entire area and found nothing. I don't even know why he was there in the first place. I thought he was going to stay home with Kaimi today." Barshaw pressed his torso into the squad car and lowered his tone, "Do you know why your father wanted to see him?"

"I can only assume it was about his missing boy. Either that or one of you messed up." Lisa gave Brent the stink eye.

Barshaw surrendered, "Hey, don't look at me! Apparently, Kalena had been communicating with Reed behind my back. My partner decided *not* to tell me he was doing some searching all on his own after work last night. I thought he was just going to do a quick drive through town, but nope, his car was found abandoned up near Pu'u Uila with a blown out a tire. Well, it turns out that Detective Takao has gone M.I.A."

"Yeah, I heard about Takao's disappearance when you called in for the S.A.R. at the base of the pali. The guy that did this to Takao is going to regret he was born. The entire station reveres that man." Lisa looked sorrowful, "So, what's your plan, Detective Barshaw?"

Brent explained, "Well, I had a motorist drive me down here in his vehicle so I could update Kalena's son about what happened to his dad and do a quick check up. When we arrived, Kaimi was being viciously attacked by someone, or something. By the time I made it into the house the assailant had jumped out of a bedroom window and stolen the motorist's car."

Officer No'eau had a look of shock, "You weren't kidding! This isn't your typical Sunday."

Barshaw flinched, "Lisa, you don't know the half of it." The detective presented his arm outward revealing Mutt and Kaimi as they descended the porch steps. "So, Marvin Mutter, the man whose car was stolen, will be taking care Kaimi until I can come back for him. I sure as hell am not letting that kid stay here all alone to be attacked again."

Lisa looked around expecting to see another body making its way down the stairs, "Where's the boy's mother? Is she not coming with us?"

Barshaw eyed the officer with an expression that was odd to her, "The boy doesn't have a mother, Officer No'eau."

Lisa placed her hand over her mouth reminded by how Mr. Lee explained that his wife "watched" over the boys. She now understood his meaning and it made her heart break even more. With a tear in her eye, she introduced herself to Mutt and Kaimi.

"Hello Mr. Mutter, Kaimi. I'm Officer Lisa No'eau and I will be your transport. Mr. Mutter, I'd like to say thank you, on behalf of the HPD, for assisting one of our detectives and offering your services in protecting this young man. If we had the man power, you wouldn't need to be put in this awkward situation, so thank you."

Kaimi smiled at Lisa and Marvin graciously accepted her appreciation, "Thank you, Officer No'eau. You can call me Mutt." Marvin ducked into the back seat with a goofy smile on his face.

Detective Barshaw helped Kaimi into the back seat with his belongings and hopped into the passenger seat of the police cruiser. "Alright, Mr Mutter. What's your address? We'll drop you and Kaimi off before we head over to get my car."

Marvin motioned to Lisa, "Would it be okay if we stopped off at Kīlauea Pizzeria before heading home? I promised Kaimi we'd have a pizza and a movie night."

Lisa's heart fluttered knowing that Kaimi was in good hands.

Kanakolu kūmākolu

Peters began to feel a little uneasy as he drove back to the station. Throughout the entire ride, Wilson watched Peters' every movement as if scrutinizing his driving ability.

"Hey, Ken. You're okay with me driving the Mustang, right?"

Wilson shot his eye from the foot pedals up to Peters' face, "Yes, why not?"

Peters looked forward to ignore his partners odd behavior. He flicked the blinker on to turn into headquarter's parking lot and accidentally rubbed the back wheel up against the base of the arm. The bump jostled both riders. Peters quickly looked at Wilson expecting to hear his iconic breath with an immediate reprimand, but Wilson just sat watching Peters' hands.

"So, what's our next step, Ken? Did we need to get something from the station? Were we called back? Was it Captain Lalau?" Peters parked the car and awaited Wilson's orders.

The senior detective pointed his finger toward the driver side window signaling to Peters to get out. The rookie hopped out of the vehicle and Wilson came around to the driver's side, "You can stay here, I need to meet someone. Lalau's orders."

Peters patted Detective Wilson on the back, "Of course, sir. Give me a call if you need me. I'll start the paperwork."

Wilson got into the car while Peters stepped onto the sidewalk and hid behind a column. He witnessed Detective Wilson slowly pull out of the stall. The car began to jostle back and forth until finally it pulled forward leaving the lot. Peters was more than suspicious of his partner's behavior.

He turned toward the precinct's entrance and spoke softly to himself, "I think I'll just have a small chat with Captain Lalau. I'm sure he can shed some light on this strange situation and Kenneth's odd behavior."

Kanakolu kūmāhā

Down at the base of the pali, the search party was hard at work scouting for signs of the lost detective. Sergeant Kinihaka lead the hunt that so far had not been fruitful. Absolutely no evidence of Detective Reed Takao had been found. To the sergeant, it started to feel like a waste of resources.

Officer Gallettes approached his sergeant, "Sir, we've covered the entirety of the pali and have not discovered anything related to the detective. We pushed our area fifty yards away from the cliff wall, searching vertically, finding nothing in the trees or burrows." The officer took a look behind him for a second and adjusted his posture toward the sergeant, "I just do not believe Detective Takao is out here, sir."

Sergeant Kinihaka stroked his dark black dyed mustache, "I believe that is the consensus of the resounding majority, Gus." The sergeant slid his thumbs into the top of his belt, "Let's do this right so we won't need to waste our time coming back out here again. We need to be thorough. We owe it to Takao."

"Yes, sir!" Officer Gallettes jumped back into the search as they pushed further away from the base of the pali.

Kanakolu kūmālima

Officer No'eau pulled up to the curb of the Mutter residence. Detective Barshaw wasn't surprised at all to see that the house was also just as colorful and happy as Marvin was. He could see a man weeding around a bed of pastel colored flowers when Mutt's voice interrupted his examination of the safe house.

"Kaimi, look! It's Joel! You guys are going to be great friends." Mutt exited the police vehicle and reached in to help the young man with his belongings.

Barshaw rolled his window down to have a short chat with Marvin. "Hey, Mr. Mutter, anything comes up give me a call. I'll be back later this evening to pick up Kaimi, okay?" Barshaw looked over at the young man, "Kaimi, we'll get to the bottom of this, I promise. I want you to hang out here with Mr. Mutter and Joel and have fun. I will be back later to get you." Mutt grabbed the pizza from the back seat. The smell wafted through the window and made Barshaw hungry, "Mr. Mutter do not let this boy go anywhere outside this house. Do not let him go with anyone other than me. Is that clear?"

Marvin could see how sincere Brent was and felt bad that he blew up at him about his car, "You got it, buddy… and detective you can call me Mutt."

Barshaw smirked and nodded his head, "Thank you, Mutt." He leaned his head out of the passenger window and called out, "Oh! And thank you, Joel!" The man that was hunched over working in the garden removed his face from the flower box and wiped the sweat off of his perplexed brow. "I'm sorry for the rudeness, for not coming out to meet you formally. We're in hurry." Barshaw looked back at Marvin, "Keep the boy safe, Mutt." Officer No'eau and Detective Barshaw swiftly disappeared from Mr. Mutter's street.

Marvin smiled at Kaimi, "Come on, let me introduce you to Curly Toed Joel." They both turned and moved through the white fenced entryway onto the rainbow colored path.

Kanakolu kūmāono

Officer No'eau was amazed at the information Detective Barshaw unloaded on her, "Brent, now I know you didn't grow up in Hawai'i, but there are things that happen here that just don't happen anywhere else in the world."

Barshaw furrowed his brow and hissed, "Oh, is that right? Like what?"

Lisa continued, "Like understanding the ancient ways."

The detective cut in with a half hearted smile, "How ancient are we talking here, Lisa?"

The officer rolled her eyes, "I'm not talking about when dinosaurs roamed the earth, Brent! I'm talking about pre-Tahitian contact."

Barshaw coughed, "And you, young lady, know about what happened on this island before man first made contact here?"

Lisa grunted, "Do you know how many times the people of Hawai'i have been told that what happened in their very own history was wrong, then how the kānaka maoli prove those scientific reports as false by the discovery of new evidence and by exposing those supposed impossible feats to the world as proof!?" Lisa straightened herself in her seat.

Barshaw read her mannerisms and offered an apology, "I'm sorry, Lisa. My brain starts to question and that's when everything just becomes a mountain of questions that form an empty pit devoid of answers. If I can't find a relation or learn facts, the hole gets deeper. The burden of proof ultimately lies with the individual that is making the claim."

Officer No'eau nodded in acceptance, "But this is one of those times that belief can help you to surpass those questions and to walk that thin rope right over that pit. You're going to try to convince yourself that monsters don't exist at the cost of losing a partner and the life of a young man who needs your help?" Lisa looked at Barshaw. She couldn't tell if it was sinking in. "Here's some straight facts for you since you can't take that leap of faith. The kānaka maoli got to experience this fertile land before all of us came here to mess everything up. But before they came, there were others that called Hawai'i their home. Creatures taller than the coconut trees and as strong as the wind. There were people that had the ability to change their forms into other natural entities, who would later use their abilities to stay hidden from the eyes of new comers, or use that ability to fight back. Some had good intentions and others did not. That's no different than today's communities, but they made it work through respect of each other. We both know that's something that's starting to disappear in today's world."

"Alright, Lisa, I have an open mind." Barshaw pondered the officer's words while she resumed her sharing.

"Let me tell you about the mo'o. Stories of mo'o were passed down through generations as a people that caused mischief, but were also known as guardians. They watched over the dead and protected kānaka and the 'āina. There was a purpose in what they did. It echoes through the communities of my ancestors and even lightly through the homes of today. The common goal shared between all of us in Hawai'i is to survive in the middle of the Pacific without killing one another. Sacrifices were made, rules were created with understanding being the true key to survival, and a very important value. These creatures, my people, our kingdom has done it for hundreds of years. We've been spoiled by the conveniences of modern technology and are forgetting about the ones that have been here from the beginning. The ones that helped the kānaka maoli to thrive so we could come and ruin it for future generations."

Detective Barshaw fidgeted in his seat, "Sorry to ask more questions, but why now? Why is it making itself known right at this very moment?"

Lisa watched the paint on the road rolling under the squad car, "Perhaps it has been happening all this time, but only now are we recognizing it because only now it is affecting us." Brent shook at the thought as Lisa pulled over to the shoulder where the fallen fir had rested throughout the majority of the day. She voiced her surprise, "Wow! I can't even tell that there was a downed tree here."

Barshaw slipped out of the passenger seat and before shutting the door he stuck his head back in, "Thank you, Lisa. I know you're very dedicated to being an officer and bringing voice to those that are suffering and those that have suffered. I appreciate your words, kindness and patience with me. I'll take what you said to heart. Thanks for the ride." The detective shut the door and jogged across the street toward the rail and looked over. "It looks like the wrecker removed the truck as well."

Lisa called out, "It's probably impounded at the station. I'll see you back there."

Brent unlocked his car and was about to make his way over to the clinics when he got a call on his cellular, "Barshaw, go ahead."

The voice on the other side of the call spoke firmly, "This is Sergeant Kinihaka, detective. We're about ready to wrap up our search here around the base of the cliff. We have made no recovery of Takao or any of his personal effects. I'm so sorry."

Barshaw had a small rejuvenation of hope, "Hey, Warren, that's great news! Anything out of the ordinary found that could be of use?"

The sergeant was silent for a moment and then finally added, "Well, the boys did happen to stumble upon a shallow cave at the far west corner of the cliff. Some got excited and believed that they found the 'Cave of Wonder.' We all had a good laugh and just carried on."

The detective asked, "Cave of Wonder!?"

Sergeant Kinihaka chuckled, "Oh, right! It was before your time, Barshaw. Back in the day a group of protesters found an ancient burial site that held unimaginable treasures. Priceless artifacts that were all in pristine condition sat in this cave untouched for centuries. It halted the development in 'Ōma'o State reserve. Days later the cave magically disappeared. It garnered the name, 'Cave of Wonders.'"

"Man!" Detective Barshaw jokingly responded, "What we could do with just one of those artifacts, right Kinihaka?"

"Well, I definitely wouldn't be out here on my anniversary getting eaten alive by mosquitos." Kinihaka let out a hearty laugh.

"Thanks, Warren. I appreciate all your efforts. Tell the guys I owe 'em a drink." Barshaw spoke with a relieved tone. He hung up his cell and took a deep breath, "It's time to check the hospital." Barshaw started his vehicle and continued his quest to find his missing partner.

Kanakolu kūmāhiku

Kaimi sat on a floral print loveseat covered in a plastic sheet, staring nervously at a small scruffy dog with eyes too big for its bulb like head. He looked down at his front paws and saw that one toe on each hand was abnormally bloated and longer than the rest of its digits. Mutt came out of the kitchen holding a couple of fancy plates in one hand, two cups of ice in the other and soda cans tucked under his arms.

Breaking the silence, Mutt let out a chuckle, "Kaimi, if you'd like to pet Joel I'm sure he'd just love it!" There was a knock at the door. "Hang on we'll start our show as soon as I answer this."

Marvin opened the front door. Kaimi could see the man that was busy outside in the garden pop his head in.

"Mutt, I'm all finished out here so I'll be on my way."

Mr. Mutter handed the man some money and thanked him for keeping his yard beautiful. He locked the door and walked over to the living room.

Mutt sat on his chair and began dishing out the pizza that sat on an ornate red wooden table with a doily separating the food container from the surface. Kaimi looked back toward Joel as he sat quivering.

"He's a well behaved little guy."

"Oh, yeah! He better be on his best behavior when we have guests, isn't that right Curly Toe Joel?" Mutt popped open the soda and poured them into the glasses. "Are we set?"

Kaimi smiled and nodded at his host. Mutt pressed a key on the remote and started their evening entertainment.

Kanakolu kūmāwalu

Peters sat receiving a lecture from Captain Lalau. "If your training officer gives you an order you should heed it."

The rookie detective pushed what the captain had to say to the side, "Sir, it wasn't what Wilson told me to do as much as how he was behaving. He didn't seem himself at all. What bothers me is how we had been separated for some time and when we met back up, he was acting as if he wasn't the same person. The man that came back to the station with me was not Kenneth Wilson."

The captain's face dropped which made Detective Peters nervous. He just looked at the rookie very, very still. It became uncomfortable as the sound of the captain's clock could be heard ticking as if counting down to Peters' professional demise. After a minute, Captain Lalau's carved face moved.

"Complete your paperwork, hand it in, and call it a day, Detective Peters. This order comes from me, not Detective Wilson, and I can assure you I am behaving exactly as I always do when I have a disobedient subordinate. I will notify your commander about my decision and I guarantee he will not have a problem with it. Are we clear?"

Rush stood up, "Yes, sir. Sorry, sir."

"Remember this Peters, you are still a trainee. I don't want to recommend that you go back to patrol, but if this is how your future interactions are going to be with your superiors, then I will have no problem proposing to Lieutenant Thompson that you are demoted to footman." Captain Lalau poked his pointer finger into the top of his desk causing a loud pop, accentuating his point. "Are we clear?"

Peters did a double take to see if the captain's desk had suffered damage and answered in earnest, "Yes, sir. Again, I do apologize for my tone." The detective flew out of the office to reluctantly follow his new orders. *I can't let this go, it wasn't my partner that drove off moments ago. I need to find out what's going on before it's too late. We can't afford to lose another good detective."*

Rush filed his paperwork and immediately left the station. He got into his car and thought about how he should proceed. *Where would Ken start?* Peters knew he wasn't capable of coming up with any leads on his own, he needed Wilson's wisdom. His head ached and his brain felt as if it were going to split. He grabbed hold of his phone and rang the only other person who he could trust.

"Hello? Detective Barshaw, I could really use your help."

Kanakolu kūmāiwa

Detective Barshaw sat in his vehicle as Detective Peters pulled into the hospital's parking area. Brent unlocked the passenger door so the young detective could get in.

"So, Rush. What's the urgency?"

Peters sat thinking about how to word the situation so as not to lose the trust of another ally.

"Rush!" Barshaw barked. "Look kid, I am against the clock here and I have absolutely zero time to waste. What did you need!?"

Peters snapped out of his self doubt and spoke plainly, "Kenneth Wilson is missing."

Barshaw scoffed, "Your supervisor is missing?" He banged his fist over the steering wheel and looked out of his window, "Okay, Peters. If your partner is 'missing' then why did I see him driving up towards the high school?"

Peters flew the seatbelt around his waist, "We gotta go to the high school right now, Brent!"

Barshaw blinked in confusion, "Excuse me? I still have two more clinics to stop off at to locate my *actual* missing partner."

Rush looked down at the chair, "Please, Brent. I need your guidance."

Barshaw could see Peters was struggling to hold it together. "Alright, fine! We'll go to the school. I'll show you everything's alright. I wasn't imagining Ken's black Mustang flying passed me. I'm not senile." Barshaw drove out of the lot thinking this was probably just a stunt orchestrated by Wilson to discipline his trainee.

"That's not it at all, Brent. I would never speak that way to or about you." Peters wiped his nose, "I believe that Wilson was cloned... or replaced, or something. Like '*Invasion of the Bodysnatchers*' replaced."

Rush knew exactly how crazy he sounded, but was surprised when Detective Barshaw held up questioning him. It was odd that he was not immediately barraged with inquiry. Peters leaned in to get a closer look at the senior detective. *Maybe this isn't Barshaw. Maybe he's a-.*

"If you are thinking I am a pod person right now, Peters, I will drop kick your butt out of my car." Barshaw gave Rush the stink eye. "If you're wondering why I haven't asked, it's because officer No'eau has widened my perspective. I am respecting what you believe you saw, for now."

"Wow! Lisa helped you with that? She's a pretty amazing woman, erm, officer... isn't she." Peters' panic began to fade away, "I guess you can teach an ol-"

Barshaw barked, "Don't you dare finish that saying, boy!" Brent began muttering as he shook his head, "Lisa! That's the thanks I get for following your advice?"

The two detectives turned onto the road that lead into the gates of the high school. At the locked entry sat a lonesome vehicle covered by the darkness of the night.

"Hey, that's Marvin Mutter's car!"

Barshaw parked his vehicle beside Mutt's and both detectives inspected the deserted transport. "Well, the car looks good."

Peters pulled the driver side door handle, "Brent, the door is unlocked." He poked his head inside to inspect. "The key's are still in the ignition and... Uh-oh!"

Barshaw called out, "What'd you find?"

Peters pointed at the seat, "Looks like blood." Rush moved over to let Brent take a closer look.

Detective Barshaw said quietly, "Scab Face Wili." Peters lowered his brow with a look of confusion on his face. Something else had caught Barshaw's eye, "Hey, what's that over there!"

Peters could make out a faint glow in the darkness coming from a small structure out near the fence on the school's field. "Looks like someone's sitting in that dugout." They made their way over to the fence. Peters placed his hand over his weapon while Barshaw took the lead.

"Hey! What are you two doing here!?" Detective Barshaw scared a couple of high school kids toking in the dark. "You are both in big trouble. How long have you been loitering here?"

One kid, Kelly, spoke very slowly, "Oh, uh, hey! We didn't mean to break da law officers. Um, let's see, wait…" Kelly looked at his bare wrist. "Yo! Bro, do you have a watch!?"

Rekka, the second kid, didn't sound any smarter but at least he spoke quicker. "Um, yeah! A watch? No, I don't have one. But, we've been here since da light was on. Yeah, Kelly?"

Barshaw wiped his face and shook his head, "Did you boys happen to see who came out of that car over there?"

Without providing anything helpful, Kelly frantically answered, "Yo! I taught dat was a hippopotamus all dis time."

Rekka swiped the joint away from his friend, "Kelly, you stupid oah what? When was da last time you saw someone come out of a hippo?" He went to wrap his lips around the blunt.

Detective Barshaw snapped the spliff away just as the boy tried taking a hit and waved it in front of his face, "I think this is making your memory a little fuzzy, maybe I should just get rid of it."

Rekka reached out as if trying to save a loved one from a capsized boat, "Wait, wait!" He looked over at his buddy, "Dis guy is just dumb, it's not da pakalōlō's fault."

Peters took his hand off his gun, "Alright, if you prove that your memory is okay and you can tell us who came out of that car, you can both have your bone back."

Rekka licked his lips, sat up straight, and wiggled his finger at Mutt's car. "Yeah, so, I saw da guy, remembah da guy, Kelly!?" He nudged his buddy in the ribs with his forearm, "Da kid dat stay in our shop class!"

Detective Barshaw yelled to get to the point quicker, "Wili!? Was it Wiliami Lee?"

Kelly nudged Rekka back harder, "Brah, no hit me!"

Rekka nudged Kelly once more, "Brah, I nevah!"

Kelly elbowed Rekka and squealed, "Brah, you just did it again!"

"Hey!" Barshaw clicked his fingers in front of their glassy-eyed faces, "You two better get your story straight or your little girlfriend here is gonna take a nap under my foot." The boys looked at the older detective with big eyes, Kelly was nearly in tears. The detective repeated, "Was it Wiliami Lee?"

Rekka finally provided something useful. "No, it was his friend. Was dat addah guy! Da one Wili hang out wit', but da buggah's face was all bus'! His sistah came an' picked him up." Rekka decided to sneak a hit. His lips cautiously approached the detective's hand as he was distracted talking to Peters.

Barshaw moved the blunt away and snapped his fingers in front of the boy's face again, "Focus! 'Alapaki and Kenani De Souza? That's who you saw?"

Rekka's eyes sparkled, "Yeah, yeah das da one! Ho, cuz, you seen Kenani's ride!? Was cherreh!"

Peters interrupted, "Kenani drove? What kind of car was *she* driving?"

Rekka struggled to remember. He was thinking so hard the detectives would've believed his life depended upon it."Ah, was one, ah... red Prius!"

Kelly nudged Rekka harder than before, "Brah, what da heck is one Prius!?" Kelly looked right into Barshaw's eyes, "Was one all black Ford Mustang, side scoops wit' low body. Da chick get good taste."

Detective Barshaw looked at Peters with concern, "We gotta go!"

Barshaw dropped the doobie and the boys leaped to the ground just as Peters passed by smearing the bomber under foot. Kelly and Rekka let out a wail as the remains of their dearly departed mixed in with the mud and sand around her.

Detective Barshaw instructed Peters, “We’ll take Mutt’s car with us, I don’t want to leave it here. Let’s head back up to the De Souza’s. Those kids have a lot of explaining to do.”

Kanahā

During the entire movie, Curly Toe Joel just sat shivering and staring at Kaimi. As the credits started to roll, Mutt stood up to turn off the the VCR, "Oh my! That was a very frightening movie! Haha, I'm so sorry, Kaimi. I hope that it doesn't give you nightmares."

Kaimi continued to look at Joel staring back at him, "Um, it's okay, Mutt. Getting attacked by Scab Face Wili took care of dat already."

Joel began to growl and it startled Kaimi. It was the first sign of life the small dog had shown besides its constant trembling. He hopped off the loveseat and climbed up on the chair by the front window.

Joel barked wildly at the window and Mutt called out from the kitchen, "Kaimi? Is Curly Toe Joel bothering you!?"

Kaimi responded, "No, it look like he stay bahkin' at da window."

Marvin emerged from the kitchen wiping the suds from his hands with a floral towel, "Joel? Joel!?" The guard dog kept barking and growling out the window. Mutt took a peek outside and saw the shadow of someone he did not know looking right at his house,

"Oh, my!" Marvin grabbed Joel off of the chair and placed him on the floor. He untied his blinds and let them fall to block the intrusion.

Kaimi watched Mutt move around the house checking the doors and windows, "Is everything okay, Mutt?" the young man asked with concern.

Marvin disappeared down the hall for a minute and came back with a huge smile and his hands behind his back, "It's all good, buddy!" Mutt pulled his arms forward revealing a board game, "Hey, buddy. Have you ever played Boggle?"

Kanahā kūmākahi

Barshaw and Peters stood in front of the De Souza residence. The neighborhood made Peters tremble. It was deathly quiet and terrifyingly still, just as it was before the sunset. The only thing Peters could hear was the slight wheeze in Barshaw's breathing. Both men turned on their flashlights and approached the front entrance. The screen door was ajar and the inner door was cracked open a few inches.

Peters looked at Barshaw, "This door was shut the last time I was up here."

A gentle breeze could be heard in the tree tops of the forest at the edge of the property. The air washed through the De Souza's home and bathed the detectives in a foul smell of decay. Barshaw threw his forearm over his face as he coughed.

"Good lord!"

Detective Peters, familiar with the smell, pulled his gun from his holster. He walked over to the inner door and tapped it inward. Barshaw flashed his hand light into the opening. A sickly grey calm reflected back in the beam of the detective's light. Both men made their way into the entrance. The opening led to the living area which was covered in dust and soot. Peters tried the light switch, but it appeared that the house was without power.

"The place is dead, Barshaw," Peters announced as his voice bounced around the empty room.

Barshaw replied, "You aren't kidding."

He flashed his torch at Peters and lead the beam down to the floor where a rotting corpse of an old woman lay with the look of pain frozen across her face.

"How long do you think, Rush?"

Peters bent over to take a closer look at the body. "Dermestids. It appears our poor soul has been gone for some time now." Rush pawed at the body, "No external punctures or wounds. The body has not been moved... could have been sudden cardiac death."

Another breeze pressed against the house squeezing more gag inducing flavor from its pores. A door from the side of the hallway creaked. Barshaw left Peters to investigate further. He moved slowly into the hallway where a stale sour taste climbed in Brent's mouth and down his esophagus. He winced as he pushed open a creaky bedroom door. His light fell upon the deformed body of Detective Peters' poor partner.

"Oh, God! Kenneth!"

Peters, hearing the commotion, stood up and followed the senior detective into the hall, "Brent, are you okay?"

"Take the next room, Peters." Barshaw scooted the young detective off to survey the rest of the home.

Peters returned after a few minutes. "We're all clear here, Brent."

Barshaw placed his hand over Peters' shoulder, "I'm sorry, Rush. It's Wilson."

Peters darted into the small room to see his partners unclothed body bent, bloodied, and broken on the floor beside a soiled single sized mattress. The small bed was covered in a reddish brown stain at one end. Peters observed that flies had recently begun to colonize on the detective's body. Rush spoke quietly staring at the remains.

"Damn it, Wilson. We should've stuck together." He turned to look at Detective Barshaw. "This means the person that I drove to the station with earlier was *not* Kenneth Wilson."

Barshaw and Peters contacted HPD to send the medical examiner and a team to close off the area.

Kanahā kūmālua

Mutt's dog started to work itself into a craze. He growled at the front windows then moved over to the kitchen and growled some more. He barked while running off to the bedroom and growled through the hallway.

"Mutt, does Joel usually ack laddat?"

Mutt waved his hand at Joel, "He's fine. I'm sure it's just because he had too much pizza."

Mutt smiled at Kaimi as they compared their word lists. Joel spun around the kitchen doing laps around the table growling and barking. He took off into the hallway at high speed and disappeared for a short while. Kaimi watched Joel fly back out of the room and straight over to the front door where he started to howl at the top of his lungs. Mutt stood up and walked over to his dog.

"Curly Toe Joel, what has gotten into you!?"

Mutt bent over to comfort his pet when he heard a deep vibration coming from behind the front entrance. He peeked through the peephole and saw two piercing white orbs staring straight at the door.

"Oh. My. Word."

The front door began to shake with a fierce vibration and the door knob clattered violently. Kaimi stood up, knocking his chair backward to the ground. Mutt turned toward the fearful young man and gave him a determined look while pressing his finger over his lips. He motioned his hand to Kaimi to move back into the kitchen. The boy backed up slowly until his waist bumped against the kitchen's counter. He watched Mutt reach inside a tall basket next to the door. There were a variety of umbrella handles sticking out, but when he pulled a decorative wooden grip upward Kaimi could see that it wasn't a parasol, it was a taiaha. Joel squirmed to free himself from Mutt's grasp and darted toward the kitchen where Kaimi found shelter. Mutt spun the Māori weapon around taking a step away from the door. He widened his stance and started to inhale and exhale deep and fierce. Curly Toed Joel faced the kitchen door and started barking. Kaimi looked at the kitchen window to see a tall shadow creeping across the backyard toward the rear exit. The handle on the kitchen door began to rattle as the door started to flex and bow. The three distressed occupants were sandwiched between two aggressors they could not see. Joel continued to bark making the whole experience much more traumatizing.

Kaimi looked back at Marvin and nervously cried, "Mutt!?"

The doors immediately ceased in motion and the entire house went dead silent. Curly Toed Joel stood shaking on a kitchen floor mat with his eyes even bigger than Kaimi thought possible. Mutt turned and looked at the frightened boy. He raised his left hand to signal to him not to move. Kaimi nodded letting out a slight exhale that set the room off once more. The doors vibrated with greater force than before and was accompanied by hard banging. Mutt could see the door frame beginning to give as the door was pulled in and out making the gap wider and wider.

Kaimi watched Mutt take two high kneed steps back and held fast to his taiaha with both hands.

Mutt started to shout at the front door, "Ka mate, ka mate, ka ora, ka ora, tenei te tangata puhuru huru!!!"

The doors finally caved in as an enormous brindle colored dog, standing on two legs, stretched its neck into the busted entry baring its sharp teeth. Mutt flashed his tongue at the intruder and swung his taiaha across the face of the brutish creature sending it right back to where it came from.

The kitchen door stopped vibrating and Kaimi could see the shadow passing each window moving back to the front of the house with haste. Mutt switched his stance as he twirled the taiaha awaiting his next victim. A second larger creature, that looked very similar to the first, snarled as it entered through the busted entrance.

Kaimi's eyes popped, "Mutt! Dat's da guy dat when steal yo' car! Scab Face Wili!!!"

Mr. Mutter spat, "Tsa!" as he swung the taiaha over his head to smash the creatures brains in, but the monster grabbed Mutt's wrist as he attempted the fatal blow and squeezed.

Scab Face Wili pulled Marvin in for a closer look and gazed at him for a moment with his one blazing white eye. He roared in Mutt's face and slashed his claws into Marvin sending him and his taiaha flying across his living room. Curly Toed Joel howled and ran as fast as he could to attack the intruder. Kaimi saw the taiaha laying on the floor in front of him, he shivered in fear and felt his knees begin to melt like hot wax. Joel gnawed at the foot of the oversized aggressor heroically defending his master. Everything started to move at half speed.

Kaimi, bewildered, began to wonder, *Is dat dog mento? What is he t'inking!?* He looked at Mutt laying face down with red liquid spreading out from his midsection moving across his pristine hardwood floor.

Everything had come to a stand still and Kaimi's thoughts became focused, *Mutt had shown courage, just like Mom did at the state reserve, facing a foe that was bigger and stronger than the both of them, but Mutt was protecting a complete stranger. Even Joel had the fire to fight.* Kaimi believed this was it. Now or never. It was time for him to make a decision; do something courageous or just give in to fear. It finally hit Kaimi, *Courage isn't about being strong for yourself and over coming fear, it's about being strong and protecting who or what you believe is important, win or lose, even if you are deathly afraid. Fear can petrify you to a standstill or it can be used to move you forward, to fight for what is right.* He looked back at the taiaha and thought, *So, what's it going to be, Kaimi? Are you ready to move?*

The large ferocious creature cast his gaze down at Joel and lifted his leg. The tiny guardian slid off the beasts foot and hit the floor with a yelp. Scab Face Wili growled at Joel then slammed his foot down hard on the small dog's head, crushing it like a kamani nut. Kaimi screamed and swung the taiaha at Scab Face Wili tearing a gash across his chest. The creature wailed as it flew backward into the other monster that had just regained its footing.

Detective Barshaw could see the commotion as he pulled up toward the Mutter residence, but once again he was late to the party. Both creatures recoiled when the detective pulled up to the house. Blaring his high beams, Barshaw took aim at the brutes with his car dashing forward at full speed. The detective came crashing through Mr. Mutters' once beautiful front gate, but the duo of terrifying life forms evaded Brent's oncoming barrage. Peters quickly pulled up to Marvin's house just in time for one of the strange animals to rub up against Mutt's car tearing off the passenger side rear view mirror and scraping the faux wood panel off of the doors. The first creature caused Detective Peters to swerve into the path of the second creature, which scurried up the front of Mutt's car shattering the front windshield and caving in the top of the automobile. The vehicle slowed to a stop after it was jolted by the monster stepping off of the rear bumper. Both beings fled into the darkness of the night howling.

Barshaw ran beside the hood of Marvin's car with his gun drawn.

Detective Peter's eyes were wide as he sat in disbelief, "What the *hell* were those things!?"

Detective Barshaw huffed, "Scab Face Wili... or whatever!"

The detective's attention was stolen away from the fleeing predators when he heard Kaimi's voice.

"Detective Barshaw! Mr. Mutter is hurt!"

Brent moved toward the house and made his way through the hole torn into the wall. As the detective entered the wrecked home, he looked down to see the remnants of a small headless animal splayed out on the floor. It nearly made Brent vomit.

Kaimi could be seen kneeling next to Marvin sobbing, "I'm sorry, Mutt! I'm so sorry! It's all my fault." Kaimi dropped down onto Marvin's back and hugged his motionless body.

Marvin let out a shriek, "Owaaawow!" He lifted his face up a couple of inches and plopped it back down into a puddle of his own blood. "Easy, buddy!"

"Kaimi, go grab a pillow." Detective Barshaw ran over to Marvin and rolled him off of his face. He took the pillow from Kaimi and carefully laid Mutt back down. Rush flew into the house eyes wide on Joel's remains. Barshaw yelled, "Peters, did you contact the station?"

Rush nodded, "They're on their way, Brent."

Mr. Mutter held his arm up. "Oh, great! My sweater's ruined. Joel is going to kill me. This was his birthday present to me from last year." Mutt crooked his neck, "Where is, Joel? Wh-Where is my little man!?"

Barshaw jerked his head at Rush, "Peters, take a look around the house for the guy..."

Marvin put up his hand, "Wait! *Guy*!?"

Detective Barshaw looked confused, "Wasn't Joel the guy I spoke to in the garden?"

"Oh, lord!" Mutt's hand waved at the wrist, "That was Koa, my gardener, dum dum. Curly Toe Joel is my chihuahua!" Marvin saw Barshaw's face veer toward the doorway.

Peters looked down beside his right foot at the red mess. He squished his face up while stepping slowly to the side giving a clear visual of poor Joel smeared across the floor.

Mr. Mutter let out a wail, "No! Not my Joel! Those son's of biscuit's are gonna pay for this. I'm gonna shove my club right up their avocado's! I'm gonna Krakatoa those mustard flickers!" Marvin's words became slurred and discombobulated.

The sound of an ambulance could be heard fast approaching. Kaimi watched the world activate around him in slow motion. He saw Peters run out of the hole the monsters tore open to receive the emergency responders. Barshaw applied pressure to Mutt's wounds with a kitchen towel as Mutt cried in pain. The EMT's flew into the house with a stretcher. The second technician slipped forward a foot and a half on Joel's brain matter. Kaimi watched it all unfold through the sound track of his beating heart. Barshaw helped to lift Mutt onto the portable bed and the EMT's carried the wounded man outside. Mutt extended his arm towards the remains of Curly Toe Joel as he passed by, wailing in sorrow. The police soon entered into the house and started to block off the doorway with caution tape. Flashes of light were intermittently sprinkled in between the murmur of commanding voices. Kaimi felt cold and everything became a big bright blur.

Detective Barshaw could see his young friend was going through shock. "Kaimi, come on. Let's go." The detective helped him up to his feet, clasping his hand around Kaimi's shoulder to help keep him propped up under his arm. Brent put the boy into the backseat of his car.

Detective Peters stood nearby trying to understand what he just saw. He surveyed his surroundings to see if he was still in Hawai'i.

"Werewolves? Ha! Who would've thought that was a thing in paradise?" Peters hoped he'd get a response from Detective Barshaw, but Brent only raised a finger to his mouth motioning to Peters to pipe down.

Barshaw spoke in a whisper, "Rush, we need to keep this kid alive! I don't know how those things found the boy, but it wasn't coincidence that Mutt's home was attacked this evening. We'll take turns staying up through the night if we have to. But, we need to find a safe house to hole up in."

The detective was interrupted by an officer holding his phone out to him. "It's the captain, sir. He wants to have a word."

"Captain Lalau? This is Barshaw," he answered in surprise.

The captain unloaded on the detective, "What the hell is going on out there, Detective Barshaw!? I don't like losing my officers. I don't like having to deliver bad news to our work 'ohana, so I think it's time to stop and call it a day. This boy, Kalena's son, you need to bring him down to the station and keep him here for the night."

The detective pinched his lower lip, "Captain Lalau, this boy has been attacked twice already. Once at his home and a second time at a location he had no relationship to. I believe someone at the station may be unknowingly leaking the whereabouts of the boy to his attackers. It might be better if..."

The captain halted Barshaw's explanation, "Leaks? Attackers!? Bring the kid in now! No one is stupid enough to mess with our precinct, detective."

"Captain, you don't seem to understand! These things-" Brent tried to explain the situation in detail but was cut off once more by a very perturbed boss.

"Get that kid here now, Detective Barshaw!"

The call abruptly ended and the disparaged man handed the cell back to the officer.

Peters shook his head, "The captain doesn't sound happy."

Barshaw grunted and walked over to the driver's side door. "Get in!" Peters hopped into the passenger seat. "I may be reprimanded for this, but I need to keep this boy alive."

Rush shrugged, "So, where do we go to keep this guy safe? You know those things are canine, right?" Barshaw flicked his hands outward questioning what it all meant. "Maybe they could smell his scent. Maybe they tracked him down."

Detective Barshaw shook his head, "No! No way they found Kaimi on this street. It's nowhere near his house, school, or town. He was safe here. Someone squealed and we need to find out who it is."

"There was only a handful of officers that knew where Kaimi was being held." Peters began poking at his fingers, "There's you and me. Mutt knew, but he was nearly killed. Wilson had no clue, but I did bring him, erm, one of those were-dogs that looked like Wilson, with me to the station, however I watched it drive away immediately after dropping me off. There was one other, but I don't think she-."

Barshaw looked at Peters and interrupted, "Officer No'eau!" Brent couldn't believe someone so sweet and caring as Lisa could possibly want to hurt Kaimi. "Okay, we need to talk to Lisa. But first, we need to get this guy somewhere safe."

Kanahā kūmākolu

Detective Barshaw grunted audibly as he climbed back into the driver's seat, "Do you think the boy will be safe here, Brent?" Peters asked with concern about the overall security of the kid's new hideaway.

Barshaw looked suspiciously at Peters, "If anything happens to anyone in this house, I will shoot *you* first."

Peters motioned a gentle nod, "We should head back to the station before Officer No'eau leaves for the day, sir."

"It's late, Peters. I think I should just take you back to your car. We can talk to Lisa first thing." Barshaw looked at Peters and found him to be quite resolute, "Look, I'm sorry about Wilson and for everything else that has happened thus far with your involvement in this case."

Peters exhaled sharply, "Kenneth was a very good detective, the world will be a far less safer place without him in it." Peters wiped his eyes and shook his head,

"He definitely had a way of making you feel terrible for trying your best, though."

Detective Barshaw reached over and placed his hand on Peters' shoulder, "Rush, I learned a long time ago that if Wilson didn't like someone, he'd ignore them completely. His reaction to your mistakes meant he cared, a lot."

Peters snorted as he wiped his nose. "That's some pretty sick passive aggressive manipulation."

"We all have our tricks to motivate the ones we care about." Barshaw slid his hand back to his lap, "Thanks for having my back at Mutter's home. It was a lot to handle. I'm still processing it."

Peters pulled his jacket tight around his chest and tried his best to pretend that what happened didn't truly freak him out, "Man, I feel so bad for Marvin. His place is a mess and his car is totaled! Even he's scraped up good."

Barshaw shook the chill from his arms, "Did you see his poor dog?"

Peters flashed back to the little chihuahua's corpse sprawled out on the floor and felt something from his stomach start to bubble upward. He pressed his hand hard over his mouth. "Harmph!"

Barshaw flung his car onto the side of the road, "Whoah, whoah, whoah! Hang on there!"

Peters pulled the handle and zipped right out the door and let out a groan.

"Son, are you alright!?"

Barshaw just sat watching the traffic cruise by. After a short while, Peters returned to the car wiping his face with the sleeve of his jacket. Barshaw eyeballed the kid to see if there was any debris.

"For a guy who makes his living off of dealing with the dead, you sure have little resilience."

Peters put up his hand, "Don't! Stop talking about it already."

Brent poked further, "I'm just saying, if a little dog…"

"Stop! Stop it. Stop it, please." Peters was taking quick breaths to restrain his convulsions. He trained his eyes on the headlights of the cars whizzing by.

Brent, having concern for Rush's state of being, gave Peters his orders, "Go straight home and check it for anything unusual. Secure your windows, doors, and whatever other weaknesses there may be. Keep your weapon near you at all times, loaded. I don't know what it is these things want, but we need to make sure we make it, so Kaimi can make it. We clear?"

Peters bobbed his head in agreement, "I didn't know this kid meant so much to you, Brent. It seems like you have a very close bond with him."

Detective Barshaw nearly choked, "I just met the kid this Friday." Barshaw looked at Peters' puzzled gaze. "From day one he was straight up honest with me. I chose not to believe him, now I owe it to that boy to keep him safe. He's already lost so much. I could have helped him from the get go, but I chose not to. It's a regret I don't expect to repeat."

Peters waved his arm around in front of his chest, "How could you have taken anything that we just saw today seriously!?"

Barshaw continued looking forward, "My intuition said otherwise. I didn't want to believe the boy and I went against my own instincts. I owe it to myself too."

Peters knew about regret. He had it since Pu'u Uila Street, where he encouraged his training officer to split up to cover more ground. He thought, *What happened earlier was a coin toss. I could've been laying dead in that musty, dilapidated house keeping an old woman's corpse company instead. Wilson didn't deserve to end up that way, no one did.* Detective Peters was all in when it came to stopping these things.

Barshaw pulled alongside Peters' car, "Please, keep safe tonight. We'll meet up before entering the station tomorrow and talk to No'eau together." Barshaw snagged Peters' jacket before he could get all the way out and said, "Shoes off!"

Peters looked at Barshaw with confusion, "Shoes off, sir?"

"It's one of the first things I learned when I moved to Hawai'i," Barshaw's face turned red, "It was my very first missing person's case here, it was when I was first partnered with Reed, we got to the family home of the missing person. Detective Takao told me, before I got out of the car, to take off my shoes when I entered the house. I didn't listen to him. I ended up disrespecting the family because I didn't understand what the culture was all about at the time. When I got to the front door and stepped in without listening to Takao, I was hit in the head with a slipper by an older Hawaiian gal. She yelled at me, 'Shoes off!' That'll be our meeting code word when we get back together, shoes off."

Peters smiled at Detective Barshaw and chirped, "I guess you *can* teach an old dog new tricks after all!"

Barshaw grinned and shook his head as he drove away.

Kanahā kūmāhā

Kaimi woke up groggy. Pain streaked across his face and it was difficult for him to breathe. He sat up looking for a comfortable position to help him relieve some of his discomfort. Water dripped nonstop from the ceiling into puddles that echoed all around him. He realized he wasn't in his bed, he sat atop a pile of slick banana leaves.

"Hello?" His voiced ricocheted off the walls of the room, disorienting him even further. Kaimi's body twitched as a swishing sound dragged behind him, "Who's there!?"

The young man started to panic and his pulse pounded deep in his chest. He could hear his heart beat vibrating off of the chamber walls. As he climbed to his feet it felt as if he plunged them into a pool of ice cubes. His eyes began to focus and the room became a bit easier to see through. A breeze hugged Kaimi and chilled him to the bone. He made his way slowly against the current of water flowing past his feet and came to an opening that was partially lit. Continuing his way forward, Kaimi found a light source in the back of the rocky tunnel. Faint voices could be heard up ahead, but he could also sense something looming just behind him. Kaimi quickened his pace, his shoes grinding the the gravel covering the floor below. His feet caused a terrible ruckus as he ambled through the tight quarters. He finally entered into a large subterranean vault. Kaimi found his brother and dad sitting and talking to each other. They were both surprised by the young man's sudden appearance. He was so happy to see them both safe that he began to cry. Before he could say a word he felt a tight grip curl around from his back and cross over his chest.

Kaimi's father leaped to his feet throwing both hands up into the air yelling, "No! Don't hurt him!"

As he struggled for freedom, Kaimi was involuntarily turned around. He found himself standing face to face with the Mo'owahine of Makalike Bridge. She shrieked a terrifying scream with eyes blazing red, glowing like embers burning through the dark.

The terrifying visual caused Kaimi to shoot straight up as he gasped for air. The couch was wet all around him and his shirt was drenched in sweat. Each breath caused his tightened chest to stretch. It gave him a harsh cough that was uncontrollable.

A light from the hallway popped on as a small framed woman, wearing a silk nightgown with her hair peeking from the top of her headband came out crying, "Oh, Kaimi! Is you alright?" She fell to his side and patted him on the back, "Oh my, you're all wet! You want somet'ing to eat?"

The woman's appearance caused Kaimi to jump. The fear of seeing the the mo'owahine in his dream gave him a panic attack, but he was soon presented with a new form of horror - a pale face, decorated with smeared mascara and bright red lipstick dyed teeth, Kaimi struggled to remain calm. She smiled a helpful grin to comfort the boy, which didn't help his situation. The two terrifying visions had caused Kaimi to forget that Detective Barshaw dropped him off with his girlfriend, Ukulani.

Regaining his composure, Kaimi answered Ukulani, "No, Aunty Uku. I'm okay, I just had one bad dream."

Aunty Ukulani rubbed the young man's hand. "You shua?"

Kaimi nodded his head up and down, "I'm sorry if I wen' wake you, Aunty."

Ukulani rose to her feet, "Let me get you some watah, laddat." Her feet slapped against her house slippers as she walked over to the kitchen sink to fill a pink glass. She returned to Kaimi with a full cup. "Here you go, boy. Go drink 'em. Go drink 'em, go!" She got up again and went into the bathroom and returned with a huge t-shirt and a towel. "Wipe off wit' dis towel den put on da shirt, okay? Okay! Now, I gotta get my beauty sleep an' I need you fo' try go sleep too. Get couple moah hours until we go skoo, okay? Okay. I leave da light on fo' you."

Kaimi changed out of his sweat soaked shirt and laid back down. He thought about his family and how real his dream seemed to be. He could still sense the cold water on his feet, he could hear the cavernous noises ringing in his ears. It didn't make any sense.

After what seemed like only a few minutes of deep thought, Kaimi saw the light from the sun painting the living room curtains a bright orange. It was almost time to get up for school.

Kanahā kūmālima

Detective Barshaw returned to headquarters bright and early. He wondered why he'd even left the parking lot the night before. Rubbing the morning crust from his eyes, he wandered over to the front of the station where he came upon Detective Peters. Rush eyed the older detective but stood poised as Barshaw made his way beside him. Barshaw looked over at Peters and cleared his throat. Peters answered back in the same manner. Barshaw placed his hands on his hips and coughed louder. Peters looked around as if he missed a memo and looked at Brent who already appeared to be fuming.

Peters questioned, "What's the deal, Brent? Why don't you say the password!?"

Barshaw's frame shook, "I made up the password! You're supposed to tell me what it is!"

Peters leaned his head baffled, "That doesn't make any sense. You told me the password, so that the next time we saw each other, you could check in with that same password!"

Barshaw bellowed, "What!? I told you the password last night so that I'd know you are who you say you are! If you weren't you, and I said the password, you could always say it was correct! *You* need to tell me the password."

Peters scratched at his head, "Well, why don't you try to trick me by saying a few fakes before saying the real one?"

"Why the heck would I go through all that trouble!? Just tell me the password!" Barshaw was perturbed but he had another solution, "Fine, on the count of three we'll say the password at the same time."

Peters had a huge smile on his face, "Great idea, Brent."

Detective Barshaw rolled his eyes, "Okay, are you ready, Peters? Alright. One. Two. Three... Shoes Off!" Barshaw's mouth dropped open, "Rush! Why didn't you say the password!?"

Peters shoulders dropped, "Ah, ha-huh, because I forgot what the password was." He threw his head to the side and winced.

Barshaw's arms flew into the air, "So, what was the point of making a password if you weren't going to remember what the darn thing was?"

"Well," Detective Peters looked as if he had something clever to share, "If I weren't who I was supposed to be, how would I have known there was a password in the first place?"

"Damn it, Rush!" Barshaw rubbed his palms against his pants and calmly stood up straight, "Do you at least remember why I chose the password?"

Peters laughed while holding a finger in Brent's facial area, "Ha! You got smacked in the head with a rubber slipper."

Barshaw slapped Peters' finger out of his face. "Ah, close enough."

Both detectives made their way into the station and checked in at the help desk. There was an older officer sitting behind the pristine white counter. Barshaw greeted him with a smile, "Good morning, Harold."

Sergeant Harold Silva was one of the nicest legacies in the department. He retired four years ago, but volunteered at the station's reception desk mostly to get out of his wife's hair.

"Mornin' Brent, how are things?"

"It's not too good, Sarge. There's a big mess that needs sorting and I have a ton of questions that need answering." Barshaw leaned his elbow onto the desk. "Hey, I was wondering, did you happen to see if Officer No'eau has come in yet? And do you know where I could find her?"

Officer Silva's eyes perked up. He watched as Lisa made her way into the station's lobby as Brent finished his inquiry. "Yup, she's right over there."

Detective Barshaw quickly turned and made a motion at Peters to catch up with Officer No'eau. Barshaw returned his attention and patted Harold's arm, "Thanks, Sarge. Say hi to Mabel for me." He darted to catch up with Peters.

"Lisa!" Peters called out to halt the officer from getting into the elevator. Lisa picked up her pace and entered into the lift that closed right behind her.

"Stairs!" Barshaw barked as he reached for the stairwell door. Peters immediately ran up. Brent watched the elevator floor indicator stall on the third floor. Barshaw yelled up the spiral staircase, "Third floor!"

Brent's voice echoed up to Rush and caused him to jump back down half a flight. Detective Peters pressed out of the stairwell door in time to see Lisa walking into the women's lavatory. He walked inconspicuously over to the elevator when he heard a loud ring. The elevator doors popped open revealing Detective Barshaw. Peters pointed his nose at the restrooms, "She went inside."

Barshaw moved closer to Rush, "Look, anything can happen, so we need to be on guard. If she changes into a werewolf-"

Detective Peters stopped Brent, "Were-dog, sir."

"Were-dog!? Are you kidding..." Detective Barshaw froze as the door to the women's toilet swung open. Lisa made her way around the two men that stood as still as statues. She took no notice of either detective as she walked over to the lounge staring deeply into her glamour magazine. "Dog!? Wolf!? It doesn't matter! We've seen what those things can do, and we don't want any civilians getting hurt here today, got it!?"

Peters nodded quickly, "Got it, Brent."

"Okay, like I said, we need to keep this contained if it all goes sideways. Keep your weapon at the ready."

Both men moved toward the lounge and witnessed Lisa standing next to the coffee pot pawing at some consumables. Barshaw nodded to Peters to head far right. He walked directly over to the young woman.

"Lisa!"

The young officer just tore open a few packets of powdered creamer.

Barshaw tried once more, "Lisa!?"

Officer No'eau looked up at Barshaw, removed her earphones and blinked with a smile, "Oh! Detective Barshaw! How's it going?" She turned to see Peters stalking her from the back. "Is everything alright, gentlemen?" Lisa reached down and stopped her portable CD player hanging from her belt.

Barshaw looked into Lisa's eyes, "Did you *not* hear about what happened last night?"

Officer No'eau glanced back and forth between both men, "No, I had to leave early last night. I went to drop my mom off at the airport." Lisa began to feel threatened, "Hey, what's going on here!?"

Without thinking, Peters blurted, "So, you didn't happen to make a pit stop on Wai'ula street before picking up your mom?"

Barshaw shook his head at Peters and continued to press the officer, "We're on to you, Officer No'eau! What is it that you want from the boy?"

Lisa was now very concerned, "What are you both talking about? What boy?"

"Kaimi Lee, Officer No'eau?" Barshaw could see that none of this was moving Lisa to react the way he was expecting. Lisa just stared at him perplexed. Barshaw took a step back and signaled to Peters to stand down.

"We're sorry Lisa, but you were the only connection we had when it came to who knew the whereabouts of our charge. No one else knew Marvin Mutter was helping us to watch the Lee boy, so when he was attacked last night-"

Lisa's eye's grew round, "Wait! What happened!?"

Barshaw gestured toward the table in the lounge. Lisa grabbed her brew and found a seat.

"Look, I need to keep this brief." Barshaw was trying his best to reveal what he knew without making a big commotion. "Someone in the department had leaked the location of Kaimi's safe house. Last night, the boy was nearly killed."

Officer No'eau sat in disbelief as the detective gave her a very quick summary of events and lowered his tone when others came nearby. "I can't believe this is happening. Is Kaimi alright?"

Detective Peters interjected, "I didn't believe it either until I witnessed it for myself. If we hadn't gotten to Mr. Mutter's residence when we did, Kaimi would've been killed by one of these nightmare inducing things."

"And the both of you believed I was one of these creatures!?" Lisa eyed the two detectives in dismay.

Barshaw put one hand in the other, "Our sincerest apologies, but from what we have explained, you could see that all fingers pointed to you. I thought this was going to be a sure thing! No offense."

Officer No'eau slapped her hand on the table, "Alright guys, so what other information do you both have!? Where do we go from here?"

Peters smiled at the idea of having another helping hand, especially since it was hers. "Well, we need to look into these De Souza kids and why they killed their grandmother. Or at the very least, why they didn't report her death."

Barshaw nodded, "That's a good start! I'll look closer into Cheylene's disappearance and if perhaps there's a collective of missing children being converted into blood thirsty monsters."

Lisa shook her head in amazement. Peters knew exactly how she felt, he sat in the same chair just a few short hours ago. "Could this be connected to those kids from back in the eighties? You remember those freaky satanic rituals from a decade ago?"

"Nothing is off the table, especially with what we've experienced over these past couple of days." Barshaw added.

Officer No'eau decided that she was all in, "I will poke around the station to see if anyone slips up and provides me information that seems suspicious. If you say there's a leak, there must be a leak."

Detective Barshaw, Detective Peters, and Officer No'eau all had their respective undertakings. With zero time to delay, they immediately got to work.

Monday

Kanahā kūmāono

Keoki watched Kaimi getting out of a stranger's car. He could see a woman communicating with his friend and she made sure everything she said was public knowledge.

"Okay, so no fo'get I coming fo' pick you up when skoo pau, yeah. Take your lunch, you need to keep up yo' strengt'."

Kaimi lumbered out of the vehicle with a face covered in bruises. Keoki saw Kaimi saying something to the strange woman, but it was too soft for him to hear. The car drove off and Keoki caught up to his pal to find out what had happened.

"Hey, Kaimi! How you doing?" Keoki asked with concern in his voice.

Kaimi sluggishly pulled one foot in front of the other as they both moved slowly toward the school.

"Sup, Keoki."

The sound of Kaimi's downtrodden voice reminded his friend about the time his mom had gotten sick. He decided not to probe, but he was worried about his buddy's injuries. He also found it extremely weird that he had gotten a ride, and concerned that his brother wasn't with him. He saw the school bus pull up and drop off the students that still had sleep covering their faces. Keoki took count of the ridership jumping off the school bus and realized Kaimi's brother was absent from the list of passengers. He also noticed that 'Alapaki and Kenani did not show up for school either.

Keoki looked over at Kaimi and downheartedly gave him details about his ride home last Friday. "So, I get into my car and Mom asks me about my day, so, I give her the run down and she just interrupts me about half way home asking if I messed myself. Her face was first-rate let me tell you! So, then I had to fast forward to the end of the day when we were told that mo'owahine story, remember that, Kaimi? The story Mr. Kahi told us?" Keoki continued without waiting for a response, "I explained what happened afterward and how I just, well, I don't need to tell you the rest." Keoki noticed their change in trajectory. He watched the door of their homeroom class grow smaller. "Yeah, so, that was cool. My mom ended up grounding me for the whole weekend. She started to get very emotional. Said something about how she's tired of always cleaning up after me, and that I'm always so messy, and it's time for me to be more responsible and that cotton was too absorbent. I told her I could clean up after myself. Then, she reminds me about the one time I tried cleaning my sheets and I broke the washing machine. But, she knew I needed glasses. So, I tell her again that I could do it myself because I'm older. She just screams like a crazy person, loud enough for our neighbors to hear, 'The stains, Keoki! What about the stains!?'" The two boys entered into the warm glowing light of the still classroom. The air was musty and made Keoki itch like a demon at church.

"Why are we in Mr. Kahi's class?" Keoki questioned Kaimi.

Kaimi just stood quietly surveying their teacher's classroom. After a moment, Mr. Kahi came out from the storage closet holding a cardboard box full of reading materials.

"I thought I heard someone come in. You boys alright?"

Keoki's eyes grew, "Good morning, Mr. Kahi. I apologize for what happened on Friday. My mother wasn't expecting that she needed to do laundry twice last week."

Mr. Kahi placed the box on a table at the back of the class and waved his hand, "Nah, it's okay Keoki. I was a bit surprised that I got a call from a concerned parent about me telling my stories. We are in high school after all." Mr. Kahi made his way around the seats to accompany the boys at the front of the class. "I guess I'll need to limit what I say when you're around, Mr. Birchham." Mr. Kahi flexed his eyebrows at Keoki which caused the young man to bare his braces. "So, what can I help you two fine gentlemen with today?"

Keoki side eyed his friend and just before he could cut the awkward silence with another nonsensical account, Kaimi spoke out. "Mr. Kahi, you know stuff, yeah?"

Mr. Kahi crossed his arms and shared a pompous look. "I've had some experiences in my life, Mr. Lee." It was at that moment Mr. Kahi noticed the strange marks on the inquisitive boy's face.

Kaimi made himself clear. "Mr. Kahi, I'm talking about spooky kine stuffs. You know, strange t'ings."

Mr. Kahi's face grew with concern. He looked over at Keoki and concluded that story time had affected more than just one student. He thought he had this whole impromptu meeting all figured out.

"Oh! I'm so sorry, Kaimi. Did my stories upset you as well? This generation just can't seem to handle anything out of their comfort zone."

Kaimi reached out his hand, "No, Mr. Kahi. I not stressing out about dat." Kaimi watched his teacher lower his defenses. "I need to ask you if you know about any addah kine monstahs dat used to live ovah hea."

Mr. Kahi smiled, but quickly threw a head waggle in the direction of Kaimi's company. Keoki popped, "Mr. Kahi, let me assure you that what happened on Friday was a complete freak accident!"

Mr. Kahi eyed Keoki with hesitation, "It's okay if you'd like to step outside for a minute Mr. Birchham." Mr. Kahi watched the young man rest into a comfortable stance. "Alright, it's your bibadeez's funeral." Mr. Kahi rested his weight over the side of his desk and cast his eyes at the ceiling. "Alright, in ancient times there were many different races that populated these small islands. Some could be found in valleys, others in the forests. Some found in the coral reef, and others right in front of your nose." Keoki looked bemused. "You're probably wondering how a being can exist without you seeing it right in front of your face, right? Well, it's because some early races had the fantastic ability to shape shift. The ultimate camouflage, am I right!?"

Kaimi's eyes lit up, "Mr. Kahi, shape shift, like da beings from da story you told las' Friday, no? Do you know any kine t'ings dat can change from somet'ing like one animal to maybe… one human?"

The boys' teacher could see Kaimi had interest in this particular talent and responded, "Yes, of course! Our ancestors called them kinolau. Some could change into a host of other more interesting things than just mere humans. Take, for instance, Lono. The akua of agriculture, he could transform into a variety of plants. He could change into a pua'a and even into the mists and rains."

Kaimi looked a bit frustrated, "Mr. Kahi, Lono is da god of peace..."

Mr. Kahi interjected, "The term god, isn't quite accurate, but continue."

Kaimi, showing his understanding, restated his point. "Lono is known fo' bringing peace, but what I wanted fo' know is if dea stay moah aggressive types of beings dat can change dea form?"

The instructor began to see Kaimi was quite serious about this fact finding, "Are you doing a report or writing some kind of story, Kaimi?" He took a peek at the clock and realized it was almost time for the tardy bell to ring. "I think we should come back to talk about this at another time, boys. Now head over to your homeroom and check in. We can meet later." Placing his hands on the shoulders of both students, Mr. Kahi scooted the inquisitive youths out of his class.

Keoki gazed dumbfounded as they headed over to homeroom to check in. "Seems like there's a lot going on in your life right now, Kaimi. Did you want to talk?"

Kaimi just quickened his step to avoid grabbing a tardy slip and ignored his friend.

"I noticed your brother and his two friends didn't get off the bus this morning. Did they cut school to hang-"

Kaimi spoke in a loud tone, "Just give me one moment, Keoki!" Kaimi had tears running down his face.

Keoki retreated from his questioning and in a soft voice added, "I'm just concerned about you, Kaimi." The boys walked into their homeroom class just as the morning tardy bell rang.

Kaimi wiped his face while Keoki found two seats next to each other. Just before the teacher began taking attendance, a couple student council members entered the classroom to make some announcements. As they addressed their classmates with school news, Kaimi spoke, "Keoki, we go Mr. Kahi's fo' lunch today. You'll get the full story den." Keoki smiled at his buddy and nodded.

Kanahā kūmāhiku

Officer No'eau scouted around the entire precinct searching for any suspicious talk and came up empty handed. She returned to the Missing Persons Division and gave Barshaw the bad news.

"Well, I flubbed it, Brent." Barshaw looked up from the computer to see Lisa wearing a very disappointed expression. "I know you said there's a leak, but for the life of me I haven't seen anything suspicious or out of the ordinary in the department," she looked at Detective Barshaw to see if he showed annoyance.

The detective grabbed Lisa by one hand and acknowledged that she tried her best. "Don't worry about it my dear. It was just a stab in the dark."

She knew Brent was trying to be nice, but his words just made her more upset with herself. "You don't need to spare my feelings just because my dad is your head honcho!"

Barshaw turned toward Lisa, "I'm not sparing your feelings because of your father. I'm telling you I am proud that you did everything that you could do. I know you, Lisa. I know how hard you've worked to try to disassociate yourself from the Lalau name just so you could make it on your own."

Detective Peters rounded the corner as soon as Barshaw stopped talking. He could feel some weird tension bouncing around Brent's cubicle. "Is everything okay? Lisa?"

Detective Barshaw turned and looked at Rush defensively, "Excuse me!?"

Officer No'eau waved her hands to try to magically erase the last twenty seconds of their lives. She looked at Peters and filled him in. "I came up empty handed. The only thing strange I stirred up was interest from Sergeant Nobriga."

Detective Peters' face became flushed, "Brandon Nobriga? From Evidence!?"

Barshaw coughed, "Can we please get back to the evidence sharing!?" He shook his head as the monitor brought up a list of missing persons that the detective did some digging into. "Alright, we've got missing children from all over these islands, so let's get rid of the ones that were found." With the click of a button over half of the names disappeared from the list. "Now let's get rid of the ones where we actually found evidence of foul play." The list became almost non existent. "Can you spot the anomaly, Detective Peters?"

Rush eyed the location of the remaining missing persons and found them all to be from their very own island home, "Wait, we're the only island with actual missing people on it!? That can't be right!"

Now addled, Officer No'eau asked if Detective Peters had anything to share that would help to alleviate this bizarre turn of events. "Help us out, Rush. Did you find anything of importance."

Detective Peters shook his head and exhaled with force, "I believe I'll just be muddying up these waters, Lisa. I found that Patty De Souza only has one solitary grandchild, a girl, and she currently resides in San Francisco."

Barshaw spun in his seat, "Who the heck are those two children living in Patty's house then!?"

Peters shrugged and continued with his facts, "I called Lorna Kepano, Patty De Souza's actual daughter, to find out if there was a hānai in the family. She said there was 'None, whatsoever.' She asked why we thought there were more children in their family and I explained the situation. She was very distraught when I informed her of the passing of her mother." Rush had a flashback of Kenneth that choked him up. He swallowed hard to clear the lump that was in his throat.

"So, I asked her if she had any clue as to who would want to hurt her mother and the woman flipped. She started going on and on about how much she hated living in that house. Lorna explained how she would see strange things in the forest behind the house, yet her mom didn't believe her. The straw that broke the camel's back was when her older brother, Corey De Souza, almost got into a car accident. He came home to tell Lorna that he saw a monster jump into the street and nearly killed him. A week later, he disappeared. She was convinced that those shadowy figures from the woods took her brother from her. She moved to Honolulu soon after, met a man named John Kepano and had their baby girl, Samantha."

Barshaw put his hand up to halt Peters, "Okay, Rush, we don't need all the dramatics. So, Lorna had one child and they live in California."

"Wait!" Peters cut his way back in, "This is the cherry on top!" Barshaw rolled his eyes and allowed the young detective to continue. "Before the Kepano family moved, quite possibly the reason behind their relocation, Lorna took her family over to Kamananui Park where a man tried to abduct Samantha from the playground. She sees her husband fighting this guy as he's trying to retrieve their daughter. John catches up to the stranger as he tries to flee with the little girl and cracks him hard in the back of the head. The blow caused the abductor to drop Samantha. John ran passed him so he could reclaim his baby. By the time Lorna made her way to the scene she could see the kidnapper getting back up to his feet. She recognized him just before he darted into the forest. Would you like to venture a guess as to who she believed she saw?"

Barshaw whined, "Just tell us!" At the same time Lisa slapped Detective Peters in the arm.

"It was Corey De Souza!" Peters nodded as his obnoxious face lit up waiting for a response from either listener. Without receiving a reaction of any kind, Peters continued, "She added that her brother's eyes glowed a fierce white. She said he looked crazed and nothing like the Corey she knew and loved."

Detective Barshaw threw his hands up and slapped them both over his forehead, "I need to call someone!" He immediately contacted the main station in Honolulu and made a request to acquire a list of names of every missing child in the state.

Kanahā kūmāwalu

Kaimi sprinted back over to Mr. Kahi's class as soon as the lunch bell rang. His friend, Keoki, was determined to keep up but was left in the dust as they approached the cafeteria. Kaimi landed at Mr. Kahi's door just as he was stepping out of the classroom.

"Oh! Why hello, Mr. Lee. I apologize if you were expecting to talk now, but I need to go and get something to eat. Those crabby old cafe workers love to shutdown the lunch line early." Mr. Kahi attempted to push around Kaimi but the boy pressed his breast into the side of his teacher to block him. Mr. Kahi could feel the young man's quickened heartbeat knocking against his arm. "Move, Kaimi, I'm being serious. If I don't eat something my blood sugar will plummet."

Kaimi presented a brown paper bag to Mr. Kahi. The aroma that seeped out of the ordinary bag smelled extraordinary.

His interest was piqued, "Okay, Mr. Lee. Let's see what you have in that sack."

Keoki stomped to a stop, jarring Mr. Kahi. The sweaty, out of breath teen just panted and curled his body in odd positions. Mr. Kahi was revolted by the young man's posture and the shrill wheezing sounds that accompanied his unpleasant scent.

"Did you need a health room pass, Mr. Birchham?"

Keoki shook his head and wandered into Mr. Kahi's classroom. Kaimi plopped the brown sack lunch onto Mr. Kahi's desk and pulled two seats closer to where their teacher would be sitting. Mr. Kahi sat in front of the bag with a smile and began to unfurl the folded opening. The smell burst forth from the unassuming container and painted the hungry man's face in its dense flavor. It triggered his stomach which started to growl.

"Sorry about that, boys." Mr. Kahi lifted a hot turkey sandwich from the pouch and his mouth watered uncontrollably. "Oh my goodness! This smells divine."

Kaimi was very happy that Mr. Kahi made such a big to do over that thing, it gave him a chance to catch his breath.

Mr. Kahi took a sizable bite and let out a startling groan. "This is exactly like the hot turkey sandwich, substitute chicken, I order down at the Uku Paila Deli. Scrumptious!"

Kaimi just sat stunned by his teacher. He'd never seen Mr. Kahi so joyous. The sandwich made the man even happier then when he would terrorize the students with his dark tales.

"Okay, Mr. Lee. You have my attention, please tell me, what was it again you wanted to know?"

Kaimi sat up tall, "Oh, Mr. Kahi, I wanted fo' ask you if dea was any *evil* beings dat could shape shift? Evil like eat yo' neighbah kine evil."

Mr. Kahi wiped his pooching lips with a paper towel, "There are accounts of kinolau ʻaikānaka in Hawaiʻi, yes."

Kaimi wanted him to elaborate, but Mr. Kahi went in for another bite. "Okay, so do you know of any evil, shape shifting, man eating, *dog* monstahs?"

Mr. Kahi took a hard swallow, causing him to sit still in an unusual position for what seemed like an eternity. An air pocket in his throat halted the movement of the tasty hoagy.

Kaimi grew impatient, "Mr. Kahi, lunch is only a half ouah!"

The air deprived educator pressed his hands against the top of his desk with his fingers splayed out in front of him. He extended his neck to allow a free flow of the obscenely large bite he took. Kaimi stood up in concern, but Mr. Kahi signaled the boy to sit by tapping a finger on his desk top.

Kaimi asked, "Eh, Mr. Kahi, you alright or what? You not chokin', ah?"

Mr. Kahi wagged his finger and slowly shook his head. Finding his composure, Mr. Kahi took a moment to catch his breath.

"Hu! That went down *HARD*!" he massaged his sensitive throat. The expression on his face read like he was just violated. Mr. Kahi looked at the sandwich, as it sat on its wrappings, with disdain. Kaimi watched the man go through all five stages of grief when he witnessed him nod at the sandwich as if to say, "I forgive you."

Once more, Mr. Kahi carefully lifted the hot turkey back up to continue his feast. Before Mr. Kahi chanced another bite he uttered a name, "Kaupe."

Keoki looked at his buddy with uncertainty. Kaimi shrugged his shoulders. "Mr. Kahi, what is a kaupe?"

A slight whistle could be heard from Mr. Kahi's nose as he chewed his sandwich. Again he wiped his mouth and explained, "Not what, who. Kaupe was a man eating chief that lived on the Gathering Isle, up on the pali. He had the ability to change from a warrior to a brindled dog that stood up on two legs. He was as nasty as they came!"

Kaimi sat forward on his chair, "Brindled? What is dat?"

Their teacher explained, "It's an animals fur coloration. Brindled fur has a mixture of brown and red stripes over a deep dark, almost black, base coat."

Kaimi's head began to throb, "Wait, Mr. Kahi, so Kaupe can also multiply?"

Mr. Kahi downed the last of the sandwich and wiped his fingers and mouth as he made sounds of joy, "Multiply? You mean like clone?"

Kaimi nodded.

"No, no, no. He was *the* one and only Kaupe. Thank God for that!" Mr. Kahi stuffed the empty brown sack with his rubbish and tossed it into the bin. "There were other brindled dog men, also known as ʻōlohe, that once protected Kahekili II, king of Maui. But, they were considered heroic, by no means were they evil. Why do you ask about cloning?"

Kaimi rubbed his hand across his forehead, "Mr. Kahi, I don't want you fo' t'ink I stay crazy."

Mr. Kahi was worried about his student's behavior and fondly thought back to his mentor, Kawika, and how he had treated him with aloha during an awkward time in his adolescence, "Kaimi, you have never lead me to believe that you're a dishonest individual. You don't get involved with drama, you're quiet. In all honesty a little too quiet, but you do your work well and complete your tasks in a timely manner. Nothing you tell me is going to change my position on that."

Kaimi took a deep breath because he knew it was going to be a lot, "Okay, hea goes. My braddah an' I went up Makalike Bridge on Friday wit' 'Alapaki. 'Alapaki tried fo' kill us. He wanted fo' feed me an' Wili to his sistah, Kenani, da Mo'owahine of Makalike Bridge. I t'ink day wen' eat Wili. An' now day aftah me!"

Keoki's eyes popped and Mr. Kahi rubbed his hand over his cheek.

"Den, on Saturday, 'Alapaki an' one missing girl when break inside my house. Two detectives came ovah fo' try help, den one of da detectives wen' die."

Keoki's mouth hung open and Mr. Kahi sat up straight in his seat.

"On Sunday, I taught my braddah was dead, but he came home wit' one smash face an' started fo' attack me. He wen' buss me up real good." Kaimi pointed at his face and continued, "Da detective came ovah an' scare my braddah away an' den da detective wen' tell me my dad got into one car accident, but no moah his body. He wen' take me to one nice man's house an' das when I seen da 'ōlohe kine guys break in an' try kill e'rybody. Now, I get one new aunty."

The end of lunch bell blared causing Mr. Kahi to jump and Keoki to let out a harsh crack from behind. Kaimi looked at his friend in disgust, "Keoki, brah, not again!?"

Keoki held his hand up and wiggled his bottom, "No? Nope, I'm still good!"

Mr. Kahi shook his head. From what he experienced in his life it wasn't hard for the man to fight off disbelief. "Just a quick question, Kaimi. I'm not saying it didn't happen, I just need a little help because that was a lot. The detectives that came to help, what were their names?"

Kaimi looked directly at Mr. Kahi and answered earnestly, "Detective Barshaw an' Detective Takao."

Mr. Kahi blinked his eyes in disbelief, "Which one of the detectives did you say died?"

Kaimi answered in the same direct fashion, "Reed Takao."

Mr. Kahi's eyes turned a bright red and he stood up with his hands over his mouth. He began to mutter, "That's why he never showed up on Sunday, oh my God."

Kaimi could see the distress his teacher was in, "Are you okay?"

Mr. Kahi leaned over with his hands on the surface of his desk, he looked at the boys and explained, "I help on the weekends at the home for the elderly as an event coordinator. This past Sunday we had an event that Reed planned to provide security for. He never showed up. I thought it was weird because he would always make it without fail. Very reliable, just like you

Kaimi." Mr. Kahi stood up, shaking his hands in front of him, with a confused look in his eyes, "Kaimi! What are you doing at school today!?"

The young man answered, "Detective Barshaw stay workin' da case today, an' I t'ink he t'ink it's safer fo' me stay hea wit' addah people around. But, Mr. Kahi, what I really need is da secret to fighting deez t'ings. How do I stop da 'ōlohe?"

The mentor shrugged his shoulders, "I'm sorry Kaimi, I'm not sure this *is* an 'ōlohe we're dealing with! I may be wrong, but it could be the offspring of the evil King Kaupe..."

Kaimi had a look of frustration, "So, how was Kaupe overthrown? What ultimately happened to him?"

Mr. Kahi took a short moment to remember what he was taught, "He met his doom when a king of Hawai'i Nui chanted a mystical oli that took away his immortality. See, Kaupe stole the king's son, it was only then that the evil cannibal king was challenged. After the chant was said, Kaupe became weakened and it was then that he could be destroyed by the king's men. Other than that, he could keep regenerating, tormenting the innocent endlessly."

Kaimi looked inspired, "Mr. Kahi, I know dat da sacred chant has been lost in time, an' when da creachah came to my house he beat me up pretty bad. I didn't feel strong enough to fight it, but one photo of my mom made me t'ink of what she said at one protest. Aftah I wen' shout doze words, I stood to my feet an' fought da monstah off!"

"I could imagine the words being spoken was just a way to fortify one's convictions, to give them the faith they need to overcome a dire situation. I could imagine it's quite like *I Kū Wa,*" Mr. Kahi spoke with a promising tone.

"Okay, so we speak a meaningful phrase an' have Detective Barshaw shoot da monstah's? Easy." Kaimi seemed a bit more confident.

"Be careful, Kaimi," Mr. Kahi warned. "If a foe holds more in terms of intimidation, mana or power in general, the ritual may not work. You need to make sure you are physically, mentally, and spiritually ready before you can succeed indefinitely."

Kaimi knew about being intimidated, he was over it. He didn't want to live in fear anymore. "I should be okay, Mr. Kahi. Da real question is, wea do we fine deez dirty buggahs?"

"If the shape shifting dog man you saw behaves like 'ōlohe, from what I remember, the creatures make their home in natural cave formations such as lava tubes. They also dig their own holes or caves in softer dirt around the base of a mountain." Mr. Kahi sat back down overwhelmed with everything that was going on.

His mind shot back to the sandwich he ate. Lunch had seemed like such a distant, fond memory.

Mr. Kahi snapped out of his stupor, "Kaimi, to tell stories about the otherworldly is one thing, but you are diving into a very serious situation using speculation as your main weapon. I am so very concerned for your safety, I would be lying to you right now if I said I wasn't a little bit afraid. You may think this is my realm of expertise, but I fear that I have failed you, my boy. Believe me when I say that I am praying for you and the safety of those that are assisting you with this. I'm sorry that I can not come and aid you, but I have so much in my life that I also need to protect."

Kaimi got up and went over to hug his teacher, "Mr. Kahi, I appreciate you sharing yo' wealt' of knowledge wit' us. No worries, I'll be alright. Now, I need fo' fine out how fo' use dis knowledge to stop deez 'ōlohe."

Keoki stared wide eyed at his friend. He thought it was like watching an episode of Jerry Springer. He had learned more about Kaimi in this one day than he had over the decade of being friends with him. It was at this point that Keoki could see how strong Kaimi truly was. He held so many losses on his shoulders, so many struggles. Keoki found a new appreciation for his buddy. He was glad to be there for Kaimi and he dedicated himself to helping his friend anyway he could. Keoki stood up as well, “I’m with you, brother from another mother! All the way.”

Kanahā kūmāiwa

Rush stood in front of a half full vending machine contemplating what kind of poison he wanted to deal with tomorrow morning. Just before he could select his snack, his cellular rang, "This is Detective Peters."

Detective Barshaw's voice vibrated lightly through the speaker, "Kid, do not say anything! I need you to stop what you're doing and meet me at the front of the station, right now. Do not take any detours. Do not talk to anyone. Do not stop for anyone. Not even Lisa." Three beeps followed Brent's ominous message signifying that he had already hung up.

Peters bent over to retrieve his treat while scanning the area. He walked a few steps backward and slipped into the stairwell like a cool breeze. Without watching where he was going, he bumped into Officer No'eau.

"Hey, Rush… uh, what's the rush!?" Lisa smiled and let out a small chuckle. The detective carefully side stepped Lisa not taking his eyes off of her. As soon as he could get around the officer, he bolted down the stairwell.

Lisa's face fell and as Peters rounded the lower level she called out toward him, "Hey! What's going on!?" The sound of Peters' shoes could be heard echoing around the spiral staircase until finally there was a bang on the exit door below.

Peters caught a glimpse of Detective Barshaw as he exited the station. He saw Brent look at him and then ditched out of sight around a parking lot column. He hurried over to the spot where Barshaw had stood and heard an engine roar. The trainee found the senior detective sitting in his vehicle waving him to enter. Peters sat in the passenger seat with his hand on his gun, "Password!?"

Barshaw raised his eyebrows in surprise, "Shoes off."

Peters buckled his belt and sat back, "What's going on? And, why did we ditch Lisa?"

Detective Barshaw stared straight ahead and drove a bit faster than the speed limit allowed. "We're grabbing Kaimi." Brent pulled out an envelope from the side of his seat and plopped it on Peters' lap. "Take a look!"

Detective Peters could see a stack of missing children files organized in a manila folder, "These are missing kids from...?"

Detective Barshaw tapped the top right side of one of the reports.

Peters looked the case name over, "Gerald Rosamund!?" Peters looked at Barshaw and back at the file. "Gerald Rosamund? Is this a lead, Detective?"

Detective Barshaw tapped his finger over Gerald's photo and revealed, "That right there, Detective Peters, is the *enchilada* of leads."

Peters thumbed through the other files. His heart just broke, "Brent, I don't know how you keep sane. All these poor kids with their families hoping for the best. How do you keep yourself from losing it?"

Barshaw now understood why Peters became physically ill when he saw Marvin's dog in the state it was in. He could see Peters had a problem with losing something innocent. "It's the hope of finding them, Rush. Dead or alive, returning them to their families is why I do it. Closure. Heartache can cause some major damage to an otherwise healthy person. A missing child is heart wrenching, but when you realize the parents, the siblings, the aunts and uncles are all affected and they're all *hoping* they will see that sweet face once more... That's how and why I do it, Peters. For all the people that the abduction affects, that's the reason I do it."

Peters started to get a sense that Detective Barshaw was only rough on the exterior. Working with the guy helped him to really appreciate who he was and what he stood for. It was something he wished he could've experienced with Kenneth before he died.

Detective Barshaw skidded around the turn and screeched to a halt just in front of the administrator's office of Lunalilo High School. Brent could see Kaimi sitting on a bench next to a pale child with curly red hair.

"Kaimi!"

The detective called for the boy, but there was no response. It appeared that the happy little fellow sitting beside Kaimi was speaking too loudly for Kaimi to hear the detective's voice. Barshaw gave a honk. Kaimi glanced up with a confused look.

The two boys walked up to Brent's window, "Eh, detective! Wea stay Aunty Ukulani?"

Barshaw pointed his thumb toward the backseat. "I called her and told her I'm picking you up. It's okay, Kaimi. Get in!"

Kaimi took a closer look at both of the detectives. "Tell me somet'ing dat only Detective Barshaw an' I would know." He looked for definitive proof.

Peters pawed at Barshaw, "See! We all needed a secret password!"

Barshaw yelled, "It didn't work!" He looked back at the boys awaiting a correct response. "Look, Kaimi, I don't know what you want me to say. Could you please just get in so we can get you somewhere safe!"

Kaimi stepped back and yelled, "No!"

It was at that moment that Mr. Kahi walked out of the office to the sounds of the commotion, "Mr. Lee, Mr. Birchham, is everything okay?"

Kaimi looked back at his teacher, "My aunty was suppose' to pick me up, an' now da detectives stay hea instead. It could be a trap!"

Mr. Kahi stepped closer to the vehicle, "Gentlemen, hi, I'm Kaimi's teacher. Could I bother the both of you for some identification."

Both detectives produced their ID's and stared back at the instructor. Mr. Kahi slowly turned to look at Kaimi as if he were out of ideas. Kaimi stood fast, "Kinolau, Mr. Kahi! Kinolau!"

Kaimi's teacher stood befuddled, "I'm so sorry to ask this, but I know you'll understand. Kaimi told me that Reed Takao was a detective that worked with the Lee 'ohana on a case."

Barshaw looked downward and sighed, "Detective Takao is my partner."

"I'm so sorry, detective. But, perhaps you could answer this. Detective Takao was supposed to make his way over to an event this weekend, but never showed up. Could you tell me what event he missed?"

Mr. Kahi hoped that Detective Takao discussed non-work related business while he was on duty.

Barshaw's lips flapped as he exhaled, "The guy was involved in so many different groups and benefits." Barshaw stretched his brain to find a date. "Ugh, ahhh. Oh!" A memory popped into Brents head, "Sunday night! He was talking about the senior home on Pūpuka place." Barshaw gazed at the three shapes standing beside the car as he peeled away the fog to see if he could reveal more.

It seemed to have been enough to convince the educator that everything was alright. He nodded assuredly and nudged Kaimi toward the car. The hesitant young man reached over to the backseat door handle and got in. Keoki snuck his way in, following his pal closely

Mr. Kahi looked at Kaimi, "Please be safe." He waved at the boys as the car pulled away from the curb.

Kaimi watched the houses fly past his window, he had never heard Keoki in such a still and quiet calm in his life. It was so unnerving that he needed to look at his friend to make sure he was still alive. He watched Keoki for a few seconds, but didn't see him moving. He looked closer, his washed out friend just stared straight ahead in a daze. The young man almost freaked until he could hear the faint asthmatic wheezing in Keoki's breath. Relieved, Kaimi shook his head and bounced his gaze at Barshaw in his rearview mirror.

"Wea we going?"

Detective Barshaw replied, "Well, we only have one point of interest at this time. De Souza residence. We need to locate these things that attacked you and stop them before they hurt anyone else. Maybe we can set up a trap for them back at the house, but with all the commotion I'm sure they aren't going back there any time soon." Barshaw's eyes cast over toward the other boy, "Is that little guy alright?"

Kaimi listened for the wheeze, "He's fine."

Thinking about what Mr. Kahi said earlier he decided to ask if there was any possible way they could find the creature's actual dwelling. "Hey, Detective Barshaw. How hahd would it be fo' fine da monstah's if I said day possibly live in one cave at da bottom of one mountain?"

Detective Peters snorted out a laugh, "I pity the fool that would be tasked in finding caves on this island. There are hundreds, if not thousands of caves and lava tubes in these mountains."

Kaimi knew that the job wouldn't be easy. He just imagined that there could be more forthcoming information from the adults in the car about maybe how to do an efficient search with island wide volunteers to help. "I just figured wit' how urgent dis mattah was people would be moah willing fo' volunteeyah, fo' come help. So, we can fine deez monstah's an' get rid of 'em."

Detective Barshaw turned the steering wheel hard to the left. The car's tires screeched across the rough asphalt pushing the vehicle away from the road and over some grass. Brent worked the sedan back onto the road. The car made its way down the offramp they had just passed. Glancing at the backseat to make sure everyone was okay, Barshaw called out, "Kaimi, are you and your awkward friend okay!?"

Everyone just scooted back into their seats and left the driving to the detective. Peters said in a concerned tone, "You alright, Brent?"

Barshaw kept his eyes trained on the road as he nodded. He had an idea, it was a long shot, but he believed it could be exactly what they were looking for. *This could be dangerous, but time is of the essence and we can't afford to waste any dropping off the boys. They are just going to have to come along for the ride.*

They continued their journey down Pu'u Uila Hill. The detective had hopes that Kaimi's new found information could prove invaluable.

Kanalima

Keoki snapped back to his senses once the car corrected itself. "What the heck!? Kaimi are we going to be safe with these guys? Please tell me you trust them."

Kaimi could see his companion wasn't handling the situation very well. "We'll be okay, we stay in good hands." He patted his friend on the knee, "Eh, Keoki, t'ank you fo' being hea wit' me, yeah."

Peters leaned over toward Barshaw, "Hey, so I understand that we are on our way to hopefully find these things, but what happens when we do? Brent, I'm not so sure that having these kids with us is the best decision."

"If you can think of the perfect hiding place for these kids while we hunt, I'll be more than happy to drop them off. The way I see it, we're Kaimi's safest bet," Brent spoke directly to his colleague.

Barshaw did more off-roading but this time it was much smoother and a lot slower. The boys watched the car come frighteningly close to scraping up against a metal stanchion. Once they passed the small gate, the car continued down a grass pathway that wasn't quite made for sedans to travel over.

Brent pointed up ahead, "This is where Kinihaka said the guys found it."

Peters looked out the windshield scanning the area above and below. He was hoping to find some kind of strange footprint or piece of clothing or even a slash mark across the bark of a tree, "What did Kinihaka find exactly?"

"The Cave of Wonders, Rush," Brent bounced his eyebrows, "The Cave of Wonders."

Detective Wilson had no words, he just unbuckled his seatbelt and swung his legs out of the vehicle.

Barshaw pulled himself out of the car and opened the door to the backseat where he saw two nervous faces. "Look, you boys need to watch each other's backs, do you understand? If anything happens to Peters or myself you run as fast as you can back to the car and get on that radio, got it? I'm sorry boys, I can't promise that we'll make it out of here, but we can damn well try to never let this happen to you or anyone else ever again." Barshaw grabbed the manila folder from the front seat and smacked it on the hood of his car. He opened the flap and on the very first page of the case files was a missing person's headshot.

Kaimi walked over and gasped, he reached over at Keoki and dragged him over to the hood. "Keoki, do you see who I see!?"

Keoki rubbed his eyes and shook his head in disbelief. He looked up at the name of the victim, "Gerald Rosamund?" He flashed a confused look at Kaimi, "It says here that he went missing just over six months ago."

Barshaw walked over to the trunk of his car and opened it up. Peters loaded his gun and and checked his secondary weapon. Kaimi was startled when he felt a stiff, heavy material slip over his head.

Detective Barshaw's face appeared from the hole at the top of the metal shirt, "These creatures may not use guns, but this vest also provides protection against knives, aka sharp claws." He grabbed another vest from the car and plopped it over Keoki. The clammy skin of the young man made pulling the vest down difficult for Brent. The detective gave it a strong, sharp tug and it finally slipped down causing Keoki to let out a forceful rip from his backside.

Peters waved his hand in front of his nose, "Good grief kid, what did you eat?" He gave Barshaw an intense look, "Thank God we weren't trapped inside the car with that!"

Barshaw could not believe the aroma this kid just produced. It was just as toxic as the smell that lingered at the De Souza's. When the air cleared, Detective Barshaw brought the conversation back to their task at hand.

"Okay, boys. You will stay at our six, which means behind me and Peters. Do not, for any reason, move in front of either of us, especially when our weapons are drawn. Don't forget how to get back to the car." Barshaw walked back over to the hood of his vehicle. "You know what this means, don't you boys?" Barshaw tapped the mug shot of Gerald Rosamund, "It means that you were right all along, Kaimi. From what I could gather, these creatures have the ability to change their appearance into any of their victims." Barshaw looked at Keoki, "Either of them could look like any of the children that they killed during their career." His gaze moved on to Kaimi, "They could even look like Wiliami." Barshaw checked the chamber of his pistol and eyed Peters, "They could even look like Detectives Takao or Wilson. We need to be alert at all times."

Keoki had started to believe that he was a part of some big budget Hollywood horror movie. When he realized that the characters that fit his description didn't last long, a chill ran through his veins. He froze in his steps and started to jitter uncontrollably at his joints.

Kaimi approached the frightened frame of his young companion, squeezing firmly at his shoulder, "You'll be alright, Keoki. As long as I'm around, you'll be alright." The words Wili spoke, that haunted Kaimi from his dream, were renewed in a vow that he would use to protect his friend. It gave Kaimi a sense of purpose and fueled his courage.

"We will take care of each other." Keoki responded as he brought up his fist.

Kaimi struck Keoki in the knuckles, "We go, cuz!" they followed the detectives cautiously into the dark foreboding woods.

Kanalima kūmākahi

"Dis is it, Keoki. If dea evah was one show down, dis is when it would happen," Kaimi spoke in a whisper to his friend.

Keoki was oblivious to Kaimi's insight. He focused on counting steps and eyeing flaws in various trees they walked past, trying his best to memorize his way back to the opening of the forest, and ultimately the police car, in case things went sour.

With every step it grew darker and quieter as the four men traveled deeper into the gloomy shade of the woods. Peters eyed the canopy for signs of life, "Brent, is it usually this quiet in the forest? Where are all the birds?"

Barshaw, timing himself between taking each step and steadying his breathing, became slightly annoyed at the interruption. "How the heck should I know? I'm not an ornithologist!"

Peters felt the sting, "I was just curious is all." The detective suddenly came under attack by a nauseating fragrance.

Barshaw was once again snapped out of his breathe-step-breathe pattern when Peters began twitching and flailing his arms about like an insane person. The old man yelled, "What!? What is it, Rush!?"

Detective Peters turned around and looked at Kaimi's comrade, "You don't *smell* anything disgusting, Brent!?"

Barshaw shook his head and continued through the tall grass. He glanced at Keoki and snarled, "Quiet! Everyone keep moving."

Kaimi tasted something in the air as well, "Detective Barshaw, Detective Peters is right. Stay get one funny smell in da ea."

Keoki caught Detective Peters gawking once more in his direction, "It isn't me! I promise. Even I find that smell revolting." The sweaty teenager looked at the forest floor as he purposefully crushed dried sticks and dried leaves underfoot.

"Young man, could you at least try to avoid giving away our position?" Peters rolled his eyes back front. "If those were-dogs get the jump on us, it'll be all your fault."

Keoki's eyes grew round and he stopped making anymore unnecessary noise.

The men found themselves at the base of the pali. Peters looked upward and eyed the steep cliff face. "That's a *long* way down," he continued his examination of the area. "Even if Takao had fallen onto the forest covering, that height would have still spelled certain doom."

Barshaw took a quick peek above and pushed on, "Kinihaka said the cave was at the end of this cliff. Make haste, gentlemen. We're almost there."

As the troupe continued their trek, Barshaw's intuition kicked in. "This has got to be it, I can just feel it." The smell that was once nonexistent to the senior detective finally revealed itself. He raised his hand in front of his face and flicked at his nose, "By golly, we seemed to have found something, boys."

An opening at the lower edge of the cliff was visible. It was a bit taller than nine feet in height and way too dark to tell if it went in a ways. Detective Barshaw stuck his arm out behind him to stop the boys from moving forward. "You kids need to keep at a safe distance." With the other hand, he drew his gun.

Peters pushed ahead of the pack, "I'll go on and take a look see, you hang back with these guys and keep them covered." The rookie nodded at Brent assuredly.

Barshaw turned toward both boys. He could see a fire behind Kaimi's eyes. It was very different than the peaceful innocence that he saw in his eyes when he first met the boy at the hospital. Barshaw felt as though the young man had come into his own. Keoki, on the other hand, seemed to be getting his strength through the determination of his buddy. His eyes darted to and fro as he tried focusing hard on their destination. Barshaw needed Kaimi to be alright so that Keoki would be alright.

"Okay, gentlemen. Let's sit tight while Detective Peters scouts the opening to the cave. Just breathe, we'll be alright as long as we keep a cool head about us." They looked on and watched the rocky mouth swallow Detective Peters. "Keep a low and tight frame. Be on the lookout for anything strange." Barshaw continued to teach the boys survival skills to calm their nerves as they patiently waited for Peters to return.

After a few minutes, the three jumped at the sound of gun fire emanating from the cavern. The multitude of shots were amplified by the walls of the cave's interior and wailed as it burst forth from the hole in the wall. Barshaw jumped up to his feet and flicked his hands in a downward motion, "Stay here!" He ran off toward the cave's entrance.

Kaimi took hold of his friend's shoulders and looked him dead in the eyes, "Keoki, remembah what you an' I agreed on?" Keoki took a moment to recall it, but he nodded to show his understanding. "Good! 'Cause we goin' include Barshaw an' Peters in on dat deal. Right?" Keoki nodded again with less hesitation. "Let's go help ouah friends!"

The boys crept around the edge of the tree line and stayed hidden in the tall grasses. They found a spot directly in front of the cave opening and could see something moving within it.

Brent held his weapon at the entrance of the tunnel. "Detective Peters!? Rush, are you okay!?"

After a moment, Detective Peters exited the hollow. His hands were up as if being held at gun point. He slowly inched away from the cavity where a second shadow could be seen emerging from behind.

Peters shook his head blurting, "Better luck next time."

His new found escort pushed the captive in his back with the tip of the gun. Kaimi could see his faux brother, Scab Face Wili, standing directly behind Detective Peters. He held the detective's gun and had it pointed right in his shoulder.

Scab Face Wili growled, "Drop da gun, or dis guy is histreh!" The creature slurped as drool slipped from the side of its injuries.

Keoki watched in disbelief, "What the heck, Kaimi!? Why does that thing look like your brother but with a smashed in face?"

"It's not my braddah, das why." Kaimi kept his eyes on the situation and snapped, "Das Scab Face Wili!"

Keoki turned with a puzzled look, "Scab? Why not Smashed?"

Kaimi was now just as puzzled, "Smashed?"

"Yeah! Wili's face looks like it's been smashed in." Keoki watched his friend continue to stare ahead.

Kaimi spent a short amount of time contemplating the scabby and smashed look of his brother's face, "Okay, fine. Smash Face Wili, den." Kaimi waved his hand in Keoki's face, "Be quiet already."

Barshaw looked closely at Peters trying to see if he was hurt. Blood stained Rush's sleeve, but something seemed off. Peters looked down the whole time so it was difficult for Brent to get a read on his situation.

"Peters, are you okay?"

Smash Face Wili took two steps closer towards his hostage, "He won't be, unless you drop da gun."

Barshaw roared, "Detective Peters!" The hostage finally looked up. "Password?"

The detained man looked at Brent and awkwardly nodded.

"Put da gun down ol' man, or yo' pahtnah going get it. Las' chance!" Smash Face Wili started to slobber over his weapon holding arm.

Barshaw yelled once more, "Password!?"

Without hesitation Brent pulled the trigger plugging Detective Peters in the chest then focused his aim at Smash Face Wili.

Both boys ducked for cover as the gun fight broke out. "What the hell, Kaimi!? Detective Barshaw just betrayed his partner!" Keoki cried while holding his head with both hands.

Kaimi shook his head, "Dat wasn't Detective Peters, Keoki. Dat was one of da monstahs. Day got Peters!"

Detective Barshaw was lucky that Smash Face Wili was a bad shot, although not terrible. He still heard the bullets flying uncomfortably close by. Brent took aim and disarmed Smash Face Wili by hitting him in the wrist. He moved toward his attacker as it cradled its arm against its chest. The breathing coming from the boy increased in ferocity as his face began to tear open.

Barshaw witnessed a dog's snout emerging from the indention of its splitting skull. It let out a fierce howl as it bore its razor sharp teeth. Barshaw raised his gun and emptied the last of his rounds into the creature's chest. It let out a shriek and fell onto its back writhing in pain, but it did not die. Detective Barshaw pulled another magazine out of his pocket to reload when he felt a searing sensation emanate from his right leg. He looked down to see Detective Peters' claws piercing through his leg as he began to morph into the second were-dog.

Barshaw yelled as he was thrown back several yards. His gun and the magazine were cast in separate directions landing in the tall grass. The creature, still not realizing there was anyone else around, intimidated the detective with its growls, slowly stepping closer licking its teeth. The Brent scrambled backwards searching the grass for his gun, when his back hit up against a tree's trunk.

Kaimi scanned the forest floor, "If only I had Mutt's taiaha!" His eyes lit up when he found a fairly straight and quite sturdy tree branch laying nearby. Keoki watched his gallant friend and followed suit. He armed himself with a club shaped branch with a rough exterior. Kaimi nodded toward Keoki and they both charged screaming at the top of their lungs. Kaimi began the war chant as they came upon the dog-man, "Ka mate, ka mate!"

The creature threw open its mouth getting ready to kill the defenseless detective when Keoki smashed his club into the creatures spine. Kaimi swung upwards microseconds later knocking the creatures fangs away from Detective Barshaw. The brute collapsed, writhing in pain from the combo, face first into the gnarled tree's roots causing it to release a shrill cry that caught her partner's attention.

Smash Face Wili rose in time to see his companion being knocked to the ground. He charged at the young warriors with rage in his bloodshot eye. Kaimi stepped in front of Barshaw and practiced Mutt's fighting stance. The beast swiped at the boy tossing him out of the way, but received a retaliatory strike as Keoki smashed its shoulder with his coarse club.

"Don't hit my friends!" Keoki screamed as he raised his club and cracked Wili right on the smashed area of the his face. A reddish brown liquid shot out with a squirt into the eyes of the young defender.

"Ew, it's warm!" Keoki tried to recover quickly, but he was slashed in the chest by the were-dog's knife like claws causing him to fall hard onto his back, blinded by the viscous suppuration.

Kaimi stood up to help his compatriot, but was blocked when the other creature got back up to face him. He once again planted his footing, readying his next strike.

"Ka ora, ka ora!"

Kaimi winced at the monster struggling to right its dislocated jaw. He took the opportunity to land a finishing blow, but the monster had feigned its injury. It dodged the boy's attack, ducking under his devastating swing. While realigning its jaw, the man-eater struck Kaimi with a strong right hook to his face, then tore its claws across his back and howled. Kaimi landed onto a dirt patch, face down. The young boy quickly flipped over in time to see the monster clawing at the earth, lunging toward him, and baring its razor sharp teeth with the goal of tearing the young man apart. Kaimi halted the fiend by propping his stick in between his fangs, pressing the branch with great force into the corners of its mouth.

The feral beast snarled and snorted, digging its feet into the ground with its powerful hind legs, fighting to get on top of his prey. Kaimi could feel the humid breath of the ravenous entity on his chest, then on his neck. It slowly inched its jaws closer and closer to his face. The wooden staff began to shake violently causing Kaimi's arms to weaken, but he fought with all his might to stay alive and keep his friends safe.

Smash Face Wili grinned as Keoki struggled to clean the rust colored fluid from his eyes. The beast leaped high up into the air and landed at the feet of the boy. Clearing most of the puss from his vision, Keoki yelped at the sight of the white eyed predator encroaching upon him. Smash Face Wili raised his foot and stomped onto the chest of the pale skinned boy, crushing his torso. The wretched being flexed his claws into the frightened child's body. Keoki's tears ran down his cheeks as he had thoughts of his mother. Keoki became paralyzed with fear.

Kaimi could see that his friend was in desperate need of assistance, but he was in a very similar situation. Kaimi fought unceasingly to find the leverage to break free, but the monster's pliability made it impossible for him to loosen its bite.

The wounded officer finally located his weapon and hoisted it out of the grass. *No bullets,* Barshaw thought as he tried his best to find his magazine.

"Damn it!" he declared at his teams current state.

Watching both boys under the duress of these unstoppable feral beasts made the detective feel as though he had failed everyone he was there to protect and bring justice to. The only thing he could do was offer a small chance for the boys to get away. If he could distract the nonhuman aggressors long enough, the two youths could get back to the squad car and radio for help.

Brent pointed his firearm at Smash Face Wili, knowing exactly what his fate would be, he screamed as loudly as he possibly could, "Password!"

Smash Face Wili turned to see the detective pointing his weapon directly at him. Preparing himself for a death strike, the monster bore his teeth and growled at Barshaw when three loud gun shots screamed through the air piercing dense fur covered flesh. Smash Face Wili looked down at his body to see there was no penetration. He turned his attention toward his partner and watched her fall over. He roared as he pivoted to see Detective Peters at the entrance of the cave holding onto his secondary firearm. The wounded detective dropped his weapon to the ground and fled back into the cave. Smash Face Wili looked at the sprawled out body of his kin and howled in anger. He took off toward the cave to put an end to Detective Peters. The beast disappeared into the the hole to seek revenge.

Keoki got up and cleared his eyes and made his way over to inspect his party. He could see his buddy safe and sound at Detective Barshaw's side and the detective sustained a massive stab wound in his leg.

"Sir, not to be a Negative Nancy, but we need to help your partner. What are your orders?"

Barshaw pushed Keoki away, "Go find my ammo." He sprayed his finger in the direction of where it could have landed. As the boy went off to find the bullets, the detective directed Kaimi, "Take your friend, get to the car and use the radio to call for help. I will hold that thing off if it resurfaces. Go quickly, before it's too late!"

The silence was ended by the sound of Wiliami's voice, "Kaimi!"

The bruised young man turned his gaze from the detective over to the cave's opening. He could see his brother approaching with a limp in his walk, "Detective, too late! It's back already!"

Detective Barshaw's eyes widened in horror as he spotted a large shadow with a tail as long as its body, clinging to the cave's wall. It looped around the ceiling and crawled into the light, yet it stayed behind the form of the missing Lee boy.

"Holy mackerel, Kaimi! You nailed it, that is a lizard lady!" The detective raised his gun and spoke from the side of his mouth, "Keoki, where's my bullets?" Brent watched as the curly red hair of the young man disappear slowly into the grass.

Kaimi could see the familiar form of his brother stop with his hands extended. "I won't let you shoot her."

Barshaw hissed, "Fine! I'll shoot you both!"

The mo'owahine hissed back at Barshaw as Kaimi looked on in a confused state, "If dat's Smash Face Wili, why play da same game as befoah?" Kaimi stood up to his feet, he looked right into the eyes of his brother, "Eh, Wili! I wen' eat yo' spam!"

Wili started to scream, "Brah, das one of da only t'ings I could t'ink about when I was stuck in dat damn cave!!!"

Kaimi ran as fast as he could and took hold of his brother, "Wili!? I taught you was dead!" As he hugged his brother, tears began rolling down his face. He then whispered in his ear, "I nevah eat yo' spam, bruddah." Wili lowered his fists and wrapped his arms around Kaimi to share in the joy.

The mo'owahine hissed in Detective Barshaw's direction which made him lower his fire arm, "Oh! Sorry, ma'am. It wasn't loaded."

Without warning Keoki popped out of the tall grass and handed Barshaw the ammo. Brent looked in fear at the mo'owahine while her mouth gaped wide open baring her fangs, her eyes blazing a deep red. She hissed as she vaulted over the twins and aimed herself in Barshaw's direction. The detective struggled to load his weapon, fumbling with the magazine.

"Good lord, this is it!" Brent could see the mo'owahine zipping through the air in slow motion. Every detail of the deadly, but astonishing, creature's features glimmering in the golden rays of the sun. Barshaw thought, *She's spectacular.* He couldn't imagine being killed by a more beautiful creature. It was a fate he was willing to accept, but to his surprise, her form continued over his head. He turned around to see the mo'owahine tackle the were-dog they thought had died by gun shot. The mo'owahine slashed at its body before stabbing her claws deep into its chest. The villain howled one last time and fell lifeless to the earth.

Barshaw looked over at Keoki, who was still on all fours hidden in the grass, and rolled his eyes up to the sky, "Good gracious!"

Keoki nodded as if he could understand Barshaw's relief, "I've sat right where you are sitting right now, sir.

Luckily, my mom is always there to help me clean up afterward."

Barshaw shook his head and smiled at the mo'owahine. He caught her surveying the cave where he observed Kalena, the boys' father, materialize. He assisted the missing detective, Reed Takao, out from the tunnel.

In complete amazement, Barshaw blurted, "Good grief, how many people are in that hole!?"

Detective Peters then staggered out from behind the two other men holding his jacket over his shoulder.

Barshaw bellowed, "All these people are making me look bad, someone help me up!" Keoki was right there to lend a helping hand.

Kaimi was so happy to see that his family was alright, "I don't undahstan', how you wen' all get hea!?"

Barshaw pointed at Wiliami, "I bet he knows exactly what happened."

Wili stepped forward and took a slow, deep breath, "Well, I guess I should staht from da beginning."

Kanalima kūmālua

Wiliami began telling the tale of that fateful Friday, "Kaimi an' I went to Makalike Bridge fo' swim wit' 'Alapaki an' Kenani. When we got dea, I wen' fine one rock in da jumping spot so I wen' push 'em ovah. 'Alapaki wanted me fo' jump first so I would buss my eggs. He was all huhū dat nevah happen. So, he wen' jump in an' fix da rock back up. He was eggin' my braddah on, but Kaimi wen' trow dat rock."

Barshaw interrupted, "Wili, we already knew that these two were trying to kill you and your brother. Can we move on to what we don't know?" The detective bounced his gaze at the mo'owahine nestled up on a tree's branch.

Wili rolled his eyes, "Das what I was getting to! Anyways, Kaimi wen' trow da rock an' all of a sudden, 'Alapaki stay pulling me into da rock's pat' when I feel somet'ing save me las' minute. Was Pa'awai, ouah 'aumakua." Wili looked at his brother while presenting the mo'owahine with his hands spread out toward her.

"Pretty neat yeah Kaimi!? Anyway, da rock wen' plop in da stream, no worries. Den 'Alapaki's teet came all sharp an' he wen' bite my leg an' nevah like let go. Brah, you nevah believe what happen nex', 'Alapaki's face started fo' change an' look like my face. Gross, yeah? Pa'awai wen' choke da guy out wit' her tail, dove in da watah fo' grab one rock an' wen' whack 'em in 'Alapaki's face. Smack!" Wili's fist hammered into his palm causing Pa'awai to flinch. "Braddah 'Alapaki wen' float down stream an' Pa'awai wen' help me climb up da tree by da bridge to go get you, Kaimi, but was too late. You was pass out on da bridge. Pa'awai carried me to dis real cool cave an' help fix my leg an' fo' keep me safe!"

Kaimi looked at Pa'awai curled up on the tree, her coloration made it difficult to see her even in the day light. "'Aumākua? What is dat?"

Kaimi's dad helped to explain, "People of Hawaiian ancestry get spiritual family guardians, 'aumākua. Yo' maddah told me when we stahted dating dat her family 'aumakua was da mo'o. All dis time I taught was da small kine gecko inside da house laddat." Mr. Lee began laughing while flexing his eyebrows in Pa'awai's direction. "So, crazy."

Wili continued, "Latah on, Pa'awai an' me wen' hea some howling, like one scary movie, eh, you rememebah da kine, Kaimi?" Wili spun his hand at the wrist. "Da kine!? Da one wit' da wea-wolves!" Kaimi's lips pulled downward as he shook his head. "Ah, das okay, braddah. So, we hea da kine howling an' Pa'awai disappeeyahs down one tunnel an' comes back wit' dis guy," Wili points toward Detective Takao.

Reed explained, "When I went to find Wili and 'Alapaki up at Pu'u Uila Street I was ambushed by one of those werewolves. It bit me and flew me into the woods. I tried running away, but it tricked me."

Barshaw watched Takao relive his terror, "I'm sorry, Reed. We searched for you..."

Detective Takao shook his head, "It's okay, Brent. I know you, I know you would never give up looking. This next part is going to trip you out." Reed winked at his partner and continued with his story, "So, I'm in the forest running for my life and I find Cheylene Hikina cowering in the woods. I covered her with my jacket and next thing I knew she changed into the monster that bit me in the first place. She chased me right off the cliff. I fell, but ended up hitting a tree branch that sprouted out of a hidden cavity up there. It swung me into the cave where I hit my head and passed out. When I woke up, I found myself in the dark on a bed made of leaves. I made my way out of the cave into the light where I stumbled upon Wili and Mr. Lee. I met Pa'awai soon after, she scared the wits out of me."

Wili said in excitement, "Eh, Detective Takao, don't fo' get da scratching we heard aftah!"

Barshaw interrupted Wili's utterance, "Wait, rewind. How did *you* get in the cave, Mr. Lee? We found your truck totaled a few miles back."

The boy's father stood tall, "Oh! Yeah, so I get one call fo' go down da Police Stations an' I wen' talk to da kine, Captain Laulau, an' he said fo' come up hea fo' help you guys fine my boy. As I was driving up da hill I see Pa'awai, she wen' push da tree onto da road." Mr. Lee paused his account to look up at the family guardian, "Eh, if you wanted my attention, you nevah need to try fo' kill me!" Pa'awai opened her mouth slightly and made a soft hiss, "Anyway, I wen' skid nearly bussin' up my truck an' I see her climbing da bed. Naturally, I freaked out an' tried to get away an' I wen' drive my truck down da hill, but before I wen' crash, Pa'awai pulled me out. My truck, totaled! Das why hahd, but she brought me to Wili. You can't imagine how happy I was to see him alive." He looked at his boys, "You two are my world. I no kid you."

Wili yelped, "Den we heard da scratching, yeah Dad!?"

Barshaw rubbed his chin interrupting Wili's admission, "This is all starting to add up, but if what I'm thinking is true, we're not out of the woods yet… metaphorically and literally." Detective Barshaw glanced at Detective Peters, "How did you survive the attack of Scab Face Wili?"

Kaimi interrupted the detective, "Da name is Smash Face Wili now, Detective Barshaw."

He shook his head, "Okay, Peters, how did you make it out of the cave without backup?"

Rush raised his hand toward Pa'awai, "I went in to inspect the cave and one of those things bit me and threw me up against the cavern wall a few times. I got up to the sounds of screaming and gun shots. When I made my way out of the cave I saw those werewolves attacking the boys, so I pulled out my backup piece and fired at the one attacking Kaimi." Peters looked over at Keoki, "Sorry, kid."

Keoki shrugged, "I probably would've done the same thing."

Peters resumed, "When my gun jammed I made a run for it. I hobbled as fast as I could down the tunnel when the dog creature tackled me down. Pa'awai showed up and just decimated that thing. Mr. Lee and Reed stopped to help me while Wili and Pa'awai made their way out of the cave to help you guys."

Barshaw looked at Wili, "So, tell me about the scratches."

The boy looked confused, "What scratches?" He stared at Detective Barshaw for a moment, "Oh! Yeah, da scratches. Remembah? Da wolf-man and wolf-lady was trying fo' fine us in da mountain, das how we knew wea day was. Day was digging aroun' da mountain tryin' fo' fine me."

Barshaw pinched his face on the right side, "Why were these things after you and Kaimi in the first place? It just doesn't make any sense. They could've had their choice of any one of us!"

A cold wind blew and made the group shiver. In the breeze was a soft snake like voice that said, "Listen."

The ensemble moved over to the tree that the mo'owahine latched onto. They could hear Pa'awai speaking over the wind as it blew through the leaves of the trees. She had much to add.

"The creatures that searched for Kaimi and Wili were the niece and nephew of Kaupe, a powerful kupua and kinolau. Their blood line was tainted by evil. Instead of honoring their purpose, they defied their design. They became twisted into rage filled beasts that could not sustain their immortality. They relied on stealing the mana from beings that descended from those with mana, but could only retrieve it from those with less than them. Try as they might to fight one with more, only to fail. I would track down these terrible abominations with the help of my family and we would destroy them before they could do more harm. Kaimi and Wili share the same mana that flows through me. They acquired it from their mother's genealogy. They were hunted because of that mana, so I stepped in. Kinolau are tough to hunt. If they're careful they could get away with living someone else's life for years without being revealed. These two were messy, lazy, and greedy. They believed that the two of them as a team, would give them enough mana to go up against an elder. We proved them wrong today."

Kaimi asked his 'aumakua, "Why did my teacha say dat you were a bad guy stealing kids fo' eat 'em latah's?"

Pa'awai slowly closed her eyes, "Oral history can be a beautiful thing. What once starts as fact slowly evolve into myth. The people of these islands have always had a flare for the overly dramatic with their kaona. Clever people, but kolohe too. I may have been seen from time to time, and on occasion, I may have had a child in my arms. I assure you, if I did cradle a keiki to my bosom, it was because I was protecting them from harm. Harm done by strangers and even harm done by 'ohana. Sometimes, our pain comes from the ones we were born to trust."

The sunlight started to fade. Pa'awai uncoiled from her perch and slithered down the tree's trunk. She made her way over to the cave and retrieved Smash

Face Wili's body and laid him beside his sister. The guardian then held her hand over the corpses and spoke in her native tongue. Their bodies transformed into Gerald Rosamund, one of their victims. The tree tops moved through a soft breeze as the mo'owahine spoke once more, "Their last victim was shared. It didn't sustain them for very long."

Kaimi's eyes lit up, "Ho, Wili, look yo' girlfrien'! I tol' you look like 'Alapaki wit' one 'ehu wig!"

Wili snapped his head away from the bodies while shucking his left fist downward.

"Times were getting harder for these treacherous creatures. They became desperate and started taking unnecessary risks to thrive. You boys need to keep your eyes open!" Pa'awai looked toward Reed Takao, "You must also be maka'ala, detective. You have koko kupua as well, which is how you survived that fall and why your 'ohana has such turmoil."

Again, her hand extended, but this time just over one of the remains. The body slowly transformed into Cheylene Hikina. She offered this as a gift of gratitude for the detectives' bravery and sacrifice. "Detective Barshaw, for your commitment to protecting the children of Hawai'i, I offer you Kaupe's niece as closure for Frank Hikina. Detective Takao, you are the protector of the heart of my family, the body of Kaupe's nephew will be returned to the Rosamund ʻohana on Oʻahu. They deserve to have their son back."

Detective Takao's face was fixed in sorrow, "Thank you, Paʻawai."

The Lee's Family ʻaumakua dropped a necklace carved from a sperm whale's bone into Detective Peters' hand. "You were willing to sacrifice yourself for my ʻohana. This will help you to build your life here so you may continue to help me, help them."

Peters looked at the Lee ʻohana, smiled, and humbly took the ancient jewelry with his hand, "Thank you, Paʻawai. I'll do what I can."

Finally, Paʻawai slithered over to Keoki. She looked him over from the top of his curly red head to the bottom of his fluorescent bare feet. She grabbed the blunt end of the club that the boy seemed to have become so fond of and spoke, "ʻŌlohe smasher. Your gift is the friendship you have in Kaimi. But, to protect your companions, you need to defend each other." Paʻawai squeezed the club tight in her hand, "This will help even the odds if you two are ever attacked again."

The blunt branch glowed a bright blue with a cool flame. The fire burned down fast, like a match stick. Keoki's weapon had turned from wood to hardened lava, but was still just as light as before. Keoki threw his arm around as the stone club cut through the air with a faint whistle accompanying each swing.

"Thank you, ma'am!" He excitedly showed off his present to the rest of his compatriots.

Pa'awai bid the group farewell, "A hui hou, ku'u 'ohana." She made her way into the hole at the base of the mountain. As she disappeared from view, the entrance collapsed behind her, making it seem as if there had never been a cave there at all.

Detective Barshaw was mesmerized by Pa'awai and couldn't believe such a majestic creature could live right here under their noses all this time without being seen by the masses. He looked over at the shredded remains of Reed's jacket that lay in the grass like a sleeping child, "Takao, go ahead and grab that will you?"

Detective Takao gave a puzzled look and snapped up the torn lump of fabric that he once used to keep himself warm. He noticed there was a slight heft to it and he began rummaging through the coat's pockets. To his surprise he came across an HPD issue cell phone. It was Detective Wilson's device.

"I think you'll find the answer to what I've suspected in the call log. Check the recently called list, Reed." Detective Barshaw took a deep breath and squinted in the light of the setting sun trying to ignore the pain pulsating up his leg.

Detective Takao's eyes bounced from the screen to Barshaw and back again. "What the hell!?" He thumbed through the recently sent and received calls and found only one contact was dialed post mortem of Detective Wilson.

The senior detective spoke quiet and stern, “This isn’t over. We need to prepare ourselves for what’s going to happen next. I fear this is going to be worse than what we’ve just faced, and we’re going to have to do it without the help of our new friend. We’ll need to be smart, because I don’t think our brawn is going to cut it.” The older gentleman held his injuries and bent in exhaustion. “We’ll need to make a plan.”

Kanalima kūmākolu

Detective Barshaw stood alone near the bodies of Cheylene Hikina and Gerald Rosamund. He leaned his weight onto Keoki's magical club and waited for the main villain to spring their trap. The sounds of the forest began to slowly drown away as if mother nature herself turned down the volume with a press of a button on a remote. The humid air began to thicken. The soupy atmosphere made Barshaw sweat around his shirt's collar. He could hear heavy footsteps pressing into the grass from the path they had used to travel into the woods.

A massive shadowy figure appeared from behind the trunk of a crooked tree. Its eyes glowed a piercing white and painted an eerie portrait that made Brent's hair stand up all over his body. Barshaw's heart beat harder and faster, his leg throbbing with each pulse. He knew he wouldn't stand a chance in this fight, he was only there as bait. The real warriors would spring into action at his command. The dark figure approached the detective, growing gradually in size. Barshaw coaxed the villainous mastermind out of the darkness as he held Detective Wilson's mobile up over his head.

A deep growl came from the blackened form as it stood at the edge of the forest, "Detective Barshaw! What a surprise." The silhouette emerged from the shade of the trees and stepped into the clearing.

Barshaw tried to bare his pain and straightened himself in defense, "Captain Lalau." The imposing height of the captain already surpassed the size of the ʻōlohe they killed and it made Barshaw nervous at how big this guy would be in his true werewolf form. "It appears we have found the missing children. Cheylene and Gerald, although we were given no notice about *this* young man when he disappeared about six months ago… Why is that?" Barshaw gripped the club tight preparing for the worst.

The captain moved cautiously toward the bodies of the fallen. "Don't toy with me, Detective Barshaw." Captain Lalau looked down as tears fell from his eyes. He cast his gaze at the man standing above the corpses and frowned as he let out a howl.

"This is my son, ʻAkākua." Captain Lalau's face relaxed as he directed his eyes at the other body, "My daughter, Pōhuli." The captain shot his face right toward the detective and snorted. "You killed them!? I should tear you apart right here and now, but, I am *not* angry at you." The captain's posture eased. "I am instead grateful to you." He bent over to reclaim his children.

"Hang on there, Captain. These corpses are going to the families that have lost their children at the hands of yours. It is only right." Detective Barshaw raised the mystical club up and pointed it at the face of his boss.

Captain Lalau's shiny white fangs stood out in the glow of the setting sun when he barked at Barshaw's command. "Tsa! They are kupua! My children bare the bloodline of the chiefs!"

"Ali'i protected their people. They didn't use them as a buffet line! Your children were savages!" Barshaw exclaimed. He could feel the adrenaline coarse through his body. He prepared to call out his war cry. But something unexpected happened.

The captain backed away and made an agreement, "Use my children to bring peace to those 'ohana. Tell the families that their remains are to be cremated and cast into the updraft of Nu'uanu."

The detective shook his head, "Why on earth would I grant such a request? That is out of the question!"

The captain made his reason clear, "If another akua searching for mana comes across the bodies of my son and daughter, they will consume them and would then be tainted by their appetite for more of that mana. The mana of man. The cycle would continue once more and I would be the least of your worries."

Barshaw nodded, "Okay, deal. But there's still a bigger question that needs to be answered. What do I do with you?"

Captain Lalau turned and faced the darkened forest, "I am finished. I will leave this realm and find my peace, finally."

Barshaw staggered around the bodies, "I'm sorry Captain, I can't let that happen. I can't allow you to leave so you can continue to prey on more innocent people!"

Lalau turned back around and faced Brent with an odd smile on his face, "You believe I also feast on the flesh of man?" Lalau let out an enormous laugh. "I will share this story with you. Many years ago, I was invited to stay with my brother, Ali'inui of Nu'uanu. His name was Kaupe. He shared in the spoils of many victories with me and we lived as kings. One day, I fell in love with a beautiful wahine and she became pregnant with twins." Lalau looked back at his keiki sprawled on the earth and sobbed, "My brother loved them like they were his own. Life was good, or so it seemed. A time came when he sent me off to Hawai'inui to steal the son of a warring chief for him. When I returned with his prize I realized something was different. While I was away from my family, my brother had fed my children the flesh of man. I did not realize my brother was consuming the bodies of the Ali'i we had slain together. He believed that in doing what he did, he would convince me to become 'aikanaka. I was so angry I took the kidnapped boy back to his father. Kaupe chased us to Hawai'inui where the chief united his army and killed my brother. All this time I've been trying to protect my children and instead have been sacrificing innocent people." Captain Lalau looked remorseful. "Brent, I can't stop you from doing what you believe is right. Just know, that you saved me no matter what the outcome. Thank you."

Barshaw lowered the club, "So, all this… just sweep it under the rug? What happens at the department? You don't think that the others won't put two and two together? What about Lisa? Is she 'ōlohe!?"

The captain raised his hands, "Lisa isn't mine. I married her mother while she was pregnant with her. My children were gone for years hunting from island to island and I took a chance at having a normal 'ohana. Well, as normal an 'ohana as a kupua could possibly have. I awaited the day that my children would return so I could protect Lisa from their appetite. She also has mana." Captain Lalau fell to his knees and eyed the club Barshaw held in his hand. "End it."

Barshaw's eyes popped. He couldn't understand what it was his boss wanted him to do. "What?"

Lalau kept his gaze at the dirt, "You're right. You're not the only person that's going to put it all together, Brent!? I wouldn't be surprised if Lisa hasn't already come to the same conclusion! Save her from suffering at trying to track down her own father! Save her from thinking one day she'll need to arrest the man that raised her! Keep her from suffering and end my..." the captain's voice cut out by a deafening knock that resembled a coconut falling from a thirty foot tall tree hitting concrete. Barshaw pulled the club out of Captain Lalau's skull and his large mass fell with a thud at the feet of his children. His blood drenched the earth as the team approached from their hiding spots. Barshaw handed the bloodied club back to Keoki, "You're going to need to get your mom to clean that."

Kanalima kūmāhā

Later that evening, Mr. Lee and his two boys made their way to the hospital. They entered room one-four-three and saw Detective Barshaw swaddled in a cotton gown, resting comfortably on his bed. Detective Takao sat on the visitor's chair right beside his partner's cot. Kaimi wandered over and took a look at the old man's injuries.

"Look at dat, detective! Now you stay wea I was when I firs' met you!" Kaimi let out a small chuckle.

Brent reached out for the boy's hand, "Kaimi, thank you. If it wasn't for you, we would still be searching the island for missing kids till… God knows when! You and your family are so inspiring. Pono!"

Mr. Lee placed his hand on Detective Takao's shoulder and pointed toward Detective Barshaw, "You gentlemen are da true heroes! T'ank you for saving my family, mahalo for protecting my boy. Dea's nutting I could possibly do to t'ank you guys fo' all you boat have done fo' us guys."

Wili hugged his dad, "You believed in Kaimi an' you held hope dat you'd fine me. You always had fait' dat everyt'ing would work out. You have always been dea foah us no mattah what. You ouwah hero, Dad."

Kaimi winked at his big brother in agreement. His eyes lit up with news, "Ho, Detective Barshaw! You would nevah believe dat Mr. Mutter was one kung-fu mastah! In fact, Wili, Keoki an' me going take da karate lessons from da guy so we can learn how fo' protec' ouwahselves!"

Detective Takao was all about it. He added, "I could also give you some training in self defense and maybe when you're older, take you boys down to the shooting range. If that's okay with your father."

Mr. Lee nodded, "Eh, as long as you teach me too!" Everyone in the room laughed.

In an odd manner, Barshaw patted himself down in search of something. Reed looked at him with a side eye, "You didn't expect that the hospital staff would allow you keep your cigarettes, did you, boss!?"

Before Brent could answer, a sultry voice breezed into the room, "Da only t'ing dat he puts his lips on dat is smokey hot is dis wahine right hea!" Aunty Ukulani flew passed everyone and went straight on over to check on her man. "Oh, Brent! If dis is da kine scares you going put me true, den we should jus' call it quits!" She threw her body onto the bed smashing Barshaw's busted leg.

Detective Takao raised his brow and stood to his feet, "Well, I guess that's our cue. Take care, boss, I'll see you tomorrow." All four men left as the sounds of smooching could be heard coming from behind them.

Kanalima kūmālima

The very next day, Kaimi and Wili sat in the middle of the bus in their usual seat. They were able to share everything they both experienced while separated. Wili shared more stories about their ʻaumakua and described what he saw in the cave. Kaimi told his brother about the story of their mother and that the cave she found was the same one Wili recovered in. Apparently, Paʻawai was there to help their mother too. Everything seemed like it was back to normal until they approached the De Souza residence. Both boys stared at the spooky home in silence. The house was still surrounded by police tape. They both felt a chill fall over them. The school bus trudged along slowly without stopping and the memory of their insane weekend began to fade as the house disappeared from sight.

The boys got to school and hopped off of their bus. Mr. Kahi had just gotten out of his car and witnessed Kaimi and his brother escaping the crowd of students.

"Kaimi! I guess everything worked out? I heard on the news that a police captain was responsible for all those kidnappings."

Kaimi smiled at his teacher, "Mr. Kahi, I got a lot fo' tell you." The young man waved a brown paper bag containing a hot turkey sandwich at his instructor. "We'll see you at lunch!"

Tuesday

Kanalima kūmāono

Detective Peters wandered into the police station all alone. There was a different tone in the air without having his mentor around to chew his butt off every time he made a mistake. *You're three minutes late, Peters!* Rush could hear Kenneth's voice ringing in his ears which was then followed by his signature sigh.

"Good morning, Detective Peters!" A soft heavenly voice whispered over the sounds of incoming phone calls.

Detective Peters snapped back from his daydream by a disappointed look from a very sweet face. "Good morning, Lisa… Officer No'eau."

Lisa threw her hands in the air, "So, are we just going to ignore the fact that you and Barshaw just ditched me!?"

"I'm so sorry, Lisa!" Peters tried his best to make it up to the young officer, "Barshaw knew it involved your father and he didn't-"

The detective was cut off, "What!? He didn't think I was trustworthy? He thought I was in on the whole kidnapping thing with my dad?" Lisa glared at Peters awaiting a correct response.

Peters dropped his hands to his side. "Barshaw didn't want you to have to deal with the arrest of your father."

"But instead he bludgeoned the man to death!?" Lisa was starting to gather a lot of onlookers.

Detective Peters pulled Officer No'eau over to the side, "He gave Brent no other choice, Lisa. He wasn't going down without a fight."

The young woman cried at the loss of the man who raised her. Her hero, her inspiration and her reason for becoming an officer in the first place. Rush leaned in to hold Lisa as she began to weep. "I don't even know who I am any more. I don't know what I should do. My father was always there to give me advice and talk me through the challenges of each decision."

Rush looked Lisa in her honey toned eyes. "Lisa, if you'd like, you could always discuss things with me."

Lisa rubbed away her tears causing her mascara to smear. "Really? I'd like that. When?"

Peters smiled at Lisa's cheeks and nose turning a bright pink, "How about tonight after work?"

The teary young woman smiled back at the detective and nodded. "We have a date, then." Lisa pulled Rush in for a long tight hug. Peters just held onto Lisa, never wanting to let her go.

Hope

Back at Lunalilo High School, Kaimi just finished summarizing the events that had transpired over the last four days to his teacher. Mr. Kahi sat in his seat staring, mouth agape, at his student. He couldn't get over how much change the young man had gone through within such a short amount of time. But, Kahi knew by experience that that's how most profound changes happen, within a short amount of time.

The boy's teacher smiled at the three young faces beaming back at him. "You guys really know how to fill a day!"

Kaimi laughed, "It's not dat we enjoyed any of it, Mr. Kahi. But, now you know what we went true, an' now you know da trute of ouah family's 'aumakua."

Mr. Kahi nodded as he wiped his hand across his forehead, "Thank you, boys. Now that I have more information, first hand accounts that is, about the mo'owahine, I can share her legacy in a different light. All this time she was like the Boogie Man, but now I know better. I will only ever say the most respectful things when it comes to Pa'awai, boys. I promise."

"T'ank you, Mr. Kahi." Wili slapped his arms over the shoulders of his brother and his new friend Keoki. "We know what dat spooky tale meant to you an' appreciate dat you stay willing fo' tell it in a less terrifying way."

"It's quite alright boys. I'd rather share a story with integrity and value, than one with just shock and awe." The boy's teacher glanced at the clock that hung at the back of his classroom and chuckled. Moving the empty brown paper bag off to the side, Mr. Kahi leaned forward intertwining his fingers together giving the small group a fiendish look. "Regardless, I do have many other terrifying tales about our island paradise to share with you fine gentlemen. Did I ever tell you three about the Huaka'ipō up Pi'ilewa Point?"

THANK YOU!
Mahalo nui loa!

Aloha to you my dear friend,

We hope you enjoyed reading this mo'olelo, story, as much as we enjoyed creating it.

We would greatly appreciate it if you could continue to support us by leaving an honest review of this book on Amazon.com.

If you don't have the time to write a review, you may also choose to click a "Star" rating which only takes a few seconds.

In either case, please use the QR code below to find our book review page and tell us your thoughts.

With much love and thanks, Del Aragon

Find us on: @Del Aragon @del.aragon

Glossary

Aloha: Love, respect or compassion
A hui hou: Until we meet again
ʻAikānaka: Man eater
Akua: Spirit, divine or supernatural
Au: I or me
ʻAumakua/ʻAumākua: Deified ancestor(s), family protector(s) or guardian spirit(s)
Auwē: Alas, oh or woe
Eō: Call, to call out or answer
Hāmau: Hush, quiet down or silence
Hānai: Raise, adopt or foster
Haole: Foreign entity, arrogant or ethnically caucasian
Hāpai: Pregnant, carry or lift
Huhū: Mad, anger or wrath
Hulō: Hurray, hurrah or cheers
I mua: Forward, progress or advance
Iwi: Bones of the deceased
Kahawai: Stream
Kahiko: Old, ancient or a time long ago
Kākou: We
Kamaʻāina: Native
Kānaka: Human being
Kāne: Man, race of man or Kāne himself
Kaona: Innuendo, hidden meaning or double entendre
Kapu: Forbidden, sacred or prohibited
Kēia: This
Keiki: Child, kid or little one
Kiʻipohaku: Petroglyph
Kinolau: Shape-shifter, having many forms
Koko: Blood
Kolohe: Rascal, mischievous or naughty
Koʻu/Kuʻu: My/My(affectionately)
Kukui: Candlenut
Kupua: Half-man half-supernatural, demigod
Lāhui: Nation, tribe or race of people
Lauaʻe: A fragrant fern
Lilikoʻi: Passion fruit

Loa'a: Find
Lua: Pit, hole or toilet, or a type of martial art
Mahalo: Thanks, gratitude or regards
Maka'ala: Alert, vigilant or watchful
Makai: Lowlands or seaward
Māka'i: Police, guard or inspect
Mālama Pono: To take the utmost care of
Malihini: Foreigner
Mana: Spiritual strength
Maoli: True, native or indigenous
Māua: We or us
Mauka: Uplands or inland
Mea'ai: Food
Menehune: A group of highly skilled people that live in Hawai'i pre-Tahitian contact. Mistakenly believed to be small fairy folk or Leprechauns.
Mo'o: Lizard
Mo'olelo: History, tale or legend
Mo'opilikua: Dinosaur
'Ohana: Family, relative or kin
Oli: Chant
'Ōlohe: Hairless, bare or brindled, or skilled in lua
'Ōma'o: Green
'Ono: Tasty or delicious
'Ōpala: Trash, rubbish or waste
'Ōpū: Stomach, belly or womb
Pa'i: Slap, spank or hit
Pā'ina: Party that includes a meal
Pau: Done, finished or the end
Pia or Hēpia: Pale yellow
Pōloli Loa: Extremely Hungry or starved
Pono: Just, fair or moral
Pua'a: Pig or pork
Puka: Opening, vent or hole
Pupule: Crazy, wreckless or wild
'Ulu: Breadfruit
Ulua: A type of deep ocean fish
Wahi: Place, location or site
Wahine/Wāhine: Woman/women
Wala'au: Talk, speak or converse
Waoakua: Highlands reserved for supernatural beings

Ho‘omaika‘i

Mahalo mua loa i ko mākou makua i loko o ka lani. Inā ‘a‘ole ‘oe, ‘a‘ole mākou e noho ma‘ane‘i.

Mahalo iā ‘oe no ka ho‘opōmaika‘i ‘ana ia‘u me ke aloha, a me ke kāko‘o o ku‘u ‘ohana a me nā hoaaloha.

Mahalo no nā kālena a me ka hiki ke ho‘ohana iā lākou.

Ke Akua hemolele, e ho‘omau i hā‘awi mai iā mākou i kou mālamalama, aloha a me kou alaka‘i ke ‘olu‘olu.

I ka po‘e heluhelu ana i keia puke, ka‘u hana aloha, mahalo nui iā ‘oukou no ke kāko‘o nui ‘ana.

Aloha iā ‘oukou,
Del Aragon

Del Aragon

Del Aragon is a creative team of the ʻOhana that shares the same family name. Together, Kiara and Gabriel pair to bring forth their best creative literary works of both fiction and non-fiction genres that deal in entertainment as well as education, inspired through the values gifted to them through their Native Hawaiian upbringings and family traditions.

Gabriel was born and raised in Waimānalo on the island of Oʻahu. Living a life through creativity, Gabe loves expressing himself through the fine arts, music, story telling, and film and shares his knowledge with the youth he interacts with as an art instructor. His moʻolelo come from a history of personal experiences that range from bizarre to life altering. He is a proud father of two beautiful girls and the husband to a genuine angel.

Kiara was born and raised in Kailua on the island of Oʻahu. Her upbringing was fortified through her daily life as an ʻŌlapa, of Pukaʻikapuaokalani Hula Hālau. She has dedicated her life to educating children, not only as an elementary school teacher, but as a loving mother of two precocious girls. She absolutely adores traveling and the thrill of visiting new places to take in the sites, flavors and culture. She is also an avid reader.

Coming Soon...

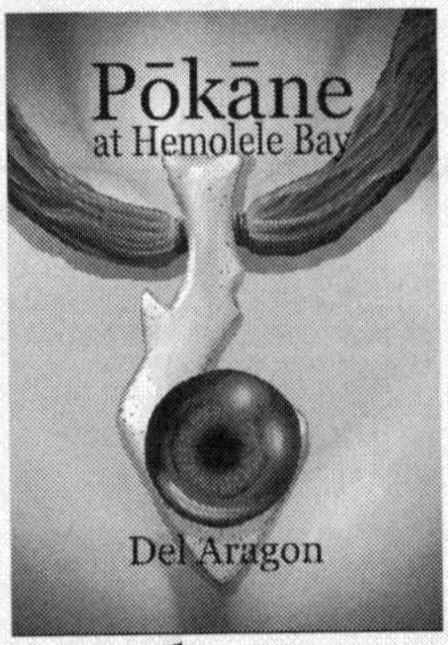

Pōkāne
at Hemolele Bay

Huaka‘ipō
up Pi‘ilewa Point

Made in the USA
Columbia, SC
29 September 2024

42397434R00209